The Dog Knows

Knows

P. X. Stratton

This book is dedicated to my dear husband, Don
Without his encouragement and technical expertise,
this book would not have been possible
He's the best

Dogs are better than people
in that they know—but don't tell

Emily Dickinson

The Dog Knows

Chapter 1

Missy, the sturdy beagle, her nose twitching, suddenly yanked the leash out of Scottie's hand. Barking loudly the dog bounded through the shrubs bordering the sidewalk. The dog walker shook her head in dismay as she stumbled after the dog, the shrubs scratching her ankles.

"Listen Missy, if you don't shape up, I'm never going to—where are you going?" Abruptly, Missy's loud barking stopped and became throaty growls. With her tail down, the dog looked back to see if Scottie was following her.

"What the—" Scottie murmured. In the yard before them she saw a man who appeared to be dead. He lay on his back with his head twisted at an impossible angle. Scottie observed that his clothes looked expensive—beige linen pants, and a cream-colored silk shirt.

"Come on Missy, we've got to get out of here and call Kevin. I don't know what happened, but it's not good."

As Scottie retrieved Missy's leash and turned to retreat to the sidewalk, a loud voice boomed out.

"What the hell did you do? Why are you in my yard? I'm calling the cops. Did you kill this guy?" The irate voice belonged to a large, ruddy-faced man with a bald pate. Sweat poured down his face, and his flowered shirt looked damp.

"I didn't do anything." Scottie huffed. "The dog and I just found him." She tugged her Tilley hat further down over her forehead, causing her reddish-brown curls to stick out on the sides.

"Oh sure. You just happened to wander into my yard. Likely story. You stay right there while I go get my phone and call 911."

Scottie and Missy watched as he shuffled off toward the house. "Like I'm going to do that," Scottie whispered to Missy. "Let's get out of here before that weirdo comes back." Sensing the urgency, Missy scampered toward the shrubs, her short, brown legs going lickity split. Scottie followed behind. When they reached the corner, Scottie stopped to call her nephew, Kevin, a police detective with the Venice, Florida, Police Department.

"Kevin, you won't believe this. The guy was dead. Missy found him. He was just lying there on the ground, and this guy came out and accused me of killing him, which of course, I didn't do."

"Whoa, what guy? What are you talking about? Slow down."

"Missy and I went for a walk and found a body lying on the lawn on the side of this house on Coconut Lane."

"Well, go home and I'll get there as soon as I can. I'll check it out. How close is it to your house?"

"About four blocks east from Palm Avenue. It's right on the corner. It's a light green house." Scottie noticed a dark-colored car across the street from the green house. It was slowly leaving. The darkly tinted windows in the vehicle prevented her from getting a good view of the occupants.

Hurrying along, Scottie chatted with Missy. "Did you see that car, Missy? Do you think someone murdered him? I wonder if he saw us. I think I should be a private detective. This isn't the first time something strange has happened. Bonita is going to wonder what kind of dog walker I am, bringing you home so soon, but I promise to take you on a longer walk next time." Scottie rang the doorbell of Bonita Bonneville's house, Missy jumping anxiously to get in.

"My word, what happened to you?" Bonita exclaimed when she opened the door. "You look like you've seen a ghost."

"Worse," Scottie shakenly responded, "a dead guy in the flesh. Actually, Missy found him. Listen, I have to get home. Kevin is coming over to question me. I'll tell you all about it later."

When she got home, Scottie poured herself a glass of caffeine-free Diet Coke, then grabbed a small notebook and a pen. Just as she was about to sit and jot down everything she could remember about the fiasco, the doorbell rang.

"I'm coming, Kevin," she called. As soon as she turned the lock on the door, it was roughly pushed open, and before she could utter a word, Scottie was shoved to the ground. She caught a quick glimpse of a big man and the flash of a big gold ring. Her head partly hit the ceramic tile and partly the entryway rug. Then, no stars, just blackness.

She came to, lying on her bed, head throbbing. Kevin was holding a bag of ice wrapped in a towel to the side of her face. "Wow, Kevin that was no way to ask me questions," she joked.

"What happened? Did you lose your balance? I found you on the floor by the front door, out like a light. I think I should call an ambulance."

"Don't you dare. I'm perfectly fine. Did you see the dead guy? What do you think? Was the fat, sweaty dude there? I saw a car pull away from across the street. Maybe he left."

Scottie rose from the bed, wobbling a little, and Kevin grabbed her arm.

"Take it easy there. I got that bag of ice for you to bring the swelling down. You're sure you aren't seeing double or triple? What happened?"

They walked to the great room, where she settled into a comfy blue and green striped recliner, obediently holding the bag of ice to her head.

"I heard the doorbell ring, and I thought it was you. When I unlocked the door, this guy burst in and shoved me down. It happened so fast, I didn't get a good look at him, just that he was big. Okay, what's the scoop? What do you know so far about the dead guy?"

Kevin looked down at her from a height of six-three, frowning with concern. "Aunt Scottie, I think maybe you got the wrong house or maybe you were thinking of a movie you just saw, but we didn't find any dead man, and the house you described is unoccupied. The owners only come here periodically. They're snowbirds. We called them, and they're at home battling snow in Michigan, but they do have relatives that stay there from time to time. Maybe you just had a little TIA and that's why you fell."

"You've got to be kidding. You think I made this all up? Come on, you know me. There were definitely two men, one dead and one alive. I wish Missy could talk. At least I'd have a collaborator. And I certainly didn't fall to the floor on my own."

Kevin backed off at the sight of the sparks in her dark brown eyes. He knew she could be a dynamo when angry. His phone rang and he promptly took the call. He listened, then replied, "I'll be there right away. Auntie, I have to go. Are you sure you're all right? Why don't you get a friend to come and sit with you for a while?"

"Just go. If I need help, I'll get it."

The tone of her voice and the exasperated look on her face sent Kevin straight for the door, just as a striking blonde was about to ring the doorbell.

"Why Kevin, what a nice surprise. It is so nice of you to visit your old aunt." She gave him a fierce hug and smiled broadly.

"Good timing, Piper. Auntie just had a fall, so I'm glad you're here. Will you keep an eye on her? I have to go." He took off in a sprint toward his car.

Scottie had watched the interchange between her nephew and Piper Foster. She and Piper had become close friends through volunteering at the library. The two women were a study in contrasts. Scottie was considerably shorter than Piper, who was close to six feet tall, with a curvaceous build and bright blue eyes. Her friendly, flirtatious behavior sometimes got her into trouble. Scottie, on the other hand, was slim and well-toned, with an infectious smile. Her husky voice would make any lounge singer envious. She hated her curly auburn hair, freckles, and slightly turned-up nose.

"Okay, what's this about a fall. I think you should lift up your feet," Piper said as she plunked herself on the sofa and stretched her long legs out in front of her.

"Don't you start on me. A guy shoved me down when I answered my front door. I'm wondering if it had something to do with what I saw. Kevin showed up shortly after that. Let me tell you about my morning. I still can't believe it."

She proceeded to tell her friend about the events of the morning, including Kevin's skepticism. "I don't understand it. Missy and I saw and heard everything just as I said. I think I'm going back there to check it out. Kevin said the house was empty, so it should be safe."

Piper walked over to Scottie and looked down at her, hands on her hips. "Well, if you're going, so am I. You're not going by yourself. Maybe someone is watching your house and waiting for you to do just that. We'll take my car in case we need a quick getaway."

Scottie eyed what Piper was wearing: a white off-shoulder blouse, pink capris, and a pair of pink wedges. Definitely not squeezing-through-the-shrubs kind of clothes. "Only if you stay in the car," she pronounced. "You're not dressed for what I'm going to do."

Chapter 2

After checking that there were no cars or strange men lurking about, Scottie hustled into Piper's bright blue Mercedes convertible. Scottie directed her to the location where she'd seen the body. Piper parked her car about a half block away from the site and insisted that she'd go with Scottie to check out "the scene." They pushed through the shrubs and looked around. Scottie was disappointed to see no crime tape or any other indication that the police had been there.

"Is this the way it looked when you were here?" Piper asked.

Scottie walked around the area where she had seen the man on the ground. "Pretty much. The grass and weeds are so short it would be hard to tell exactly where the body was. But I don't think it looks like anyone was dragged away. We haven't had any rain recently, so it would be hard for footprints or tracks to show up. Either there were two guys who carried him off or one big creep."

Piper looked at her watch and said, "I don't think there is anything to see here. Why don't we go have lunch somewhere and just forget about this?"

Scottie, however, had started to walk toward the house. "Come on, girlfriend, let's take a look through the windows. Since the owners aren't here it shouldn't be a problem. If anyone shows up and asks what we're doing here, I'll tell them you're thinking about buying it."

"Don't go getting me involved in this—whatever it is. Plus, I'm getting hungry. Let's go have lunch."

"Stop whining and let's look around. This is really a nice yard, except for the weeds. Being a corner lot makes this area quite large, and all the shrubs provide a lot of privacy, a good place to put a body."

Scottie walked up to the pool cage and opened the door. "It's open. Let's peek in the house." Piper glanced nervously around before following her into the lanai. Scottie was already peering into the sliding glass door of the house.

"It looks okay from what I can see," she said, her face up against the window. She tried to push open the slider and was surprised to find it easily slid open. "See? It's meant to be. Someone left the door unlocked just for us. Whoever is taking care of the house should be fired. Let's check it out."

"Are you out of your mind? I'm not getting arrested for breaking and entering." Piper hovered outside on the lanai, watching as Scottie walked into the house.

"We're not getting arrested. Besides we didn't break, we just entered. Get in here. It's not a bad looking house. Wow, they must have a lot of dogs. There are four crates lined up here in the kitchen and a bunch of dirty dog bowls in the sink. They're apparently big beer drinkers too. There are a lot of empty beer bottles around. I'm going to just take a quick tour of the house. If you're going to stay out there, let me know if you hear someone coming."

Scottie walked through the great room, taking note of the empty pizza boxes and more beer bottles. The furniture looked well used, and the rug under the coffee table was stained. "What slobs. I can't believe they went off leaving their house like this," she mumbled to herself. She poked her head into a bedroom, which didn't appear to have been used. The bed was neatly made, and the carpeting looked clean. Further down the hall she looked into a bathroom. Everything looked normal. Next bedroom was okay. She thought she heard something from the kitchen, but decided it was just her imagination.

Piper continued standing guard at the open slider, wishing her friend would hurry up so they could leave. Suddenly she heard the sound of the garage door opening. "Someone's coming!" she whispered loudly into the house. "We have to get out now." No answer and no Scottie. Piper heard the kitchen door being opened and ducked behind a storage box on the lanai. Her heart was beating so fast she thought she'd have a heart attack. Ducking down low, she risked a peek.

A big man with a red face and pot belly stood at the kitchen door. "Jeez, Carlos, you are an idiot. You left the farking lanai door open. What the hell were you thinking? Forget that, you weren't thinking. We've got to get our stuff out of here before someone starts snooping around. You pick up the trash, and I'll haul out the dog cages and bowls. And don't forget whatever's in the bedroom and bathroom."

"Dammit, Ruben, I'm not your flunky. So, stop treating me like one. We're in this together partner, fifty-fifty. I don't understand why we have to leave this house, anyway. Tell me again what Tina said."

"Just that we have to get our stuff together and get out."

"Then you pick up the junk, and I'll take out the dog stuff."

Carlos huffily went over to the dog crates and easily picked up one in each hand. Giving the stink eye to Ruben's back, he stormed out to the garage.

Upstairs Scottie continued her search for any clues that might give information about the dead guy. "Holy moly," she exclaimed on entering the master bedroom. Fast food wrappings, beer bottles, and a plate of dried cheese and crackers decorated the dresser and nightstands. The duvet and top sheet on one twin bed were half on the bed and half on the floor. The other twin bed only had a pillow on it. A chaise lounge appeared to have been baptized several times by a dog. Dirty clothes were piled in the corner of the room. *This doesn't make sense,* she thought to herself. *The other bedrooms were neat and tidy, this one's a total mess. Something's wrong here.*

Scottie was about to check out the en suite bathroom when she heard a loud voice yell, "The leashes are in the pantry. Don't forget them." Panic struck her as she realized it was the voice of the fat, sweaty guy who had told her to get out of his yard. And he was coming down the hall to the bedroom she was in.

With adrenalin fiercely coursing through her veins, she glanced around the room. No room under the bed. She needed something to protect herself. A lamp? No time. It'd have to be a beer bottle. Grabbing one off the nightstand, she scrambled behind the bedroom door. She discovered the bottle wasn't empty when, holding it up near her head, beer ran down the arm of her blue jean shirt. Oh brother, now she'd smell like a brewery. His footsteps continued down the hall toward the master bedroom.

Piper's legs were beginning to go numb as she crouched down behind the storage box. She peeked around the box and saw a dark-haired man rummaging around in the pantry. "I don't see any leashes. They must be somewhere else," he mumbled to himself.

He left the room, and Piper decided this was the time to leave and get help. She duck-waddled to the side lanai door, then ran down between the neighboring houses, tripping once. She hated to leave Scottie, but she needed to call the police. Her legs were so wobbly she could hardly run. Getting to the sidewalk, she hoped walking would make her appear less suspicious than running. Besides, her ankle hurt. She must have twisted it when running between the houses. She had to lean against her car when she reached it. It was then Piper realized she'd forgotten to take her purse. It was still behind the storage box on the lanai!

Piper hadn't even thought about her purse and the cellphone in it when she hid behind the box. Hiding from bad guys wasn't her forte. What if they found her purse with everything in it: her phone, checkbook, credit cards, and everything else? Sitting down on the curb and crying was really tempting. But she had to get help. What to do and where to go now? How was she going to explain everything?

———————————

As Scottie felt the bedroom door move a bit she leaped from her hiding spot, and swung her arm with all her strength, and smashed the beer bottle against the big guy's head. He managed a quick look at Scottie before he went down. "You," he managed to say. "I'll get . . ." His eyes closed, and he slowly crumpled to the floor. Scottie carefully walked around him and peered out the door. Not seeing anyone, she had just started down the hall when she heard the second guy holler, "Ruben, what's taking so long? Do you need help? I can check the bathroom there. We've got to get out of here."

Scottie thought quickly. *Should I go back in the bedroom and crawl under the bed? No, that won't work; not enough space, and besides, Ruben—that must be the fatso's name—might come to and see me. I'll have to take my chances and see if I can get to one of the guestrooms before the other guy comes to check on him. I hope Piper is okay. If anything has happened to her . . .*

Chapter 3

As Piper stood on the street pondering what to do, she noticed a car, kitty-corner across the street, starting to back out of a garage. She hobbled over to the driveway and waved frantically to the driver. An elderly man stopped the car and got   out.

"What happened to you?" he asked surveying her disheveled visage, the snagged blouse, dirty knees of her capris, and a couple of leaves in her messy, long blonde hair. "You look like you've been in a fight. Should I call the police?"

Piper wiped away a tear and shook her head. "No, but if you could give me a ride to the police station, I would really appreciate it."

He gave her one more appraisal and said, "Sure I'd be glad to. Hop in."

Piper got in the car, and they drove off. At the end of the block the driver frowned and asked, "Ah, did you just have a little accident?"

Bewildered Piper said, "What do you mean?"

Appearing cross, the man wrinkled his nose. "It's the smell."

Piper sniffed, and sure enough there was a poop smell. "Oh, my God," she exclaimed. "It's my shoes; they're full of dog doo. I'm so sorry. I'll get your floor mat cleaned. I had no idea about my shoes, and they're new too." She wiped another tear away.

The old man shrugged. "Just glad it's not the car seat. The floor mat is no big deal. Don't worry about it."

At the police station, Piper thanked the driver profusely and declined his offer to walk her to the door.

At the front desk, Piper asked Sergeant Maria Gomez if Kevin Shelton was available. "Please tell him it's urgent." The Sergeant told her to take a seat. She plunked down in a chair and closed her eyes.

After what seemed like forever to her, Kevin showed up. She threw her arms around him and began sobbing. The desk sergeant raised her eyebrows and smiled. Kevin shook his head and gently pushed Piper away. "Let's go somewhere where we can talk. I want to hear all about whatever it is. I'm sure it has to do with Auntie Scottie."

Kevin ushered her to an empty conference room and instructed her to take a chair at the table. Indicating that he'd return immediately, he left briefly and returned with a box of tissues and a cup of coffee. Piper took a tissue and dabbed at her eyes and blew her nose.

"Kevin," she sniffled, "I think this is possibly one of the worst days of my life." She proceeded to tell him about everything she knew thus far. "And Scottie is still there in the house with them. They must be the killers. And my purse is there," she wailed. "And look at my new shoes."

As if fearing she might break into hysterics again, Kevin said softly, "Look, let's go to the house, find Scottie, and get your purse. If the men are there, I'll take care of them. You can take your coffee and drink it on the way."

Piper looked aghast at black liquid in the Styrofoam cup. "Oh heavens, I'd never drink that."

Carlos was about to walk into the master bedroom when he noticed Ruben sitting on the floor near the door, moaning and rubbing his head. A huge lump was beginning to form.

"It's that woman again. I knew she was going to be trouble," grunted Ruben. "She's here somewhere. Check the bathroom."

"What woman? I don't know what the hell you're talking about. There's nobody here." It took great effort, but Carlos finally managed to help Ruben to a standing position.

"She's the real reason I'm so anxious to get out of here. I didn't tell you about her because I knew you'd go berserk. She saw 'you-know-who' in the yard before we hauled him away. Tina doesn't know about it. She didn't say we have to get out of the house."

Exasperated, Carlos glared at Ruben. "And you call me an idiot. There's a witness? We're screwed. You totally ruined everything. Get your crap together and let's get out of here. I wondered why you wanted to clean up the house and get on the road so fast. I already put my things in the van. I'm going to check around; she's probably hiding here somewhere." He checked the bathroom and then stormed out of the bedroom, leaving Ruben to clean up the garbage and grab his stuff.

Hearing the men talking, Scottie crept down the hall and through the kitchen. She had just closed the lanai door leading from the kitchen when she heard footsteps. She had no time to run across the lanai to the screen door that would take her to the lawn, so she ducked behind the storage box. There, she was totally flabbergasted to see Piper's purse. What had happened to her? She wouldn't leave her purse. *Now what?* She had to get out of there.

Scottie peeked around the corner and didn't see the men. Then she heard the sound of the garage door going up. Grabbing Piper's purse, she held her breath until she heard a vehicle leave, then ran out of the lanai. Skipping over dog poop, she moved between the houses and headed for the sidewalk. There was no sign of any vehicle, but Piper's car was still parked down the block. She hurried over to it, jumped in, threw the purse on the seat, and headed for the police station.

Kevin followed Piper's directions to where she had parked her car. No car there.

"Kevin, it's gone!" Piper wailed. "It must have been stolen. I've got to get my purse. I think I'm going to have an attack of some kind." More tears began to roll down her face.

"Now, don't panic. We'll figure it out. I'm sure there's a good answer for everything. I'll check out the house, see who's there, and get your purse." He drove to the house and parked out front. "I want you to stay in the car. If you see anything suspicious, honk the horn." Working with a drama queen was as almost as bad as drug dealers.

He rang the doorbell and waited. No answer. He walked to the back of the house and went into the lanai. Everything appeared to be okay, except there was no purse behind the storage box. Finding the back door open, Kevin went into the house and shouted out, "Anybody home?" Again, no answer. He checked out each room, including the closets. Obviously, no one was home. And Scottie wasn't in the house. Where was she, and what was really happening?

Carlos Garcia and Ruben Rumsey headed east out of town. Both were silent as Ruben drove. Finally, after several miles Carlos said, "We're going to have to tell Tina what's been going on, and she's going to be really pissed. You know how she is. I'm going to let you tell her. It's your fault."

Ruben, his face growing redder than usual, took his eyes off the road to glare at his co-worker. "My fault," he snarled. "Listen you, you . . ."

Seeing that Ruben was getting extremely agitated and afraid he might get them in an accident, Carlos calmly said, "Okay, okay. Let's tell her only about the woman being in the house and not the guy who was in the yard. There's really no reason she needs to know about him. We'll tell her we cleaned up the house, got the dog stuff out, and left."

"Isn't Tina going to wonder what the big deal is about that woman being in the house? After all, wasn't she some sort of intruder? What was she doing there, anyway?"

"How the hell would I know? I don't think we need to worry about her. What's she going to say? 'I broke in and saw two guys cleaning up the house?'"

"Yeah, I guess you're right. The less Tina knows the better. And she should be glad we got the stuff outta the house. I think we should get extra pay for our quick thinking."

Carlos laughed, "Like that's going to happen. But living in that house was a pretty sweet deal. We're going to have to do some fast talking to convince her we did the right thing moving out."

After an hour of driving, they pulled off the highway onto a dirt road leading to a small, white ranch house. A couple of old cars and a tractor were parked permanently in the side yard. Weeds were growing happily around them. Ruben drove around to the back of the house and parked near a large metal pole barn. The big door to the barn was open, revealing four stacks of cages piled three high. The larger bottom cages were housing adult dogs. A fenced-in area near the barn contained six puppies, jumping and barking when they saw the van drive up.

As the men got out of the van, Carlos yelled over to Ruben, "That barking is going to drive me nuts."

"They're probably hungry and thirsty. You'd be barking too. Here comes Tina."

A rotund woman in neon green capris and a too-small T-shirt emerged from the back door of the house. "What took you boys so long?" she bellowed over the barking. "Get in here and tell me whatcha been doing."

Scottie parked Piper's car at the police station. She had to let Kevin know about the house, the men, and that Piper was missing without her purse. She went to the desk and explained the situation to Sergeant Gomez, adding that Kevin was her nephew.

Sergeant Gomez sighed and said, "Is she tall and blonde and somewhat of a bimbo? She sure hung onto Kevin."

Relieved, Scottie couldn't help but smile a little at that comment. "That's her. Was she hurt? What did she say?"

"He took her into a conference room, so I'm not sure. I don't think she was injured, but she was a mess. Lots of crying."

"Are they still here? May I see them?" Poor Piper, she'd probably never speak to her again.

"No, they left. I'm not sure where they went. Kevin did say he wouldn't be gone very long."

Just as Scottie was about to ask another question, in walked Kevin and Piper. At the sight of them, Scottie rushed over to Piper and gave her a quick hug. Stepping back, Scottie took in Piper's appearance. and exclaimed "You *are* a mess; are you hurt? I'm so sorry I got you into this fiasco. Then looking down she asked, "Where are your shoes?"

Piper narrowed her eyes in fury. "Kevin made me throw them away because of the stink. I guess I stepped in dog doo. He wouldn't let me in his car otherwise. And my ankle hurts, my blouse is ruined, my capris are dirty. I am not a happy camper. I notice you have my purse. Thank God for that."

Kevin looked from one of the ladies to the other, then hurriedly said, "Listen, I have to get back to work. Are the two of you okay? Aunt Scottie, I assume you drove Piper's car here, since you have her purse."

Scottie knew he was anxious to get on with his job. "Just go, we'll be fine. And thanks for your help. We really appreciate it. I do have to speak with you later, though." She patted his arm and gave him a quick kiss on the cheek. Noticing the smile on Sergeant Gomez's face, Scottie went over to her and knowingly whispered, "Maria, you know he really is a great guy."

She turned to Piper. "Okay, girlfriend, here's your purse. I'm keeping the key fob and driving you home. I'll get the car and pick you up out front."

Scottie delivered them both to Piper's house and declared, "You go take a shower. I'll fix us some lunch."

"Yes, Mother," Piper said sarcastically as she padded off barefoot to the bedroom.

In the kitchen, Scottie browsed through the pantry and the refrigerator, finding ingredients to put sandwiches and a salad together. She had just finished setting the table on the lanai when Piper came out looking refreshed and lovely in a yellow sundress and white sandals.

"Just in time," Scottie announced. "For one person you sure have a lot of food in the house."

"Well, you never know who might show up. I see you found the open bottle of wine."

"We deserve it after our little adventure. You were really brave though. I'm proud of you." Scottie decided her friend needed some positive feedback after what they'd been through.

"Really? I was never so scared in my life. Do you think those guys were visiting there or what? Something seemed weird about them, and they certainly weren't getting along well."

"I agree something wasn't right. They definitely were in a hurry to get their things out of there. They even tried to pick up some of the mess they made. And the fat guy sure doesn't like me, especially after I hit him on the head with a beer bottle."

"You what? Are you crazy? Now it's breaking, entering, and assault. You're going to jail. And I'm not coming to visit. Or is he dead? Maybe it's murder."

"Don't be silly. He's perfectly fine. I had to do something so I could get out of there before his buddy showed up. I'm sure they're involved in some nefarious activity. They had all that dog stuff but no dogs. That was weird. You didn't happen to see their vehicle or get the license plate number, did you?"

Piper snorted. "Are you kidding? I had all I could do to get out of the lanai and out to the street. And I even forgot my purse." She shivered and took a big swallow of wine.

After lunch Scottie put the dirty dishes in the dishwasher, then asked Piper, "Could I please get you to drive me home? I have to check on Marshmallow and Miss Chablis. They're going to want their dinner later today."

"I suppose. And what are these critters you're going to visit?"

"Cats. Marshmallow is sweet, very friendly. The other one is a grouch. I could think of a better name for her."

Chapter 4

Ruben and Carlos eyed each other before Ruben plunged into telling Tina their tale. "It's like this. Some idiot woman broke into the house. A big nasty woman, really mean looking. We didn't know who she was, but she hit me on the head with a beer bottle and ran out. Probably planning to rob the place, so we figured we better get the hell out of there. It was a good thing Lenny had already taken the dogs. We cleaned the house, took the dog stuff, and here we are." Feeling quite pleased with his story, Ruben glanced over at Carlos and nodded.

Carlos shuffled his feet and said, "Yup, that's why we had to leave. She might have stolen something; you never know."

"She had a big bag with her, so she might have grabbed some stuff before she hit me," lied Ruben.

Tina scowled. "Well, that puts us in a real pickle. I am not happy with you two. Maybe you shouldn't even get paid. Now we have to come up with another place to keep the dogs temporarily. It's not going to be easy. I've got six puppies ready to go. Having them in town with easy access for Lenny to take to the pet store and referral customers in Miami is much better than people coming out here nosing around."

"Come on, Tina, we do a really good job for you. It wasn't our fault," Ruben whined. "What if that woman blabbed about us being in the house? We had to get out."

"Okay, okay. I'm gonna call my friend Buck and see if he can put you and the dogs up for a couple days. He's out fishing quite a bit, so maybe he won't mind too much. Sit down, boys." She waved a hand at the guys who remained standing.

Ruben glanced at the chairs in the small kitchen. Tina was sitting on one, and the other two were loaded with stacks of magazines and newspapers. He and Carlos moved them carefully to the floor, then plunked down. Tina lit a cigarette and fished her cellphone out of her tight capris.

"Hello, Buck," she hollered into the phone. "Tina here. How've ya been? Doing a lot of fishing?" She listened, nodding her head, and puffing away on her cigarette.

"Sounds like good eatin'. Hey, I got a question. My boys here need a place to stay for a few days. Would it be okay if they bunked with you until their next place is ready? They'd be bringing a couple of dogs with them. You don't have your old dog anymore, do you?"

After listening a considerable amount of time, Tina smiled and said, "Buck, you're a good guy. I owe you one. They'll be there later today."

Stubbing out her cigarette, she lit another one and blew out a smoke ring. "You two are lucky I have such good friends," she said. "Your accommodations aren't going to be as palatial as last time, that's your fault, but Buck's place is on the beach. We'll get the pups and you're good to go. There's one that has some health issues. If it looks like he's not going to make it, you know what to do. And you better keep Buck's place clean, or I'll hear about it."

Ruben rolled his eyes at Carlos and shook his head.

They loaded the six puppies into a cardboard box and put them in the van. They had empty crates in the van, but they decided not to take the time to put the puppies into them. They also threw in a big sack of puppy chow.

Ruben was in a hurry to get to the beach. "That yipping and barking back there is going to drive me crazy. I can't wait to get rid of these little monsters," he groused. He picked up speed when they left the dirt road, tires screeching.

"What are you trying to do? Kill us?" Carlos snapped. "Slow down."

Just as they rounded a curve, a pickup truck swerved partially into their lane. Ruben turned the wheel, and the van skidded onto the narrow shoulder of the highway. The cardboard box with the puppies tipped over, and they scrambled all over the back of the van.

"Maybe we should stop and get them back into the box. No telling what they'll do," said Carlos, glancing back into the van "They're digging into everything."

"Nah, I just want to get to the beach. They'll be okay. It's not that far. I can't believe that guy almost ran us off the road. What a butthead." Ruben continued to drive over the speed limit but considerably slower than he had been.

After driving down several streets they finally located the house where Tina wanted them to stay. They backed into the driveway of the small yellow bungalow. Carlos hopped out and opened the back door of the van. "Holy Mother of God," he hollered.

Ruben climbed out of the van and went to see what Carlos was yelling about. His face turned even redder. He shoved Carlos aside and growled, "I'm going to kill those fu…" Six pairs of innocent eyes briefly looked at him and resumed their activities. The bag of puppy chow had been torn open and was scattered all over. Four of the puppies were scarfing up the puppy chow like there was no tomorrow. A little labradoodle, tail wagging, was happily chewing on Ruben's black leather loafer. Obviously, he was a grazer and found the shoe more enjoyable than the food. The rest of Ruben's clothes were all over. Apparently one dog had already eaten too much and gotten sick on a shirt. The sixth puppy, the one with a large open wound, was curled up in the corner on Rubin's polyester sport coat, gazing sadly at all activity going on around him.

"No, you're not. We have a job to do, and we need the money. If we'd put them in the box or the crates or you hadn't driven so fast this wouldn't have happened. So, settle down and let's get busy. I'll put the dogs in the crates, and you can take care of your clothes and clean up the mess." Carlos picked up his bag of neatly packed clothes and turned his   back   on   Ruben   to   hide   a   snicker.

Chapter 5

Scottie was glad to be back home. She showered, put on fresh clothes, checked her email and phone messages. There was one phone message to which she immediately responded. Her long-distance boyfriend, Blake had called today to say he wouldn't be able to fly to Venice for the weekend. She'd really been looking forward to seeing him. Hoping everything was okay, she left a return message asking him to contact her. She loaded her phone, wallet, key fob, and a bottle of water into her large tote, locked the house, and drove over to check on the cats.

Using the garage entry-code she'd been given, she entered the house and called out, "All right you two, I'm putting out your dinner." Immediately a large, white fluffy cat was purring and weaving in and out of her legs. "Well, hi there, Marshmallow, where's your partner? Are you hungry?" She dumped out the cans of cat food into one large dish and added water in the other one. Taking her tote, she went into the living room and just sat down on the sofa when the doorbell rang. She looked through the peephole and saw an ordinary looking man standing there. "Who's there?" she called.

"I'm Fred, I live a couple doors down. I saw your car and was told to come and check on the water heater when you got here. They've been having some problems with it."

Scottie opened the door a bit, and he gave a flash smile and entered the house before Scottie had a chance to do or say anything.

Scottie checked him over. Big guy, average looking, brown hair, brown eyes, nose too large for his face, neatly dressed, blue polo shirt, gray pants. Why was she feeling a chill? Something wasn't right. Suddenly both cats were in the room. With tails swishing and their cat eyes staring they casually strolled over to Fred. He moved a couple of steps closer to Scottie. The cats started rubbing against Fred's legs.

Scottie's phone sang out, and as she reached to answer it, he tightly grabbed her wrist. "Oh no you don't." Alarmed, she glanced down at his hand and noticed a large gold ring. And then it happened.

Sneeze, sneeze, sneeze, sneeze, sneeze. "You rotten, no good pieces of . . ." His eyes started to tear up and turn red. He released Scottie's wrist, and as he was about to give Marshmallow a fierce kick, the wheezing began. He bolted to the door and ran out. Scottie raced out the door after him, but there was no sight of him. Where could he have gone? She hurried back into the house and locked the door. Standing and shaking in the living room, she pondered what to do.

She needed to see if there was a car parked nearby. She ventured down the street, past four houses, but saw nothing suspicious. No cars racing by or parked on the street except for an Amazon truck and driver making a delivery. Where the hell did the guy go, and how did he know she was going to be taking care of the cats? There was no point in calling Kevin. What could she say? There was possibly a bad guy who might have done something to her, maybe it was the same man who had hit her, and the cats made him leave? She might as well just go home and crash. Later she'd ask her friends about their water heater problem and their neighbor Fred.

Scottie had just arrived in her kitchen when her phone rang. She was relieved to see it was Blake. "Hi, is everything okay?" she said. "I was worried about you. Why can't you come this weekend? Are you sick?"

Blake chuckled. "No, I'm not sick. Just a lot of work to do. Being a prosecutor takes a lot of time. You know how busy I always get."

After a long silence, Blake quietly added, "It isn't working, is it? Flying back and forth is expensive and it's a long drive. I can't quit my job, and you don't want to live here. Should we just think about it for a while?"

"That won't change anything. I understand what you're saying, but it makes me sad. We get along so well." Scottie grabbed a tissue off the counter and dabbed at her eyes. They'd been dating for about three years and always had a wonderful time together.

"Scottie, this is going to be hard for me too. You know I'll always be here for you. Just call me if you need anything. Who knows, some day we may be living in the same area again. I'm definitely not feeling great about this. I do miss you."

"I guess this is for the best. But we'll still keep in touch, right?"

"Absolutely. I have to go. Work calls. We will keep in touch. Bye."

"Bye," she said to empty air. He was gone. Scottie sighed, a sad, lonely feeling coming over her. She knew things weren't the same with Blake. She didn't want to let go, but it really was time. How could so many bad things happen in one day?

She poured herself a glass of white wine and sat down in her favorite chair. Her phone rang again just as she was about to take her first sip. It was Bonita, Missy's owner.

"Hi Scottie, I've got some good news. My niece Harper has moved to town. You know, the writer. She bought a condo not far from the beach and moved in already. And guess what? She bought a puppy. I told her about you and your business. Are you busy tomorrow? I thought it would be fun to see her condo and the new puppy. And how are you, by the way? This morning when you brought Missy back you didn't look too good."

"Oh, Bonita, I'm happy for you. Tomorrow morning would be fine. I'd love to see Harper again. And you know how I feel about puppies. It's been a hell of a day. I'm just about to have a small pity party because Blake and I have called it quits. We both found having a long-distance romance was too hard. Maybe neither of us cared enough to try harder. Of course, the rest of the day has been a mess, starting when Missy and I went for a walk." Scottie went on to fill Bonita in on the happenings of the day.

After Scottie finished talking, Bonita asked if she needed a friend to join the pity party. Scottie chuckled and replied, "Thanks for the offer, but I'm going to just have my glass of wine and watch some stupid show on TV and turn in early."

The next morning Bonita picked up Scottie and they drove over to Harper's new condo. On the way Bonita explained to Scottie that Harper's boyfriend of many years was recently killed in a plane crash. He'd been a test pilot in the air force, and apparently there was some malfunction with the plane. Harper, being a successful freelance writer who worked mostly from home, had moved to sunny Florida to be closer to Bonita, her only living relative.

"I was totally surprised when she called and told me about moving to Venice and now buying a puppy. It's great she did, but it just seems like such an impulsive thing to do," Bonita said.

"I kind of understand it," Scottie responded. "I sort of did the same thing. I couldn't continue living where I was. The memories were too horrible." She didn't elaborate, and

Bonita tactfully didn't ask. They continued the ride in silence, each with their own thoughts.

Bonita pulled up to a small, six-unit complex a block from the beach. Two lovely pink hibiscus trees and a variety of bright-colored flowers graced the grounds in front of the building.

"Wow, what a great location, and apparently they have parking underneath the living area," Scottie exclaimed.

Harper met them at the door and gave them hugs. "You both look great. It's been a while since I've seen you, Scottie. Come on in and see my new abode and my new furry kid. There's a bit of a problem there, I'm afraid. Oh, and please excuse the mess. I've unpacked some boxes, but I've got a long way to go."

She ushered them into a partially unpacked kitchen. "Come and see the puppy first, then I'll show you around the condo after. I'm hoping you can give me some advice with him. I was so anxious to get a dog that I didn't do the research I should have. And he's so darn cute. I just fell in love with him the first time I saw his little face."

She gestured to a small pet bed, where they saw a little black and white puppy quietly lying on its side, gazing at them with brown eyes. He gave a couple of weak tail wags. His left back leg had a huge open sore. The fur around it was matted and dirty.

"Oh my God, what's wrong with his leg?" asked Bonita, looking super concerned. "It looks like it's infected or something. Does he have some nasty disease or was he bitten? I hope he doesn't have rabies. What did the seller tell you?"

Harper sighed and led them to the living area. "Have a seat, ladies, and let me tell you what happened. And please don't advise me what I should have done. I know better. There was an ad in the *Venice Gondolier* advertising this puppy. It's the paper that comes out semi-weekly. There was this cute little picture, the price, and a phone number. So, I called the number and a guy said he could bring him right over for me to look at, but he wanted cash because he'd been stung before with checks. Well, I don't usually have cash on hand, but I had sold a lot of furniture from my house before I moved here. I put the money for the puppy on the little table in the entryway. When the guy got here, he shoved the dog in my arms and wanted to know if the money on the table was his. I told him it was, and he grabbed it and was gone. I barely had a look at him. It all happened in a flash. The only thing I really remember about him is the extremely strong smell of cheap cologne. I actually had to open the windows to try to get the smell out."

"That poor puppy definitely needs some help," said Scottie. "I'll give you the name and number of a vet I know. I think it's the same one Missy goes to. He's excellent. If anyone can fix up that little guy he can. Bonita, maybe you could call the vet and tell him the situation." Getting no response, Scottie turned to Bonita, who was sitting on the sofa, her face totally white and her eyes full of tears. "Bonita are you all right?"

"It's just that I can't bear to see that dog suffering. What do you think happened? And to think he actually sold it to you knowing what condition it was in. What kind of person would do that? I'll phone the vet right now and see if we can get an appointment immediately."

Bonita called, and best she could do was an early morning appointment the next day.

Scottie quickly said she would drive Harper to the vet's office with the puppy, knowing Bonita probably wouldn't be up to it.

———————————

Early the next morning Scottie picked up Harper and the puppy. "I did get him to eat a little bit, but not much," Harper commented as she settled into the car with the puppy on her lap, a small blanket under him. "His nose is hot and dry, so I just know he must be really sick."

"The vet we're taking him to is great, so if anyone can help, he can." She glanced in the rearview mirror. "Is there a car following us? It's a black sedan. I think it's two cars behind us. Maybe I'm just being paranoid. Harper, would you keep an eye on it? I'm going to go a couple blocks off our route to see if it follows us."

"Why would anyone be following us?" Harper asked, watching the mirror. "What's going on?"

"This place ain't bad, but it is kind of small," Ruben said. "I'm glad Buck left on a long fishing trip. It's too crowded when he's around. I still can't believe you sold that little sicky. You really should give me half of the money because he ruined my sport coat. When did you say the pups get picked up?" He poked his head into the lanai, where the dogs were running around. "And what the hell is that smell on you?"

"I used some of Buck's cologne. I didn't think he'd mind. And I'm not giving you any of the money. I placed the ad and made the sale. So just get over it."

"Some friend you are. See if I ever share any money with you. With the way you stink, even fire ants wouldn't come near you. When did you say we get rid of the pups?"

"I didn't say, because I don't know. Tina is supposed to call and let us know. The last time she called, she said she had some exciting news for us when we get back to her place."

"Yeah, I bet. She's probably going to fire us."

Carlos scowled in exasperation. "I'm going for a walk. All you do is bitch." And with that he stomped out.

"Okay, guys." Tina said. "The puppies will be picked up about noon tomorrow. Just like before, some of them will be sold to individual owners, and a couple will go to the pet store in Miami.

Tina had long ago decided Ruben and Carlos didn't have what it takes to work with rich clients, and she had just as much told them so. Consequently, she had an alternative plan.

She'd met Lenny Ortega ages ago at a motorcycle rally and had gone into business with him, knowing he had several questionable financial venues. She didn't know what they all were and didn't want to know. He was slick and a smooth talker; tall, slim, lots of black hair worn quite long, and piercing black eyes. Women loved him. Tina knew a really bad boy when she saw one.

He and Tina had made a deal. He would take the puppies to Miami and sell them for her, and in turn she would store locked crates of his in her storage buildings, which were also locked. Lenny paid her handsomely for the locked storage space and the fact she was closed-mouthed and didn't ask questions. Periodically, Lenny would ask her to organize a motorcycle rally at her place, which she loved.

Tina and Lenny found Carlos and Ruben to be the perfect middlemen. Fairly reliable, but not the brightest. Tina provided them with a place to stay and a modest income. They took care of the dogs. When Lenny came to town, he would pick up the dogs and give Carlos and Ruben his locked crates to take to Tina. Lenny usually didn't want to take the time to drive out to the country to take the crates to Tina, and plus, he always met with his other business partners in town. Ruben had asked Lenny once what was in the crates. He never asked again.

Chapter 6

"Is the car still behind us?" Scottie asked as she rounded a corner. "I can't imagine why anyone would follow us."

"I think you lost it. There's no one behind us at all now. Maybe you just thought there was." Harper continued watching the side-view mirror until they stopped in front of the vet's office.

Dr. Gary checked out the puppy and decided he indeed did not look good. He thoroughly cleansed the wound and inserted a drip IV line to get him started on antibiotics. The doctor suggested that the puppy stay overnight rather than be moved again. Harper said she would be back in the morning to see if she could take him home.

"If I get to take him home tomorrow, I'll have to give him a name. I just couldn't for now," she added.

Seeing Harper's down-cast expression, Scottie patted the young woman's shoulder. "He's in good hands, so we'll think positive thoughts. I have a feeling everything will work out. Unfortunately, I can't help you tomorrow. It's going to be a busy day. Maybe Bonita can go with you to pick him up." She drove back to Harper's condo.

"I'm so thankful that you could help me today," Harper told her. "I'm sure either Aunt Bonita or one of my neighbors will go with me to pick him up. The next time you come over I am going to fix you lunch or dinner, and if all goes well there will be a doggy in my house that is feeling great."

Scottie left Harper, hoping the puppy would survive. As she drove home, she couldn't help but wonder if she just imagined a car following her. But on arriving at her house, she was shocked to see that her front door was open. *What the hell!*

She knew she hadn't left it open. She would never do that. There could be someone in there. Snakes could have slithered in or some other critters. Should she call someone, or just take a chance and go in? No, she didn't want to get anyone else involved. She hadn't always been using the alarm system lately. Running late and always being in a hurry can cause problems like that. It really was her own fault, and she needed to chin up and go inside.

Before entering, she took a small can of Mace, and her phone out of her tote. Scottie shoved her phone in her back pocket, prepared to call for help if necessary. Quietly pushing the front door further open she crept inside the house. She didn't hear anything unusual, just the air handler humming away. Her great room appeared to be empty. She put her tote on the sofa. Examining the dining and kitchen areas and finding them empty of any intruders, she ventured down the hall to the primary bedroom. All clear.

Just as Scottie was about to walk out of the room, she glanced at the large window that overlooked the lanai and the pond beyond. Something caught her eye. On the floor, sticking out from the panel of the long, pale blue grommet drape on the right side of the window, were the toes of a pair of black shoes. Someone hiding behind the drape! She froze, heart pounding. The material was fairly thin. How could anyone be behind the drape and not create a bulge?

Holding her breath, she moved the drape aside. Nothing but pair of men's shoes. They were scuffed and obviously well worn; one was missing a lace. A small piece of white paper stuck out of the right shoe. Crazy. Someone had broken into her house and left a pair of smelly old shoes, and she wondered what else. No way was she going to touch anything. Scottie grabbed her tote, locked the doors, put the alarm on, and got the hell out. She'd call Kevin from her car. Poor guy. He probably hated to hear from her.

Carlos and Ruben had been glad to hand the dogs over to Lenny in exchange for the wooden crates. At least there was no barking, peeing, or pooping. When they arrived at Tina's, she was in a good mood. They hadn't seen her so happy in ages.

"Hey boys, I made us lunch," she announced. Lunch consisted of bologna sandwiches on white bread, potato chips, and beer. While they ate their lunch, Tina smoking in addition to eating, she told them her good news.

"I am so excited about what's going to happen. Do you remember my cousin Shonalee? Actually, you probably don't. You weren't around when she was here last. Well, her husband died recently. I think he was her third, maybe fourth, I can't remember. Anyway, all her husbands had money. She's been to Florida many times and loves it, so she's moving here from Kentucky. And guess what? We're all going to be working with her." With that announcement, Tina cracked open another beer and beamed at Ruben and Carlos.

"What do you mean, working with her?" asked a dubious Carlos.

"I have to tell you; this gal is a real businesswoman. First, she's an astrologer, how cool is that? And she's going to buy a big house that will have to be in an area zoned so she can do business in it."

"I still don't see what this has to do with us," said Ruben.

Tina ground out her cigarette stub. "Let me finish. She'll not only be running her astrology business, but also have comfort dogs to sell and CBD treats that she's going to make for dogs. With my help, of course. And you two are going to train the comfort dogs."

"Train the dogs! We don't know anything about training dogs. No way," Carlos exclaimed, starting to pace around the small messy kitchen.

"Why don't you let us make the CBD treats instead?" Ruben asked.

Tina shook her head. "I know what you're thinking. You don't make the treats with stuff you get high from, so get that idea out of your head. Plus, my recipe is a secret."

"Does she know how to do all this stuff? Seems like a lot of different kinds of things will be happening at that house," commented Carlos.

"She's a super smart gal. This is going to be a great experience for all of us. You'll be staying here for a couple of months while you get the dogs trained. You can't stay at Buck's forever, and that wouldn't be a good place to do the training. You should get along fine in the guest room."

"Doesn't the guest room have bunk beds? I'm not sleeping on the top one. I don't think I could get up the ladder," Ruben groused, opening another beer.

Carlos halted his pacing hands on his hips. "Don't expect me to sleep on the top one. I had enough of that as a kid. And I don't think those beds would fit us, especially you, Ruben. Tina, this isn't going to work. We have no idea how to train dogs, and we can't sleep in your guest room."

"Stop this whining, you buttheads. If you think you can find a cushier job somewhere else, hit the road. You'll have to walk, though, because the van is mine. It's your choice. Make up your mind, I've got work to do." Tina stomped out of the kitchen, slamming the back door behind her.

"Shit, now what?" Carlos asked Ruben "She's come up with some crazy ideas before, but this is the worst. What do you   think?".

Ruben took a swig of beer and looked around the kitchen as if hoping to see the answer on the wall. "Hell, I don't know. She's right about the job. It has been pretty good, and the pay isn't too bad. I really liked staying at that house in town, except for finding the body and the rest of that stuff."

Carlos glared at Ruben. "Keep your mouth shut about that. Don't *ever* mention anything about it. You never know who's listening. Back to our current problem. Let's think about it. Sleeping in the guest room in the bunk beds is out. As for training dogs, I don't even know what she wants them to do. Jump through hoops or what. I think we should tell her we'll do the job if she can find us a better place to sleep, and she'll have to show us exactly how we're supposed to train them. I'd rather be in town, but I guess I can put up with staying   out   here   for   a   while."

Ruben finished his beer, wiped his hand across his mouth, and threw the empty can into an almost full large plastic tub. "Guess we better go find her. She won't be in a good mood, that's for sure."

Chapter 7

Shonalee Benson drove into Tina's yard and parked her new red Cadillac convertible. She surveyed the outside of the house and the grounds, wrinkling her nose at the sights and smells. Only knowing she didn't have to live here and that the place would benefit her new business made it bearable. She flipped back her long, straight blonde hair and strutted up the rickety steps to the back door of the house.

"I'm here, Tina," she yelled as she opened the door and sashayed in. She stopped short when she saw two unsavory-looking men sitting in the kitchen. One fat and bald and the other skinny, with slicked back, black hair.

"Where's Tina, and who are you?"

Tina entered the kitchen and engulfed Shonalee in a tight hug. "I'm so glad you're here. You look great. The surgery obviously went well." She glanced over at two men to see if they were staring at Shonalee and her low-cut white tank top, which provided an ample view of her new breasts. Also, the short skirt and high red heels made Shonalee second-glance worthy.

"Shonalee, I'd like you to meet these two guys. They work for me and will also be working for you. This here, is Ruben."

Ruben stuck out his fat, sweaty hand, which Shonalee reluctantly accepted with the tips of her fingers.

"And this is Carlos."

Carlos did the same, without making eye contact, stammering, "Pleased to meetcha."

"Okay, guys, you can go and get the barn cleaned up. It looks like a mess. Shonalee and I have business to discuss." Tina waved her hand toward the door for the men to leave.

Tina was happy with the way things were progressing. After Shonalee left she'd called Carlos and Ruben back in the house. The guys agreed that if she could squeeze twin beds in the guest room they would sleep there. She explained to them that the comfort dog work would consist of making sure the dogs were trained to pee and poop outside, not crotch sniff, and not bite. How hard could that be?

Now that Shonalee had arrived, they started discussing how they would be involved in her business activities. Plus, Tina had another business plan in mind. But it was going to take a little research and a fair amount of planning. She'd talk it over with Lenny the next time she saw him.

Scottie tried unsuccessfully to reach Kevin. After leaving a message on his phone to call her as soon as possible, she decided to go to Piper's. She needed to talk to someone who knew about most of the weird things that had been occurring. She saw no point in going to the police station. Chances were whoever had broken into her house didn't leave any fingerprints, and the police would admonish her about not making sure her alarm system was activated.

Driving into Piper's driveway, she observed Jack's car was also parked there. She hoped she wasn't interrupting anything. Piper and Jack had been an item for ages, but still lived in their own houses. But Piper smiled broadly when she opened the door and saw Scottie. Noticing her friend's solemn face, she gave her a quick hug. "All right, what happened now?" she asked. "Come on in and tell us about it. We just ordered a pizza, and I was about to make a strawberry salad. Jack, look who's here."

Jack got up from the kitchen chair he'd been sitting on and gave Scottie a hug. "It's great to see you. I understand you two have had some recent, shall I say, excitement in your lives?" He grinned and pulled out a chair for Scottie.

The kitchen chairs that Jack had designed were reminiscent of the clean modern style of Arne Jacobsen. Jack was an architect/designer and had injected some interesting and colorful contributions to Piper's house.

"Someone broke into my house," Scottie told them. "And listen to this. Someone put a pair of men's shoes behind my bedroom drape, so at first, I thought a guy was standing behind it. Sort of like you see in the movies. I almost had a heart attack when I saw them."

"Did you call the police?" asked Jack. "Could you tell if they took anything? Someone is obviously trying to scare you or worse. This could be a dangerous situation you've gotten yourself into."

"She's already been knocked down. I'm really getting worried about you," added Piper.

Scottie was glad she hadn't told her about the guy who apparently had cat allergies. No telling what he would have done. "I'm fine," she said. "I'm not going to let some weirdos scare me. I left a message for Kevin. He knows about what's been going on. It would take too long to explain everything if I just called the police station. Besides, nothing has really happened."

Piper knit her brows; her blue eyes full of concern. "I don't care what you say, this is all very strange and nasty. You're staying here tonight. And I don't want any arguing. Jack and I won't take no for an answer."

"But—"started Scottie.

"No ifs, ands, or buts. It's a done deal. When Kevin calls, he can do whatever needs to be done at your house. He knows how to get into your house, right?"

Scottie sighed. "Yes, he does. Jack, how do you put up with this pushy broad?"

Jack gave a little smile and winked at Piper. "It's tough, but she's my girl."

Chapter 8

Lenny was back in Venice, to pick up the dogs and deliver the crates to Carlos and Ruben. After that he conferred with his business partners, Tony, and Pete. The meeting occurred in the same restaurant where they always met. The Coffee Cafe was a favorite among the locals. It was noted for a variety of coffees, and the selling of several different newspapers. The smell of freshly baked bread and pastries always permeated the air. Lenny got there early so he could get the table in the back of the room which provided more privacy. After Tony and Pete arrived, they began planning the motorcycle rally at Tina's. The same special group of bikers and their friends as they'd had in the past would be invited.

The partners set a date that would give them enough time to have sufficient inventory of their products to sell to their buddies. Cyclists who always came to the rallies would be more than happy to line up some bands to provide the music.

Tina would get the food and beer again. They were sure she'd overcharged them significantly the last few times, but there really wasn't another good option. Lenny told his partners that Tina would be having some comfort dogs trained shortly, which could also be sold for big dollars. Some would be sold from her cousin Shonalee's shop when she got it going, and Lenny would take some to Miami. It was great cover. The pet store there was doing a bang-up business in addition to the dogs Lenny sold himself.

As the meeting wound down, Lenny asked, "Is there something that's been going on here that I should know about? I get the feeling that you guys are keeping something from me." He narrowed his dark eyes as he stared intensely from one partner to the other. The silence was palpable.

Finally, Tony cleared his throat and said, "Okay, it's like this. You remember the guy we met awhile back who started working with us? Called himself Phil Thomson?" Not waiting for a response, he went on, "We thought he was working out quite well. He really knew the business. I know you didn't see him that often."

"I think I only saw him at one of the rallies and a couple of times here in town when we all met. What about him? Where is he now?"

"It turned out he wasn't what he seemed to be. So, he had a little accident."

"What the hell did you do?" Lenny hissed quietly between his teeth. "If you've messed up everything . . ."

"No, we just did what we had to do. He was a Fed. We found out when the three of us were walking to this restaurant and a couple who knew him just happened to also be coming here. They greeted him like a long-lost pal and the husband said, 'What are you doing here, Mr. Federal Agent? On vacation?' Phil pretended he didn't know the couple, but we both knew then he had to be a Fed."

"Holy crow," said Lenny.

"Yeah, we realized when we thought about everything, that we hadn't caught the little things. Like how he just happened to run into us here and asked to join us at our table. Sure, the place was packed, and we had room at our table, but then he started asking us if we knew where he could buy certain things. It all fits. We didn't have any choice when we discovered who he really was. We dumped the 'item' in the yard of the empty house you said belonged to a couple Tina knows. Remember, you had even considered renting it to store some of your stuff? That way it wouldn't all be at Tina's."

Pete continued the story, his voice low. "We just backed the car in the driveway and quickly put 'it' in the yard. We didn't see anyone. Since it's a corner lot with a big side yard and lots of bushes preventing a view from the street, it was a great place. After, we parked across the street to watch the house to make sure no one was there. All of a sudden, a woman comes out of the bushes with this dog. She looked like she was going to scream or something, but she saw our car, pulled out her phone, and took off like a bat out of hell. So, we left. We both got a good look at her."

Lenny glowered at his partners. "And you couldn't bother to tell me this before? I can't believe it. We're screwed. Did the woman see you?" His voice continued to get louder.

At that moment the waitress came over with the coffee pot, asking if they wanted a refill. They all responded with a quick "No."

Pete said, "Quiet down. We don't need to tell everyone in town our business. I don't think she knows anything about us. Hell, the car windows are tinted, and we weren't there long. We followed her and got her home address. We think she's a dog walker, with nine lives like a cat. Every time I make a move on her, something happens."

Tony shifted in his seat and said, "But one piece of good news. We went to get the 'you know what' later in the day and it was gone. We don't have a clue as to who took it or why. There's been nothing in the paper or on TV. So maybe we're in the clear. I don't know if we should just forget about this woman or not. We've probably rattled her cage enough so maybe she won't do or say anything."

Lenny shook his head in disgust. "She might not, but I can't believe the government will just forget about him.

We'd better think this through carefully before we take any other action."

_____

Tina sat on her front porch in a dusty wicker rocking chair, smoking, and drinking a beer. She barely noticed the tired look of the porch itself, the missing areas of gray paint on the floor and peeling white paint on the railings. Tina was musing about her various business ventures. Because of the dogs it was too noisy to sit outside on the deck in the back of the house. You couldn't hear yourself think. Still, she really was quite a businesswoman, she thought. She had the dog business, the deal with Lenny renting the storage buildings and holding the motorcycle rallies on her property, plus going into business with Shonalee.

It was a good thing she'd inherited the big chunk of land. One day she planned to sell it to some greedy builder. She was getting sick of the dogs always barking and whining. Never did like them that much. And now Lenny had the nerve to say she needed to have more dogs for him. Tina told him about her new plan to get more, and he was a little skeptical. Said they needed a trial run. But some day, after her property was sold, Lenny could find some other place for hiding and selling his stuff.

As for Rueben and Carlos, they could fend for themselves. Just a couple of idiots anyway. She'd move into town, get a snazzy car, and fancy house, and just help Shonalee, or maybe move in with her, assuming she didn't have another husband by then. Feeling quite pleased with herself, Tina ground out the cigarette on the floor of the porch and kicked the butt into the grass. Ruben and Carlos needed to hear about the new plan. They probably wouldn't be   happy   about   it.

Chapter 9

Scottie found out from Kevin when he returned her call that the intruder had jimmied the side door of the garage to enter the house. As she suspected, the alarm hadn't been set, or it would have gone off. No fingerprints were found. Scottie breathed a sigh of relief when Kevin told her he locked up the house, and said he'd get the door repaired the next day. He took the shoes that were behind the drape. They both agreed the shoes probably would be of little use in finding the culprit. Written on the piece of white paper tucked in one of the shoes was "Mind your own business or else." Scottie decided to take Piper up on her offer to spend the night at her house after Kevin told her he didn't think she should spend the night in her own home.

Scottie, Piper, and Jack chatted late into the night. When Scottie got up in the morning and looked at the clock on the nightstand next to the bed, she couldn't believe the time. She'd slept soundly until 9:30 am! She quickly took off the night shirt Piper had loaned her, got dressed, and went into the kitchen. Both Piper and Jack were gone. A note on the kitchen table said she should make coffee and eat whatever she could find.

Scottie shook her head. Canceling an appointment or showing up late to see a new client would not be good. She hurried home, took a quick shower, filled an insulated cup with coffee, grabbed a breakfast bar, and then drove off to meet her new client. She was glad the woman lived in the neighborhood.

The woman who answered the door smiled broadly, her hazel eyes twinkling. She wore an ankle-length purple dress with raglan sleeves and a long string of pearls. Her gray hair was pulled back with a purple ribbon.

"I'm Candace Tyler, but most people call me Candy. And you must be Scottie. Come in and meet my little one." As if on cue, a barking white bichon wearing a blue plaid scarf scampered up to Scottie and gave her a lick on the ankle.

"I think he approves of you. His name is Buster. He's been such a comfort since my husband passed away. I broke my ankle a while back and I haven't been able to walk long distances ever since. I know he needs more exercise. Our mutual friend Bonita recommended hiring you to take him for walks. Come and sit down. How about a cup of coffee or a soda?"

"I'll have a Diet Coke if you have one," Scottie replied as she sat down on one of the stuffed chairs. She'd left her coffee in the car. Buster jumped on her lap, gave her a quick lick on the face, and sat down.

"Buster, maybe Scottie doesn't want you on her lap," said Candy as she went off to get the drinks.

"Oh, I don't mind. I like getting to know my little friends. He's very handsome." Scottie looked around the comfortable living room. The furniture was a pleasant mix of antique and contemporary. A large colorful landscape painting hung over the white sofa. A purple throw covered the sofa, no doubt to accommodate dirty little paws. A triptych of black and white photos hung on another wall, views of a younger Candy and an attractive man on a sailboat.

"Okay, Buster, time to get off Scottie's lap. And I have a treat for you." Hearing the magic 't' word, Buster, tail wagging, jumped down and sat alertly in front of Candy.

After she'd set down the tray with the drinks on the coffee table, she fished out a small doggie treat from the folds of her caftan. Buster flopped down on his stomach and received his treat, which was gone in a gulp.

Candy smiled at Scottie and said, "Tell me about yourself. Have you always lived in Florida? And how did you get into the doggie business? It has to be challenging at times."

"It's true, sometimes it can be. But I've always liked animals, and I lost my own dog. It was devastating, so rather than get another dog I decided I'd care for other people's pets. I used to live in northern Florida, but I just couldn't stay there." Scottie's face turned pale, and she gazed away, remembering what had happened.

"Oh, Scottie, I didn't mean to upset you. You don't need to talk about it if you don't want to."

Seeing the sincere, kind look on Candy's face, Scottie decided to tell her why she'd moved. It had been so long since she'd spoken to anyone about it.

"It was a couple of years ago. My sister Liz was visiting me at the time. I was living in northern Florida with my dog, Mindy. It was quite windy outside, and there was the threat of a hurricane south of us. I was fixing dinner, so Liz said she would take Mindy for a short walk before the weather got any worse. My good friend Blake was also going to join us for dinner. When I glanced out the window, the sky was dark and nasty-looking; the wind was already playing havoc with the palm trees, bending them sideways. It hadn't started raining yet."

Scottie stopped talking and took a sip of her soda. She wondered why she was telling Candy about Liz and Mindy.

Candy nodded her understanding. "I can tell this is difficult to talk about, but sometimes it's better than gunny sacking it. You know, keeping those thoughts to yourself. Somehow just talking about it can often help. What happened to them?"

Scottie set her Coke down, twisted her hands, and took a deep breath. "The table was set, the dinner was ready, the wind was getting stronger, and it had started to rain. Liz had said they would be gone just a little while, so it seemed like they should have been back, especially since it was raining. A short time later Blake showed up. He was soaking wet, and I could tell from his face something was wrong. Behind him stood a policeman. Blake had found Liz and Mindy when he was driving on the way to my house. A huge frond from a king palm tree had fallen on them. Liz apparently was killed immediately when the force of the frond hit her. Mindy died shortly after."

"Oh, Scottie, I'm so sorry, said Candy. "I can see why you left."

"The hurricane eventually made its way to the Panhandle," Scottie said with a sigh. "My house suffered minor damage, at least compared to others. So many were completely destroyed. After I got the house repaired, I put it up for sale. I was fortunate that it sold quickly. The art gallery I had been managing was demolished. Blake understood that I just couldn't continue living there. So, I moved south. We had dated for three years before I moved and then took turns visiting each other for the past two years. It wasn't easy. As a matter of fact, we just recently decided that the long-distance romance wasn't working. Boy, I'm being a real motor-mouth. Thanks for listening to me. Now tell me about you and Buster."

At the sound of his name, Buster, who had been quietly lying on the floor with his nose between his paws, got up and hopped onto Scottie.

Candy shook her head and chuckled. "You certainly have a new friend. Just push him off if you don't want him there. He can be rather annoying sometimes, but I love him anyway. Buster has been my best buddy since Marty passed away. That was five years ago. Marty and I were avid sailors." She gestured to photos on the wall. "We'd often be gone for months at a time, sailing around the Caribbean. Close friends and relatives would spend their vacations here, renting our house while we were gone. Sometimes they'd go sailing with us. It worked out beautifully. I think life is kind of like a wind chime; sometimes it's active and noisy and other times it's quiet and still. And I think some of both is the best. After Marty was gone life was too quiet for a while." Buster jumped off Scottie's lap and went to sit beside Candy.

"I can certainly see how he'd be good company," smiled Scottie

"Buster and I have quite a few friends, both because I'm living here all year long now and we both enjoy people and dogs. Cats not so much. Also, I've joined a church and a couple of organizations. Listen, I didn't mean to keep you. I'm sure you've got things to do. If you're willing to take Buster on as a client, I'd really appreciate it."

They discussed times when Scottie could walk Buster and what fees would be charged. Most importantly, Scottie and Candy both knew they'd just made a good friend.

Tina had phoned Lenny about her new dog idea. He hadn't thought much of it. He felt it was too risky, not profitable enough, and the people involved not competent enough. Tina felt otherwise. After all, it was her idea, her business, and she was going to do it. He was just jealous he didn't think of it.

She listened through the kitchen window. Carlos and Ruben were both outside trying to train two labradoodle/who-knows-what puppies to be comfort dogs. Both puppies happily ran around sniffing and barking, totally oblivious to any commands made by Ruben and Carlos.

"At least we got one of the requirements down," Ruben said.

"We do? And which one would that be?" asked Carlos.

"They both know how to do their business outside," replied Ruben.

Carlos looked over at him to see if he was serious. He was. "Has it occurred to you that they've only ever been outside? You have no idea what they'd do inside a house. I wish Tina hadn't added making the dogs learn to sit. They sure don't want to do that. And we need to give them names, so they'll come when they're called."

"Then, I'm going to train the black and white one. And I'm going to call him Killer," Ruben said.

"You sure you want to do that?" Carlos asked. "For one thing, it's a female, and I'm not sure Tina would like the name."

"I knew that. Just kidding," Ruben said.

"R-i-g-h-t," drawled Carlos as he ran after the tan and white puppy. "Come here you little . . ."

Tina looked out the window and shook her head. *They're hopeless idiots*, she thought, *both the men and the dogs*. She wondered if she should even add the new sideline to the business, but it might be worth a try. She waddled over to the kitchen door and yanked it open. Seeing the door open, the puppies ran to get in the house. "Oh no you don't, you little demons. Guys, get these critters and put them in their crates and then come in. I've got something to tell you."

After some scrambling, the guys managed to corral the wiggling puppies into their crates, which they put in the pole barn.

Tina had the three of them sit around the kitchen table, which was a mess. Two overflowing ash- trays, an empty coffee cup, several empty beer bottles, and a large open pizza box pretty much covered it. There were a couple of cold pieces of pizza slices left over from the night before. Tina caught Ruben eyeing the pizza.

"Go ahead help yourself," she told him. "I was just going to give it to the dogs. Listen, I wanted to ask how the training is going with the comfort dogs? I know you just started, but do you think you could have them ready to go in a couple of weeks? Shonalee has her house almost ready, so she could take them. I'd like to make some money as soon as possible."

"Jeez, we haven't even named them yet," Carlos complained. "A couple of weeks sounds kinda soon. What do you think, Ruben?"

Ruben with his mouth full of pizza, mumbled, "I donno."

Tina gave them both the stink eye. "Well, they'd better be ready. Actually, I have another little plan I want to try. You're going to have to squeeze this project in between your dog training and delivering dogs to Lenny. This will take place in town. Before you say anything, I'm telling you I don't want any whining or complaining. Got that?"

"How can we complain when we don't even know what you want us to do?" whined Ruben.

"This is the plan." Tina paused to make sure she had their attention. "The two of you will take the van to town and drive to fancy housing areas, where there are always people walking dogs. After you deliver dogs for Lenny you could do this."

"But lots of them are gated housing areas. How are we supposed to get in?" asked Carlos.

"They're not all gated. The house you were living in was a super neighborhood that was ungated. Let me tell you what you're going to do," continued Tina.

"So, do we have to go back there? What if someone recognizes us? I don't think it's a good idea. I mean, what about the woman who broke into the house? She saw me." Ruben's expression grew more worried with each question.

"Jeez Louise, if you two don't shut up and let me finish . . .," said an exasperated Tina.

Carlos held up his hand. "Okay, okay we'll be quiet. But can we get a beer first?"

"Go ahead, and bring me one too. And not one more word or you two can pack your bags and get out of here. Understand?"

Ruben opened his mouth to say something but after a quick glance at Tina promptly closed it.

"As I started to say, you drive to a good neighborhood and look for someone walking a well-groomed, healthy-looking dog. Some of the dogs we have here aren't exactly in the best condition. When you spot a dog like that, one of you jumps out of the van, runs up behind the person walking the dog, shoves 'em down, snatches the dog, and scrams back into the van. A healthy, pedigreed dog is worth a lot more than those we have in the pole barn. I think we can get really good money with this plan. I call it the 'Shove, Snatch, and Scram' plan. Doesn't it sound great?"

No answer. The kitchen went totally quiet, except for Ruben sucking on his beer.

"So now you have nothing to say. What is it with you guys?" Tina said through the side of her mouth as she lit up a cigarette. "First I can't shut you up and now you clam up."

"You told us not to talk. So, we didn't," explained Ruben.

"Well, now you can. Isn't it a terrific plan? What do you think?" asked Tina.

Carlos pursed his lips. "Let me see if I've got this straight. We're driving down the street, we see someone with a dog that looks good, Ruben jumps out of the van, runs to the dog walker, pushes her over, grabs the dog, and races back to the van, and I hit the gas."

Ruben pushed his belly away from the table and went to get another beer. "I'm not a very fast runner. Why do I have to be the shover?"

"You're not the best driver," explained Carlos patiently. "I think I could handle that part better."

Tina considered Ruben, with his red sweaty face, rotund body, and the bright red, flowered shirt that was unbuttoned halfway down his hairless chest. No way Ruben could do it. He'd probably trip before he got to the sidewalk, and he'd never make it back to the van before he was caught. It'd have to be Carlos. He was skinny and quick.

"I think Ruben should drive the get-away van," she said. "Carlos, you're in good shape and can move fast. You'd be in the van like a flash."

Ruben smiled smugly at Carlos, "Go get 'em cowboy."

Carlos shook his head and rolled his eyes as if to say, "Why me?"

Chapter 10

This was the second time Scottie had walked Candy's dog Buster. He was a terrific walker, marching along right beside her with only the occasional stop to read some pee-mail. Scottie was deep in thought thinking about all her friends, old and new. She was glad Bonita had introduced her to Candy and Buster. Candy was perceptive and kind. You couldn't help but like her.

Bam! Suddenly she was on her hands and knees on the sidewalk, the leash yanked out of her hands and Buster picked up by a guy who ran down the street carrying him. "Stop!" yelled Scottie as she attempted to get up. A man who was walking toward her had seen it happen and ran after the dog snatcher and Buster. It didn't take long before he caught up to him, grabbed Buster, and before he could do or say anything, the culprit raced around the corner and was gone.

The rescuer returned to Scottie, who was now sitting on the curb, dolefully examining her bloody knees and palms. She perked up when Buster strode up next to her and attempted to lick her knee. She gave him a hug and said, "Oh, sweetie, I'm so glad you're back. I don't know what Candy would do without you. Why would anyone try to steal you? I know you're super handsome, but . . ." Scottie then realized she hadn't thanked the stranger who'd recused Buster and was standing next to her.

"Are you all right miss?"

She gratefully accepted the hand he offered to help her up from the curb. Then she took a good look at her helper. A good-looking guy, tall, slim, dark eyes, salt-and-pepper thick hair. *He can come to my rescue anytime*, she thought.

"Thank you so much for helping us," she said. "Buster's owner would have been so upset if he'd been stolen. I really appreciate it."

"Boy, I'm a mess," she added. "I should have worn long pants today instead of shorts. I've got to get him home."

She felt a trickle of blood was running down one leg from her knee, and the other one was beginning to bleed. Her palms were also bloody, especially the right one.

"Let me drive you. My car is right over there. You've got to get some bandages on those knees. My name is Charlie Marshall. I was in the neighborhood, visiting my dad's friend who is not doing well. I'm a semi-retired medical doc. I have a few friends at the Urgent Care center."

"Thanks, but I don't want to get blood all over your car. I just can't believe this happened. Why would anyone try to nab Buster?" Getting into a car with a stranger. How stupid can a person be? Walking at least two and a half blocks with blood running down her legs wasn't a good idea either. Her rescuer looked okay, but then a lot of killers do. Oh, what the hell.

"There are a lot of strange people out there. You never know," said Charlie "Come on, let's go. Also, I've got a clean gym towel in the car you can put on your legs. Don't worry about the car. We'll get Buster home, and then you're going to the Urgent Care facility."

The three of them got into Charlie's car and drove to Candy's house. Buster was happy to get home, as if sensing that he'd just avoided something bad. Candy was shocked when she saw Scottie. "My word, what happened to you. Did you trip? Did you get tangled up in his leash?"

Scottie held the towel to her knees, not wanting any blood to wind up on Candy's expensive rug. "Candy, this is

Charlie. He saved us. Some guy pushed me down from behind and grabbed Buster. He was fast, but Charlie was faster. He raced after the creep and saved Buster."

"I saw him push . . . hey, I don't even know your name," Charlie said to Scottie.

"I'm sorry. Guess I'm a little out of it. My name is Scottie Shelton, and this is Candy Tyler. She'll probably never let me take Buster out again after this episode."

Buster sat looking at the three of them, wagging his tail occasionally when his name was mentioned.

"Don't be silly, of course I will," Candy said. "The important thing is to get those knees cleaned. I do have a few medical supplies here. We can get them taken care of right away. It looks like your hands need a little work too."

"Thanks, Candy, but I told Scottie that I would take her to Urgent Care," Charlie said. "The seashells that were mixed in cement on the sidewalk really cut up her knees. They'll get them cleaned up there. But thanks."

Scottie was feeling guilty and angry about what had happened. She planned to ask Charlie if he could remember any info about the dog snatcher that would help catch him. Bent over, still holding the towel on her right knee, she said to Candy, "I apologize that Buster didn't get his entire walk in today. At least he got a short walk."

"Don't worry about him. We'll play fetch later with his favorite ball. He'll be fine." She worriedly glanced at Scottie and then Charlie. "So, you two just met? Are you sure you don't want me to fix those knees?"

"Charlie is a semi-retired doctor, and he knows some people at the clinic, so it's okay," Scottie explained.

Charlie smiled. "Really, she's safe with me."

"I just don't want anything to happen to my new friend. Scottie, give me a call when it's convenient. I want to know how you are. It was nice meeting you, Charlie. Buster and I both thank you for your help."

"Well, that went great," Ruben grumbled facetiously. "All you had to do was snatch the dog and jump into the van. How hard is that? What are you going to tell Tina?"

Carlos was hot and sweaty. He'd worn all black clothes, including a black wide-brimmed hat pulled low on his forehead. He hadn't planned to have to run down the street and also around the corner of the block. "Listen, birdbrain, you're the one who drove around the corner. I barely had a chance to get in the van. You weren't supposed to do that. And I couldn't help if some guy comes up and grabs the dog back. Why'd you want to come to this neighborhood, anyway? Somebody could have recognized us. And we're not telling Tina anything about this, you hear?"

Ruben hesitated a moment before he spoke. "It's like this. The bimbo that saw the dead guy in the yard and then was in the house must walk her dog around here. I thought if I saw her, that dog would be the one for us to get. She deserves to lose her dog. And guess what? She was the one I saw. How lucky was that? It was a different dog, but it looked good. I will say you did a good job of shoving her down, at least from what I could tell. Too bad you couldn't hang onto the pooch."

Carlos threw the black hat back in the van and ran his fingers through his hair. "You are really starting to piss me off. First of all, she probably recognized you, and if that's not bad enough she'll be telling the cops if she hasn't already. Now we have to find another dog, and what about the guy who took it from me? He could probably ID me. This is a total—"

"Oh, get over it. We'll find another dog. They'll never find us." Ruben drove several blocks to another area of attractive houses. Just then they both saw a small blond-headed boy walking a dog of pitbull/labrador heritage.

"Aha, this'll be a snap," said Ruben.

"I don't know. I think a smaller dog would be better. Just keep driving."

"Nah," said Ruben, slowing down the van so they were almost side by side with the boy. "Get your butt out there and nab it."

Carlos gave him a rude finger sign and jumped out of the van. He ran over to the boy and shoved him aside. Immediately the tan and black dog started growling and baring its teeth. It stood protectively near the little boy, who'd started to cry.

Seeing the situation could quickly turn ugly, Carlos wisely ran the short way up the street and hurriedly clambered into the van.

"I told you we should only go for small dogs. Jeez, I could have been eaten alive. That dog is a killer. You should have seen its face. I swear, the teeth were longer than most dogs that size. They were enormous! And the eyes were flashing red. If you want a big dog, you go get it. I think we'd better get back to the farm. Tina is going to have a cow when she sees no new dog today."

"I guess so. We'll just tell her we didn't see any worth picking up."

Chapter 11

Charlie drove Scottie home after she'd been taken care of at the clinic. She invited him into her house and made them both cups of coffee, which they took out to the lanai. They sat in comfy wicker chairs, Scottie with her feet up on the foot stool.

"You've got a great view here," Charlie said, admiring the slow movement of the water in the pond and the soft rustle of the palm fronds. "Very peaceful."

"It's where I sit whenever I need some time to relax and just think good thoughts," said Scottie. "But lately there have been so many strange things happening . . ."

"What's been going on, if you don't mind my asking? Today was certainly strange. Someone trying to steal a dog like that."

Scottie studied Charlie. He seemed to be easygoing and calm. And trustworthy. He had known several of the people working at the clinic, like he said he did. And they appeared to like him. That was just what she needed right now. She decided here was another new friend. And who knew what might develop?

"Can you stay awhile, or are you in a hurry?" she asked. "Because it may take some time to tell you the whole crazy story. And believe me, I'm not making it up."

"I have nothing else to do. I'd really like to hear about what's happened. How about I get us another cup of coffee? You just sit there and rest. Your knees will thank you for it."

While sipping their second cup of coffee, she told him about finding the dead man in the yard and all the other weird things that had occurred.

Charlie's eyes widened as he listened to her. "Wow, something strange is definitely going on. Have you been to the cops? This is sounding really dangerous. What're you going to do?"

"My nephew, Kevin, who is a police detective, knows about most of it. The problem is evidence. There really hasn't been anything of significance. Maybe if I could figure out how the events are tied together . . . if I made a diagram of the times, people I saw, what they did, etcetera, it would help. You know, like they do on television. I've got to get this figured out. It all started when I saw the dead man."

"I still think the police should be more involved, but if you're going to work alone on this, I'd like to help—although I'm not sure how much good I'll be. Your idea of a chart or diagram makes sense. You're thinking like a detective."

Scottie smiled. "Thanks, I'd love some help."

"Great! You got it." Charlie stood up. "But right now, I think you should just rest. Fortunately, we were drinking decaf. How about I pick you up later and we go to dinner? After that we can think about putting together some sort of chart."

They decided on a time for Charlie to pick her up and where they would go for dinner. Scottie's knees were feeling stiff and achy, so a short rest sounded good. She gave Candy a quick call to let her know Charlie had brought her home safely and he'd just left. She could hardly believe he was interested in helping. It felt wonderful having a man around again. *Don't get ahead of yourself girl,* she thought. *You just met him. For all you know he's married or has some kinky quirks.*

———————————

Ruben skidded the van to a screeching halt next to the pole barn in Tina's yard. They waited in the van for the dust to settle.

Carlos *glared* at Ruben as he climbed out of the van. "Jeez, do you think you can drive any faster? I thought you were going to drive through the barn."

"Oh, shut up," mumbled Ruben.

The men had been bickering all the way back from town. Not having grabbed even one dog to give Tina wasn't going to go well. First, they'd agreed they were going to tell her it was just too difficult and the few dogs they did see didn't look that great. But then they decided, after much arguing, they'd say they simply didn't see any dogs.

They went into the kitchen, ready for Tina to throw a temper tantrum. But no Tina. "Tina, you here?" yelled Ruben. No answer. Just as they were about to go outside, she walked in. Both men gaped at her. Her normally bright red hair was now coal black as were her eyebrows.

"How do you like it? Pretty cool, hey? I decided I needed a different look," Tina explained. She twirled around the kitchen so her newly colored tresses would float out about her shoulders.

"Well, you certainly got it." snickered Carlos. Tina's eyes narrowed. "What I mean is, it looks really good on you," Carlos lied. Ruben wisely kept his mouth shut. He just grabbed a beer out of the fridge.

"Okay, you two. Show me what you got," demanded Tina, starting for the door.

Ruben took a swig of beer and sat down. "It's like this, Tina. We just didn't see any dogs."

She turned back and sat down. "What do you mean, you didn't see any dogs? How dumb do you think I am? There must be a bazillion dogs in town."

"What he means is we didn't see any really special dogs," chimed in Carlos, seeing that their explanation wasn't going to work. "They didn't look any different than the dogs here."

"I am really disappointed in you two. Can't even handle a simple chore like that. You'll be glad to hear I have another exciting plan that even you two should be able to handle. That's in addition to getting dogs to Lenny and training the comfort dogs."

"We're pretty busy already, Tina. I'm not sure we can handle more work," Ruben groused.

"Then I guess I'll have to lower your salary and get someone else for this project."

"Tell us about your new plan, Tina. Don't listen to Ruben. I'm sure we can handle it." said Carlos, not wanting a cut in pay.

"You know what an avid reader I am. I came across this article about dogs in China being dyed to look like pandas. There was a picture, and they looked really cute. Shonalee said she'd be glad to sell them in her store. What do you think? I'll see if I can find the article later. It's around here somewhere."

Carlos eyed the stacks of old tabloids around the kitchen. "That would be really helpful, especially seeing a picture."

"Do we start with all white dogs or all black dogs? asked Ruben. "Because I don't think there are any like that in the barn."

"This is where you'll have to use your creativity," Tina explained. "I mean, look at me. I change my hair color frequently and I've had several different businesses, which I won't go into. It should be a piece of cake for you to do this."

"We'll have to get some dyes and stuff. Do you have any more of your black hair dye? What do we do about the parts that need to be white?" Carlos asked.

"Carlos, like I said, this where you have to be creative. I do have some dye left, but not enough. You'll have to buy some when you go to town to deliver the comfort dogs to Shonalee. Think of what stuff you're going to need, and I'll give you some money to buy them."

Carlos looked over at Ruben, who appeared to be just gazing out of the window, totally ignoring the conversation. "My comfort dog isn't quite ready for prime time. Maybe Ruben's dog is."

"Ruben is your dog ready to go to Shonalee?" asked Tina.

"Kinda," replied Ruben.

"What does that mean? Either it is or it isn't," said Tina.

"I'd say it's 82% ready," Ruben said, making up a number.

Tina shook her head in exasperation. "I'll give you another week, and you'd better be done with them. Shonalee has a couple of customers already interested in them." With that Tina did a shooing motion with her hands, indicating she wanted the guys out of the house. "Don't forget to check out the dogs in the barn to see which ones would make good pandas," she yelled as they left.

"Oh brother, she gets the craziest ideas," grumbled Carlos as they started walking to the pole barn.

"I think making dogs look like pandas sounds easier than training the dogs. The dog I'm trying to train just isn't getting it. Maybe I'll just tell Tina it's all trained. She'd probably never find out."

"I wouldn't count on that. She gave us another week to train them. We'd better get at it. But before we take the comfort mutts out, let's see what dogs we can turn into pandas."

They looked into all the crates. There was only one dog they felt would actually qualify. It was a mixed breed of unknown heritage. The fact it was mostly white was good. The long, floppy ears, not so good, nor the fact it was skinny and short-haired. Ruben pointed out a couple of other dogs that might work, even though they were not just black or white.

"They'll take a lot of dye," Carlos said. "By the way, is there a white dye, or will we have to use paint?"

"How the hell would I know? We'll have to ask Tina. We can put together the list of stuff we'll need later. I want to finish training my yapper now."

They got the comfort-puppies-to-be out of their cages and put leashes on them.

"What did you name your dog? asked Ruben.

"Waldo," replied Carlos.

"That's a stupid name. My dog's name is Wilma."

"How'd you come up with that ridiculous name?"

"She kinda reminds me of my aunt Wilma."

"Whatever. Funny we both picked names that start with W. The people who buy them will probably change the names anyway."

They spent the rest of the morning trying to get the puppies to sit and to come when their names were called, without much success. However, the dogs were amazingly successful in peeing and pooping outside.

After a lunch of leftover cold chicken wings, Cheetos, and beer, the guys asked Tina for some paper and a pen so they could list the supplies they'd need to make the dogs look like pandas. Somehow it was hard to believe people would want to buy a dog that looked like a panda. Then again, it takes all kinds.

Chapter 12

Scottie was having difficulty deciding what to wear. It would have to be something that didn't rub on her banged-up knees. She finally decided on a long green skirt with a pale-yellow top. Looking at herself in the mirror, she decided she didn't look too bad. With the soft fabric of the skirt covering her knees, they shouldn't hurt too much, and they wouldn't show.

At the sound of the doorbell, Scottie hurried to open the front door. Charlie, looked at her appreciatively. "You look terrific."

"Thanks. Come on in. I'm almost ready. I just need to get my purse and my hat," Scottie said, feeling a rosy blush rise on her cheeks.

They drove to Pop's Sunset Grill on the intracoastal waterway and sat outside, enjoying the view.

"I just love watching the boats sailing along and the wakes they create. It's so peaceful most of the time. Still, there're always one or two sailors who feel the need to speed," Scottie added as she watched a speeding boat almost upend a kayaker.

"I agree. There's something relaxing about it. I guess that's why we love having easy access to the water."

Scottie adjusted her hat to keep the setting sun away from her face and asked, "Where do you live, Charlie? Tell me about yourself. I really don't know much about you."

"There's not all that much to tell. My wife passed away about three years ago. I have one son, Mark, who is currently living in Germany. He works for an international company and winds up living in different locations around the world. He's divorced. His wife didn't care for the vagabond life, having to move frequently, so she basically just spent most of the time in this country. Needless to say, absence didn't make the heart grow fonder. They didn't have any children. Mark's a great guy. We get to see each other several times a year. Wish it were more often but that's just the way it is."

"I'm sorry to hear about your wife. It's tough. And I know so many people who've lost their spouse. Trying to appreciate and enjoy every day becomes a priority. And now suddenly my life has become so . . . I don't know what to say, unsettled."

"It certainly seems that way. But between the two of us, Scottie, we'll solve what's happening, with the help of the police if need be."

"Back to you, Charlie. Have you lived in Florida long?"

"About twenty years. Always on the Gulf Coast side. Same area, several different houses. I downsized after Angie died. Our house was way too big for one person. I found a house on Siesta Key that's fairly new and just the right size. I really like the location, although because of traffic, it can sometimes take a while to get anywhere."

"Is your house on the gulf or intracoastal side?" Scottie asked.

"It's on the intracoastal side. The only negative about the house is the stairs. It's built up, with the garage below. The stairs don't bother me now, but someday they probably will. How about you? You've told me about the current happenings, but what about before?"

Just then the waitress brought their grouper dinners and glasses of wine. Between bites and sips, Scottie gave Charlie an abbreviated history of her life. She had Charlie laughing at some of the situations she'd experienced. She didn't want to spoil their date with a discussion about the current mysterious happenings they were going to chart.

After a lengthy dinner Charlie drove Scottie home, and they parted at the front door after agreeing see each other the following evening. Scottie suggested dinner at her house, to which Charlie readily agreed. As Scottie closed the door her phone began to ring. It was Piper, wanting to know how the date had gone. Scottie had previously told her about how she'd met Charlie and that they were going out to dinner.

"Is he still there? Is he staying the night?" Piper asked in a hushed tone.

"No and no," Scottie replied. "We had a great time, but that's it. No kissing or anything else. However, we are going to see each other tomorrow night."

"Well, that sounds promising. When do I get to meet him? Maybe the four of us could get together somewhere."

"Not yet. It's just too soon. We're having dinner here at my house tomorrow night. We'll see how that goes."

"You're cooking! Are you sure you want to do that? Cooking isn't exactly your forte. Maybe you can order something and have it delivered. Or I could come over and pretend to be your live-in chef. I could make my famous chicken cordon bleu and cheesy potatoes and—"

Scottie interrupted, chuckling, "No way. I know you're an excellent cook, but I'm going to put something together. Don't ask me what. It'll be a surprise even to me. If he can stand my cooking, I think that will be a real test of a possible relationship. I promise to keep you posted on how it goes."

When they hung up, Scottie got her computer and started looking up recipes. This could be a real challenge. Maybe takeout wasn't such a bad idea after all.

———————————

Bonita's doorbell chimed, and Missy started barking. When Bonita opened the door, Missy stopped barking and sat down. Standing outside the door were two men in dark suits and white dress shirts.

"Sorry, I already belong to a church," Bonita told them.

"No, ma'am. We're not here for religious reasons. We're with the FBI. I'm Agent Myers, and this is Agent Lowell. May we come in?"

Bonita nervously asked for some identification, and after briefly looking at it, invited them in. The three of them sat in the living room. Missy snuggled close to Bonita on the sofa, staring at the men, who had selected the two recliners.

"We understand there was a guy renting a house in this block. Unfortunately, he seems to be missing. We've been checking with your neighbors to see if anyone has seen or heard from him. He hasn't paid his rent, and all his personal belongings are still in the house. His name is Luca Martini. How well do you know him?" asked the older of the two agents.

"If this is the man, I think you're referring to, I only saw him once. It was at a neighborhood cocktail party at the Smiths. I think that was his name. There was also a new couple who just moved into the neighborhood. Everyone was there. Kind of a meet and greet deal. I don't think I spoke more than five words to him. He seemed nice, well dressed, pleasant. There was a big crowd, everyone mingling around, sipping drinks, and eating appetizers. Why aren't the local detectives working on the situation?"

"They are aware of this matter, and we are just assisting," explained Agent Lowell.

"Anything you might recall would certainly help. Maybe you'll run into him somewhere else or hear something. Here's my card," Agent Myers said as they both stood. They shook Bonita's hand, thanked her for her time and started for the door.

Just as they were about to leave, Bonita thought about Scottie and the man she'd seen when taking Missy for her walk. "Wait a minute, guys, I don't know if this is relevant or not, but I have a friend who thought she saw a dead man in a yard not too far from here. But the thing is, after she notified the police and they checked the yard, there was no one there. The whole thing was crazy. I sort of forgot about it because nothing was ever on the news or in the papers. Maybe my friend never did see a body. But she's really not a dingbat, and I've never known her to make up stories. She's really quite bright."

"I think it might be good if we could speak with her. Would you give us her name, phone number, and address?" Agent Lowell said.

"She may be hard to get a hold of. She takes care of pets—takes dogs for walks and things like that. Let me get the info."

After the men left Bonita called Scottie. She didn't answer, so Bonita left a message about the visitors she'd just had and for her to expect a call from them.

"Missy, I sure wish you could talk. You could have given those guys some scoop." Missy cocked her head, and her dark brown eyes appeared quizzical, as if to say, "I don't have the faintest idea what you're talking about, but it sounds interesting."

Chapter 13

Scottie had just driven into her garage when her phone rang. The caller identified himself as Agent Myers. She was glad Bonita had left her a message about the agents wanting to speak with her. Otherwise, she certainly wouldn't have believed an agent from the FBI would be calling her. Myers said they would be at her house later in the afternoon. Scottie hoped they wouldn't come too late or stay too long. She had a dinner to make. She hauled in the groceries she'd bought for dinner that night. One of the recipes she'd found online looked good, but sounded rather complicated and would need some prep time.

Scottie had asked Charlie to come about six. They could have drinks and appetizers first and then a leisurely dinner. After that maybe they could talk about the weirdness she'd been experiencing. She'd thought about buying a portable dry erase board on which to note the dates, times, and events. Unfortunately, she hadn't gotten around to it. Asking Charlie if he could remember anything about the dog thief would be important. She wondered why they hadn't talked about it before. But she figured she had been upset and had just met Charlie. He'd definitely been a distraction.

The agents didn't show up until close to six, after Scottie assumed they weren't coming. up. Just as she ushered them in, Charlie arrived.

"We have extra company, Charlie," she announced. To the agents, who'd sat down, "This is my friend Charlie Marshall. We're having dinner here tonight." Hopefully they'd get the hint and wouldn't stay long. "Charlie, these men are with the FBI. Bonita called and said they have some questions for me about a missing man. Is that correct? Agents, you'll have to introduce yourselves. Though she told me, I don't remember your names."

Agents Myers and Lowell introduced themselves and confirmed that they wanted to know about the man she had seen in the yard when she'd been walking Bonita's dog. Scottie gave a description of not only the dead man, but also the one who had accused her of doing the killing. She noticed the agents looked at each when she described the dead man.

She said she had notified the police and they determined there was no body. Scottie wondered what to say next. *Should I tell them about going in the house that was supposedly empty but wasn't? And that I clunked fatso on the head with a beer bottle? Maybe I'm going to be in big trouble, like Piper said. And I certainly can't tell them Piper was with me. She'd have a heart attack if she was contacted by the FBI.*

Scottie was quiet for so long, Agent Lowell asked, "Are you okay? Did you remember something else about that day?"

"Just a minute; I have to put the dinner in the oven. I have some appetizers ready. Would you like some? I know you don't drink on the job, but I have sodas and other things." Straightening her long periwinkle sundress, she went to the kitchen area, and put the Italian meat pie in the preheated oven, and got the cheese and shrimp out of the refrigerator. The crackers were already in a basket. Suddenly there was a movement behind her. It was Agent Myers.

"Ms. Shelton, we really don't want anything to eat or drink. We'd just like you to tell us what else you know. Come back and sit down."

"Well, since I have appetizers here, I might as well put them out. Charlie, would you like a drink?" In addition to the appetizers, she also put plates and napkins on the coffee table.

Charlie, sensing there was something she really didn't want to talk about, said gently, "No, I'll have a drink later. I think you should just sit down and let the agents do their job."

Realizing that she'd stalled as long as she could, and that lying to the FBI was definitely a no-no, Scottie sighed, sat down, and then stood up. "I need a drink of water first."

Agent Lowell rolled his eyes.

"After I was told there was no corpse and no one was living in the house at the time, I went back to confirm this with a friend," Scottie announced.

Now the tricky part. She hadn't even told Charlie about going into the house. Everything but that. Time to put on her big girl panties and tell everything. *Oh boy.*

Scottie shakily made a point of saying the doors were unlocked when she entered the house, and her friend never went into the house. She went on to tell them about what a mess the house was—the dog crates, beer bottles, and dirty dishes.

Seeing the rather shocked look on Charlie's face, Scottie took a drink of water and continued, about the men coming into the house, and her hitting one of them with a beer bottle.

Agent Myers, grim-faced, said, "This is very curious. Both the local police department and the FBI have examined the house and did not see any dog crates or the other items you mentioned. I do agree with you it wasn't exactly clean. By the way, what is your friend's name? Was it you?" he asked, looking at Charlie.

Charlie shook his head. "No, and this is the first time I've heard about Scottie going into the house." Scottie glanced at him guiltily. Charlie went on to say, "She did tell me about seeing the man in the yard and several things that have occurred since that time. Scottie, you have to tell the agents the rest."

"What about fingerprints in the house?" Scottie asked. "Any useful information there? That fat guy is probably on one of your lists?"

"There were a lot of prints in the house, but no one with any record, at least not so far. So, what did Charlie mean when he said you should tell us the rest?"

Scottie looked at Charlie. *Poor guy, he must be wondering what he's gotten himself into.* "Charlie, help yourself to the snacks. And you can get a glass of wine if you want." She took a piece of cheese and put it on a cracker. "Come on, guys, you might as well have some too. This may take a while." They both said "No thanks" in unison.

Partway through telling the agents about everything, Agent Lowell sniffed the air and exclaimed, "I think something's burning."

"Oh, my God," Scottie yelled as she ran to the kitchen. "The dinner!"

She yanked open the oven door. "I think the air is going to get even bluer. It's totally ruined." Cursing under her breath she waved away wisps of smoke coming from the blackened pie. She slammed the oven door shut, turned off the stove, and dejectedly walked back to the men.

This was all she needed. Charlie was not only going to think she was the break-and-enter type, but she couldn't cook a dinner. And to top it off, the FBI was on her case.

The three men watched Scottie as she slouched down in her chair and closed her eyes.

"Ms. Shelton are you all right?" asked Agent Myers. The men waited for Scottie to respond.

Finally, she opened her eyes and sat up straight. "I'm fine, I guess. It's just these past few weeks have been so unreal. And I haven't even told you about the other things. Excuse me, but I have to open the door to the lanai. The burnt dinner smell is getting to me." She started to get up when Charlie said he'd open the slider.

Agent Lowell put his notebook and pen into his pocket and both men stood. "Ms. Shelton, we have another appointment, and you obviously need to make other dinner plans. Are you and Mr. Marshall available tomorrow morning? Also, your friend who was with you. We'd like to hear the rest of your story."

"This is not a story; I'm not making anything up," Scottie said indignantly. "And I don't know if my friend is available tomorrow. If she is, I'll see if she'll join us. She's always super busy."

"If she can come here, that would work. Otherwise, she can come to our office in Tampa. We'll be here at nine tomorrow morning. Thank you for your time today. I hope you have a better day tomorrow, Ms. Shelton."

The agents, standing straight in their dark suits, sternly shook hands with Scottie and Charlie and left.

Scottie gazed woefully at Charlie. "Oh Charlie, I'm so sorry about all this. I'll understand if you want to leave. They said they were were going to come earlier in the afternoon, and I thought they would be long gone before you got here. Now dinner is ruined, and I didn't tell you about going into the house. It's because I didn't want you to think badly of me and—"

"Hey, it's okay," interrupted Charlie as he took Scottie's hand. "It's not the end of the world. Why don't we take the appetizers and wine outside? We can go out for dinner later." Chuckling, he shook his head as he picked up the cheese and crackers and carried them out to the lanai.

As they sat on the love seat, sipping wine and munching on the appetizers, Charlie shook his head at Scottie's solemn face. "You're obviously really worried. Is it because you went into that house? I don't think it's that big a deal."

"I don't know. They didn't say anything about it. But I also hit the guy with a beer bottle. Maybe they could get me for assault. And Piper is going to have a fit when I ask her to come here tomorrow. She's going to say 'I told you so.' Thanks for staying, Charlie, I really appreciate it." Scottie gave him a weak smile, and he put his arm around her.

"Well, I must say things have been pretty exciting since I met you. And I've loved every minute. We'll see what happens tomorrow."

Chapter 14

Shonalee had constantly been asking Tina when the comfort dogs would be ready. Tina was sick of it. It was time Ruben and Carlos delivered the dogs to her whether they were trained or not. She'd sent her cute pictures of the labradoodle mix puppies, hoping that that their good looks would suffice.

She called to Ruben and Carlos, who were giving the dogs their food and water. "Hey guys, come on in the house. I got something to tell you. It's too damn noisy out there."

Immediately when they came inside, Ruben went to get a beer.

Tina scowled at him. "I'm sure glad you buy your own beer. By the way, it's only ten in the morning."

Ruben wiped a dribble of beer off his chin. "I've been working hard; I deserve it."

Tina rolled her eyes, then said, "Shonalee has been on my case about those puppies you've been training. She wants them like yesterday. She's got some buyers who're really interested in them. They got excited when she showed them the pictures I sent her. It's time you take the dogs to her. I know they're not totally trained, but it shouldn't matter that much."

Carlos didn't say anything. As Ruben went to the refrigerator to get another beer, he gave a little chuckle and said, "You're right they're not totally trained."

"Whaddya mean by that?" asked Tina suspiciously.

Carlos gave Ruben the stink eye. "He means they could still use some work, but I think Shonalee will be happy with them."

"Well, she better be. I'm going to tell her you'll be bringing them this afternoon. How dirty are they?"

"They might need a little wipe up," said Carlos.

"See that they look good before you take them. I don't want to hear from her about dirty dogs. Got that?"

Both men nodded.

"I'm going down the road to see Gretchen. Her daughter is there with her new baby. I shouldn't be gone too long."

"Is this the same daughter you told us had an ugly, fat baby? She got mad when you called it a Michelin baby because of all the rolls." Ruben laughed. "Maybe this one will be just as ugly."

"I never said that to her," exclaimed Tina. "And this is her other daughter."

"You did so say that. I remember—"

"I'm going outside," said Carlos, leaving them to their petty arguing.

After lunch Ruben had been filling dog bowls with water from a hose outside the barn when his phone began chirping. He walked away while speaking on the phone, totally ignoring the hose, which was pouring out water on the sandy soil.

The two puppies he was supposed to put in the van were playing outside. When they noticed the lovely mud puddle being made by the water running from the hose, they immediately went for it. By the time Ruben noticed them splashing in the puddle, they were a mess. Muddy water was dripping off both of them. "Get out of there right now," Ruben screamed, his face getting beet red. They both stopped playing and stood still. Then they ran over to him and gave the proverbial wet dog shake, mud flying generously over Ruben. "Shit, now you got mud all over me." Fuming, he roughly grabbed them and threw them in their crates.

"Carlos, where are you? You've got to come and help. These monsters are driving me crazy," yelled Ruben. No answer. "Where the hell are you?" Figuring Carlos must have gone in the house, Ruben waddled in to see.

Carlos was sitting at the kitchen table, making the list of supplies for creating the panda dogs. He looked up when Ruben entered and laughed.

"What have you been doing? Painting yourself with mud? I don't think Tina would want you dripping mud in the house."

"Oh, shut up. If you'd been out there watching those no good—"

Carlos interrupted, "And if you'd helped me make this stupid list before you went out; you'd better change your clothes before Tina gets back. Where are the dogs?"

"They're in their frigging crates and a frigging mess. I was hollering for you to come and help. We can't take them to Shonalee the way they are. We're going to have to hose 'em down or something."

Exasperated, Carlos tore the sheet with the list off the notepad and shoved it in his shirt pocket. "So now the crates are dirty too. You really know how screw things up. You'll have to wash out the crates too."

"What do you mean, me? You're going to have to help. One of those dogs is yours. You trained him. I'm going out to get my dog cleaned up. You can do whatever you want with yours."

Ruben hoisted up his muddy pants and left the house. He brought the crate with the puppy in it over to the hose and proceeded to spray both the dog and the crate together. Uncomfortable and scared, the puppy started whining. Unfortunately for Ruben, Tina drove into the yard at that time. Seeing what Ruben was doing, she clambered out of her truck and gave him a swift punch on his shoulder.

Startled, he turned to see who'd hit him. As he did so, he wound up hosing down Tina.

"You stupid son of a b . . . What the hell do you think you're doing?" she sputtered, wiping the water dripping from her face on her sleeve. You got me all wet, and that isn't the way you wash a dog. Why are they so dirty anyway? No, don't tell me. I don't want to know. And you're filthy. Those dogs just better get properly washed and dried now. And that goes for you too. Like I told you, Shonalee wants them this afternoon."

"You didn't have to hit me," Ruben said defensively. "It's not my fault you got wet. I didn't even know you were there."

Narrowing her eyes, Tina hissed, "Don't even go there."

Chapter 15

The FBI agents showed up at Scottie's house right on time the next morning. Charlie had come about a half hour earlier and had coffee with her. She was feeling more like her upbeat self. It was a beautiful sunny day; Charlie hadn't given up on her; and hopefully Piper would come as she'd promised. It hadn't been easy to convince her it was really important and she wasn't in any trouble. The fact she would finally get to meet Charlie was the clincher.

"Is your friend going to join us?" asked Agent Lowell, checking his watch. It was 9:15. "We don't want to start before she gets here."

Just then Piper breezily strolled in, sporting a bright pink jumpsuit. She hadn't bothered with the doorbell. "Hi, everyone, sorry I'm late. You know how the traffic can be. So, tell me what's happening."

"Actually, we were waiting for you," Scottie said. She made introductions all around, noticing how Piper thoroughly checked out Charlie.

Agent Myers nodded to Piper. "I understand you went with Ms. Shelton into the—"

"No, no, I just went into the lanai," Piper nervously explained. "Scottie did go into the house, but it wasn't locked. She didn't break in. She just wanted to look around. After seeing a body in the yard, you know, and then it disappeared. How crazy is that?".

"What did you see and hear when you were in the lanai?" asked Agent Lowell.

"I just got a peek at a thin guy in the kitchen. I was hiding behind the storage box. He had dark hair. I didn't get a good look at his face. He was looking for dog leashes. In the pantry. Totally bizarre. I heard two men, but I just saw the one. Apparently, they wanted to get all the dog paraphernalia and their personal stuff out of the house. I didn't stick around to find out anymore. I went to the police station for help. This whole episode was really scary, and I wound up ruining a very expensive pair of new shoes."

"Ms. Shelton, do you have anything more to add to this?" asked Agent Lowell.

"I've told you what I remember about the house and the body, but there are a few other things that have happened to me I'd like to tell you about." Scottie went on to describe the other strange incidents she experienced. "Who was the dead guy anyway?"

Ignoring her question, Agent Lowell looked at Charlie and asked, "What was it you observed?"

"I saw a man push Scottie and grab the dog she was walking. I ran after the guy and got the dog back. He was thin, the man I mean, and totally dressed in black, including his hat, which was pulled way down on his face. He ran around the corner and was gone. I think I heard a vehicle speed away, but I guess I was more concerned about Scottie and how badly she was hurt. I took the dog back to her, and here we are." Charlie smiled at Scottie.

"So, I see," said Piper, grinning at the two of them.

"Did either of you happen to see the make of the vehicle that may have been involved?" asked Agent Lowell.

"I did see a dark-colored van drive by, and then a gray Cadillac sedan came after that. But I couldn't tell you if either one was used in this dognapping," replied Charlie.

"And for all I know he may have had a car parked anywhere around there that he could just jump in and drive off," Scottie added.

Piper looked at both agents, tossed back her long, wavy blonde hair, and stood up. "Listen, guys I'm concerned for my friend here. There are definitely some bad characters who are after her. I'm afraid she'll really get hurt one of these days. What are you going to do about it? This can't continue."

"I agree," Charlie said. "And I have a feeling it has something to do with the guy she found in the yard."

Scottie was amused watching Piper go into her diva mode. She'd thought Piper might be totally intimidated being questioned by FBI men. But if she had been, she'd obviously gotten over it. Scottie thought how wonderful it was to have friends who cared about her. She knew they'd be around to help if any other nastiness occurred.

The agents wanted assurances that they would be kept informed if other episodes occurred like the ones Scottie had experienced. She asked them as they were leaving when they would let her know about the case. They gave a rather noncommittal answer and left.

Piper moved from the sofa to the recliner that Agent Myers had been sitting in. "That was an interesting visit, and they were certainly a cheery couple."

"I think it would be strange if they were laughing and joking around," Scottie said. "I assume everything they're working on is pretty serious."

"By the way, how was dinner last night?" asked Piper, changing the subject and smiling at Charlie.

Scottie frowned and opened her mouth to explain about the burned food, when Charlie spoke up. "We had a great dinner. Everything was delicious." He neglected to mention they had gone out to the local Italian restaurant.

"Really. Glad to hear it," Piper said in a shocked voice. "Listen, I have to take off. It was nice meeting you, Charlie.

I'll make plans for the four of us to get together. Scottie, behave yourself. No more adventures. See you soon." With a flourish she was out the door.

"She's a whirlwind." Charlie chuckled. "Is she always like that?"

"Oh yeah, that's Piper. She's a great friend though. She'd do anything for you. Thanks for not telling her about dinner last night. I'm not sure she believed you, but we did have a good dinner. Just not the one I made. I'm blaming those FBI guys for the ruined meal, although I do have to confess a lot of cooking doesn't get done in this house. Living by myself I haven't seen the need for it. I'll try making dinner for us another time if you think you're up to it."

"Definitely, and I'm sure it'll be delicious."

Scottie grinned. "For now, I'm going to make us lunch. I know I make great sandwiches and salads. And I'm hoping there are no more strange goings-on. But we wouldn't have met if it weren't for Buster being nabbed."

"Right, something positive did happen. So, do you still want to make your chart or graph?"

"How about we talk about it after lunch? I keep thinking there are facts I'm missing. Going through it all will help. Those creeps don't know what they're in for. I wish the FBI guys had shared what they have on the case. But I knew that wouldn't happen. I wonder if Kevin has been in the loop. Maybe I should ask him what he's heard. I do know he has other cases he's working on."

"You certainly can mention that you had a visit from the FBI and see what he says. He may not know anything, other than the aspects than involve you. Also, anything he does know may be confidential."

Scottie looked coyly at Charlie and chuckled. "I guess you're right. But maybe I can get it out of him anyway. He loves his auntie. We'll see. Let's go make lunch."

———————————————

While Tina was at home planning for the motorcycle rally, Carlos and Ruben drove the two puppies to Shonalee.

"I still don't think they look that clean," Carlos said, looking in the back of the van at the dogs in their crates. "And they're not fully dry yet."

"She wanted them today, so she's getting them today. Just the way they are," said Ruben, picking up speed.

When they arrived at Shonalee's boutique, the two potential buyers were sitting out on the lanai waiting to see the puppies. One customer wanted a male and the other wanted a female, so Shonalee was ecstatic. She and Tina would be selling their first comfort dogs for a nice profit.

The guys took the crates with the puppies out of the van. Carlos regarded the anxious puppies. "Maybe we should let them pee before we take them in the house. You know how excited they get when they see people. Although, other than us and Tina, they haven't seen anybody else."

"Oh, they'll be fine. They went before we left the farm."

"If you say so. I have my doubts."

"We're going to leave right away, as soon they're in the house. They'll be Shonalee's problem."

"They'd better not be a problem, or we'll have both Shonalee and Tina on our necks," said Carlos.

"Shonalee can be on my neck anytime," Ruben said, snickering. Carlos rolled his eyes.

Holding the squirming puppies, the two men hurried to the front door. Carlos rang the doorbell, which was promptly answered by Shonalee. She looked stunning, wearing a gauzy white top, green patterned leggings, and five-inch-high heels.

In a whisper Shonalee said, "Oh, my God, they were supposed to be really clean. They look like they need a good bath. They are cute, but now my clients might not want to buy them. I'm not sure you should leave —"

Ruben pushed his way into the hallway, setting his puppy down. "They'll be fine. Your buyers will love them."

Carlos followed behind him and put his puppy down also. Waldo was off in a flash, racing into what Shonalee called the Pet Boutique. Wilma followed behind him.

As Carlos started for the door he said, "We're going to take off now. Good luck with the puppies. By the way, we named them Wilma and Waldo. But you can change the names." He didn't want to stick around to see what would happen with the dogs on the loose.

"Have to do some shopping for Tina before we go back to the farm. Good to see you again, Shonalee." Ruben gave her one more leering look.

The 90's ranch house Shonalee bought had previously contained a good size hair/nail salon attached to it. The set up was perfect for her purposes. There were two rooms. One led into the next. The first she turned into the Pet Boutique, and the other room she used for her astrology readings. The astrology room opened onto the lanai, which she could also use. The Pet Boutique carried a variety of dog items for sale: leashes, water and food bowls, soft fuzzy beds, dog crates, cute doggie clothes, and soon-to-be-on-sale the yummy special treats.

Shonalee and Tina had been trying to make their own marijuana dog treats, which currently they weren't pleased with. Tina had several plants behind the barn they incorporated into the recipe. They thought it would be cheaper than buying a commercial product. Tina dried the leaves and crushed them as much as possible. However, the dogs they had tested the treats on promptly went to sleep. They concluded the next batch shouldn't contain as much pot. Currently a shelving unit stood empty where the treats would be displayed. The shelves temporarily held cute photos of different breeds of dogs in attractive frames that were for sale. To celebrate the grand opening of the Pet Boutique, Shonalee had decorated with balloons and streamers, making the room look festive.

The puppies gave a quick perusal of the boutique, then noticed that beyond the astrology room, the sliding door to the lanai was open and people were sitting there. Totally excited, Waldo ran to them barking. Three clients, a middle-aged couple and a young woman, were sitting on comfy chairs around a firepit. The couple had been having marital difficulties, and the husband thought having a comfort dog might help. The wife was totally skeptical. For her part, the young woman was going through a patch of trying to "find herself" and felt a comfort dog would aid in the quest.

Waldo promptly ran to the husband and began sniffing his crotch. The husband pushed him away, and his wife just laughed. Her laughter immediately stopped when Waldo walked over to where she was sitting, lifted his leg, and peed into her open leather tote bag, which was sitting on the floor. The papers that were sticking out of the tote were dripping wet.

"That dirty beast just destroyed my bag and everything in it," she wailed, grabbing the bag. "I told you this was a stupid idea. You never listen. I'm out of here." She stormed past Shonalee, who had entered the lanai, just in time to witness the disaster.

Waldo sat next to the husband, gazing up at him innocently. "You know, I really like this dog. Does he have a name?" he asked.

"It's Waldo," replied Shonalee. "It's just a temporary name. You can change it to whatever you want."

"Waldo, I like it." Hearing his name, Waldo jumped onto the husband's lap and began licking his face. "Waldo, you and I are going home together. I'm going to need to buy some supplies for him, Shonalee. What do you suggest?"

While Shonalee was getting together a hefty array of doggie items to sell to the husband, Wilma was cowering behind one of the chairs in the astrology room. The experience of being hosed down while in the crate had been traumatic for her. She had just done her "business" on the new carpeting behind the other chair. The "business" wasn't discovered until considerably later.

The young woman noticed Wilma had gone behind the chair, so she walked over to see her. Noticing how scared the puppy was, she carefully picked her up, and returned to the lanai, and sat down. Softly petting the dog and whispering to her seemed to have a calming effect. "You're the dog for me. We both need some loving. And you need a good bath," she said to the puppy. "I'm going to call you Serenity." With a satisfied smile she carried Serenity to the boutique to make the puppy hers.

Shonalee had filled two large bags with all the purchases the husband had picked out. The new halter and leash were on Waldo, who was leaping at the check-out counter. A new crate had been put in the car and the husband was paying the large bill. Shonalee had made a point of saying all sales were final. She visualized the wife having a fit seeing Waldo coming home with her husband. It was a good thing they'd come in separate cars, and she left before he did. Shonalee, feeling a little guilty, even asked him if his wife would be upset when she saw everything he'd bought, especially Waldo. Rather gleefully he said he didn't care. If she didn't like it, she knew what she could do. With that, he and Waldo happily left the shop.

"Serenity is coming home with me," the young woman announced, walking into the boutique cradling the puppy.

"Serenity, what a great name," gushed Shonalee. This day was going much better than she expected. "I'm sure the two of you will get along wonderfully. Do you need a leash for her or anything else?"

"No, I'm all set. My brother gave me all his dog's things when it passed away. All I need is Serenity."

When Shonalee called Tina to tell her what a successful day it had been, Tina was totally shocked that both dogs had been bought, although she didn't say that to Shonalee. She knew

Carlos and Ruben hadn't really done a good job training the dogs. Actually, she wasn't sure they were trained at all.

"Tina, when can I get the next comfort dogs? Even though the puppies weren't exactly clean, and I don't think particularly well behaved, my customers loved them. I had no idea how easy they would be to sell."

"Right now, I've got so many projects I'm working on I can't give you an answer," Tina replied. "I'm trying to get everything organized for the rally, you and I have to get doggie treats made, and then there are all the dogs to take care of, and . . ."

"Can't Ruben and Carlos do a lot of that?" asked Shonalee.

"I wasn't going to tell you until I was sure it would work, but Ruben and Carlos are going to make panda dogs."

"What are you talking about? Make panda dogs. I never heard of such a thing. It sounds ridiculous. Just how do you do that?"

"It's all done with paint or dye. You paint the dogs to look like pandas. They look adorable. They do it in China. I thought you could sell them in your shop."

"I don't know," Shonalee said doubtfully. "I'd have to see them first. Changing the subject, when is this rally? I've never been to one. I think I'd like to come."

"I don't know if they'd let you. I'd have to talk to the organizer. It's pretty much by invitation only. I'll let you know." The last thing she wanted was for Lenny and Shonalee to meet. That would be trouble with a capital T.

Chapter 16

Lenny called Tina to find out when the next batch of puppies would be ready to go to Miami. He told her he'd be bringing some supplies to the Puppy Farm, and he could take the puppies on his way back to the city. In reality he wanted to see if Tina was getting the preparations for the motorcycle rally done as promised. She couldn't always be relied on when it came to getting things done on time.

"I've got about four dogs ready to go. When would you be coming here to get them?" Tina asked. Since she hadn't accomplished much regarding the rally, she hoped it wasn't soon.

"I'm not sure yet. My calendar is pretty full. When I come, we can also discuss the rally. We have quite a list of attendees. Let's hope it's the best one yet. I'm sure you've been busting your butt getting stuff organized."

"Absolutely, you know me," lied Tina. "I even got a nipple ring to get ready for the rally. My boob is kind of sore, but it's really cool."

"Listen, I've got to go," said Lenny. He tried not to visualize Tina with a boob ring, which he was sure she'd want to show to everyone.

Two days later Shonalee was in Tina's kitchen. They were in the process of making a new supply of doggie treats, not as strong as the last batch. Tina had even given Ruben one, to see what would happen. Ruben thought it was delicious but didn't get particularly sleepy. Of course, he wasn't told it was a doggie treat or that the recipe was improved by using marijuana with THC instead of CBD.

While the two women were waiting for the last batch of treats to bake, Tina showed Shonalee her boobie ring. Shonalee tried her best not to appear totally shocked. She didn't even have a tattoo, much less a piercing. Her last couple of husbands were older and rather stodgy, so no tattoos or jewelry in unusual places, if you please. To Shonalee buying new boobs and showing an ample amount of cleavage was one thing, but a ring stuck through her nipple, no way.

"That has to hurt like hell," she said. "Why would you do that?"

"Oh, I did it for the rally. I wanted to do something different this year. That's why I dyed my hair black too."

"Wow, what did you do last year?"

"Just the complete body paint. Lots of girls do it. There's always a wonderful artist who will paint whatever you want."

"And it's your whole body? You're, nude? You'd have to be. I'm not sure I could do that."

"What are you? Some kinda prude? It doesn't matter, you won't be at the rally anyway," announced Tina.

"I didn't know you'd checked with the guy in charge. What did he say? Why can't I come?"

Before Tina had time to make up an answer, there was a knock on the kitchen door. It was Lenny!

Holy shit. I didn't expect him to be here today. This won't be good, thought Tina.

Chapter 17

Scottie and Charlie were putting together the facts about the people she'd encountered and the happenings since she saw the dead man in the yard. She was convinced the missing man must have been someone important since the FBI was involved. She asked her nephew Kevin what he knew. He was reluctant to talk about it, saying he had been questioned by the agents and provided them with the little information he had, but was given little in return.

Scottie had taped a large piece of white butcher paper across the sliding glass door to her lanai. On the table next to the slider, she'd put small a basket of felt-tipped colored pens.

"I'll do the writing on the paper," said Charlie.

"I don't think so. I've seen how doctors write."

"I can print. I'm pretty good at that."

"Okay, we'll give it a try, but I'm going to make some coffee for us first. Some stimulus might help me remember some itty-bitty details I didn't think of before."

They began by creating a timeline, starting with the date she saw the body and everyone she encountered that day. Scottie suggested that any strangers and their appearance should also be added with each date. Using the calendar on her phone and the small notebook where she kept additional client information, they began the project. She was glad to see Charlie was right about his printing. It was quite legible.

"Now that I think about it," Scottie said, her brow furrowed, "there was a black or blue colored car that pulled out from across the street. The windows were tinted really dark. I wonder if the driver had something to do with the body. Maybe it was the guy with the cat allergies. That guy is definitely a bad actor. Maybe he's behind all the mayhem. Or he or she could be a buddy of the two in the house. Of course, I'm just guessing."

"Should I note that on here?" asked Charlie as he pointed to the paper with his pen.

Scottie nodded. "What I can't figure out is why anyone would be harassing me. And somehow, I can't see the fat guy in the yard and the dark car having anything to do with each other. I'm not sure why I say that. We did find out fatso and his partner shouldn't have been living in the house. Apparently, they were some sort of squatters. Who knows where they're camped out now. Probably living uninvited in someone else's house. They could easily be the ones who killed that guy."

Scottie's phone rang. It was Harper, asking if she was available to come for lunch the following day. She wanted Scottie to see how her puppy was doing and how her condo looked after she'd finally gotten it organized.

"Let me check my calendar. Things have been pretty hectic lately," Scottie answered.

"That's what Aunt Bonita said. She mentioned her neighborhood was buzzing about the missing guy, and everyone being questioned. What the heck's going on? I remember you thought someone was following us on the way to the vet. Are you somehow involved in that?"

"I don't think so other than seeing the dead man when I was walking Missy and telling the police about him. The FBI did question me about it. Looking at my calendar, Harper, I'm totally booked tomorrow. Darn! But I do want to see your condo and that furry little guy of yours. May I take a rain check?"

Scottie wasn't about to tell Harper about her lunch plans with Charlie the next day. After walking Buster in the morning, she and Charlie planned to sail out of Sarasota Bay to have lunch on the Le Barge sightseeing boat. Scottie didn't know if Bonita had told Harper about her new friend Charlie, and she didn't want to talk about it right now.

Scottie and Charlie continued working on the timeline. "I'm so glad I have you to help me with this," Scottie told Charlie. "This is serious stuff, at least to me, but I have to say it's fun doing it with you."

"Well, that goes for me too," said Charlie as he kissed her lightly on the lips. "You are a most interesting woman. We'll have to see where this takes us."

Chapter 18

Lenny walked into Tina's kitchen and stopped dead in his tracks to stare at Shonalee, just as Tina had feared. And she stared at him. The electricity between them was palpable. Coincidently they were dressed alike, in skinny blue jeans and white T-shirts. However, Shonalee's T-shirt had a deep V neckline.

"Tina, you have to introduce me to this gorgeous woman. Why didn't you tell me about her?" asked Lenny, never taking his eyes off Shonalee.

"This is my cousin Shonalee. We're business partners. She just sold two comfort dogs from her shop that were trained here. And we're making dog treats right now.

Lenny, why don't we go outside and discuss our business," suggested Tina.

"Hey, Tina, you didn't introduce me to this gentleman. I'm not a potted plant," said Shonalee, pouting.

Tina was totally flustered. This was exactly what she did not want to happen. Shonalee was really like a babe in the woods. The men she had been married to had mostly been retired respectable businessmen. Lenny was a businessman, but you wouldn't necessarily call him respectable. He was a bad boy: charming when he wanted to be, the sultry, dangerous looking type, and at times ruthless.

Tina was sure Lenny would love to have Shonalee working with him in his various businesses. With her looks she would be a definite asset. Losing Shonalee as a partner wouldn't be good for Tina. She had visualized them making loads of money.

"This is Lenny. I do business with him too. Come on, Lenny, let's go. I have some things I want to show you." Tina started for the door. Lennie didn't budge. "Why don't we discuss the rally here in the house?"

Shonalee caught the reference immediately. "Are you in charge of the rally?" she asked prettily. "I'd really like to come to it, but Tina said it's by invitation only and she didn't think I could get invited."

Lenny put his arm around Shonalee's shoulder and said, "Sweetheart, you can come to any place, any time with me."

Tina glowered. "Shonalee, you keep an eye on those treats in the oven. They should be done in about fifteen minutes. Just put them on racks—"

"I know what to do," interrupted Shonalee. "I've done all this before." She turned her back on Tina and stomped over to the stove to look at the treats.

Lenny admiringly checked out Shonalee as she bent over to look in the oven window at the treats. "Shonalee, I'm glad we had a chance to meet," he said. "I'll be sure you get the info on the rally, and I know we'll have a rollicking good time." He gave her a kiss on the cheek when she stood up from the oven before Tina could steer him outside to discuss the rally, store the supplies he'd brought, and get the puppies crated that were going to Miami.

Ruben and Carlos were in the barn, trying to find the dogs each had previously picked out for the panda project. They had bought a variety of supplies that they planned to test: hair dye, acrylic paint, poster paint, spray paint, and brushes. The one grocery store they went to didn't have black and white food coloring.

"I don't see the dogs we were going to use anywhere," complained Ruben.

"No, I don't either."

"I bet they went to Miami or Tina took them to some other pet store."

"Guess we'll have to find a couple more. This isn't going to be easy."

After much debating they chose two mixed breeds. Both had some black and white coloring. The legs on one, however, were mostly tan. Carlos and Ruben left the puppies in their crates while they hauled out two well-worn wooden tables from the barn and set them up under a large live oak tree. The expansive shade it provided would make a more comfortable work environment than the poorly lit, noisy barn.

"I'm taking the bigger table because my pooch is bigger," Ruben declared. He'd chosen the

dog with the tan legs and a long, fluffy white tail.

"Whatever," replied Carlos, rummaging around in one of the sacks of supplies on the ground. He found the bottle of black dye and set it on his table. "We need something to put the supplies on. I'm not going to keep bending over to dig for what I need, and these tables aren't big enough. There's nothing in the barn that would work. At least nothing I can think of."

"I'll go look in the house. Maybe there's some sort of smaller table we can use."

Fifteen minutes later Ruben, huffing and puffing, was trying to haul out a rather large wooden chest. The polished walnut wood and brass hinges made it an attractive piece of furniture. The chest rested on four sturdy legs.

"You could come and help. This thing is heavy," he yelled.

After helping Ruben get the chest near the tables, Carlos, paused and shook his head. "I don't think Tina would want us to use that. Did Shonalee see you take it?"

"Nah, she was talking on the phone and messing with the dog treats."

"I still don't think we should use it."

"We can put some newspapers on the top. It'll be fine."

They spread a couple of newspaper pages on the top of the chest and then unloaded the supplies. Ruben claimed the black poster paint and a fat brush. "Do you think we need some rags to wipe the brushes with? You know, if you change paint color."

"Yah, I think so. Maybe some water too. You know, to wash the brushes off. Like when going from black to white."

"Why don't you go get that stuff. I got this," Ruben said, pointing to the chest.

"Which I had to help you carry. Guess I have to do most of the work around here."

Ruben just gave Carlos a finger gesture again. Carlos got some rags from the barn but didn't find a suitable container to wash the brushes in, so he went into the house. Shonalee had just cleaned up the kitchen and was getting ready to leave.

"I have to leave sooner than I was going to. Two clients called wanting me to do readings today. I hadn't planned on that. Tell Tina I took the treats to sell in the boutique, but I left some for her to try on the dogs in the barn, okay? Oh, and please tell Lenny I'm sorry I didn't get to say good-bye, but I'll see him at the rally. Maybe you could help me carry this to the car." She dumped a big bag of treats into Carlos's arms.

Walking Shonalee to her car, Carlos asked, "Do you know if Tina has a bowl or pot, you know, to wash brushes in? I couldn't find what I wanted in the barn."

"Sure, she's got all kinds of things in the bottom cabinet near the stove. Don't forget to put it back where you found it. I'm really looking forward to seeing those panda dogs. You guys must be so-o-o talented to do that sort of thing." Giving a little wave, she backed up the car and was gone in a cloud of dust.

Carlos looked in the cabinet Shonalee suggested and grabbed a large ceramic bowl decorated with flowers.

Ruben and Carlos finally organized all the supplies, and the puppies were on the tables, ready to be turned into pandas. Ruben's puppy was excited and tried to jump off the table a couple of times. Frustrated, Ruben yelled at him several times and the scared dog peed on the table. Ruben used the entire bowl of water to rinse off the table.

"You better go get the bowl filled. We're going to need that water," Carlos said. "You shouldn't have used it all."

"You're a real pain in the ass, you know that." Ruben shuffled off to fill the bowl from the hose outside the barn, leaving the puppy on the table. Fortunately, Carlos glanced over just in time to see the dog about to jump off. He grabbed the puppy, put his leash on, attached it to the table leg, and set him on the ground. He quickly turned back to his table to make sure his dog was still safely sitting there.

Ruben came back with the bowl of water and saw his dog on the ground. "Why the hell is he on the ground tied to the table leg?"

"He was about to jump off the table, you idiot."

"Would have served him right." Ruben opened the jar of poster paint and dipped in the brush. Putting the dog back on the table, he decided to start with the tan legs. That should be the easiest. He smeared a healthy amount of poster paint on the right back leg. Suddenly the puppy hunched his back and did a colossal poop. "Oh, shit!" Ruben, jumped back from the table, threw the brush as far as he could, then put the dog on the ground and stormed away. The puppy stood in the grass unsure of what to do. He looked back at his sticky back leg and decided this was the time to roll around on the ground. He managed to get paint in quite a lot of places on his body, as well as several oak leaves that stuck to the paint.

Carlos watched the puppy on the ground. What a mess! Not his problem. But now he felt a few drops of rain. He clipped the leashes onto both dogs and started to hightail it to the barn. The rain became torrential, and by the time they got to the barn all were drenched. The poster paint on Ruben's dog was dripping off, and Carlos's dog just looked strange with big circles of black dye painted around the eyes. Carlos gave both dogs a bowl of water and put them in their crates.

He briefly thought about the supplies sitting out in the rain and also Tina's walnut chest. "Let 'em sit there, what do I care," he mumbled to himself. "Ruben's not here to help. He's probably in the house drinking beer and watching TV, and here I am dripping wet." He sprinted to the house through the rain. The panda dog project had not gone well. "No surprise there."

Chapter 19

Lenny's other business partners, Pete and Tony, were getting more freaked out by the day. As far as they knew the body they'd left in the yard at the house had never been found, but they were sure the FBI was on the hunt. They kept telling each other "No news is good news," but figured it was only a matter of time before something, literally, showed up.

The dog-walking woman was the only one who'd seen the body, so she must have taken it, or she knew who did. Why else would they have seen her come out of the shrubs with the dog? After tossing around a variety of possible scenarios, they concluded grabbing her and making her tell them what she did with the body was necessary. Their plan had been to pick up the body later, when it was dark and permanently dispose of it. They'd only temporarily put it in the yard. Bodies didn't just disappear like that. At least not usually. And this body was one Pete and Tony wanted to make sure wouldn't be found. Finding out what happened to it was critical.

Having been involved in several nefarious activities in the past, kidnapping didn't seem like that big a deal to Pete and Tony. It was just a matter of when to do it and how. They thought they'd keep Lenny out of the loop. He'd go ballistic for sure if he knew about it. Since the rally was taking place in about a week, and they'd have to be there, grabbing her would have to take place after. That would give them time to do some planning. They knew where she lived, but her schedule taking care of dogs and cats didn't lend itself to being on a rigid timetable. From what Pete and Tony could tell, it was basically a daytime job. Although apparently, she did check on cats in the early evening sometime. Pete had followed her to the house where the cats had sent him into an allergic fit.

"She must be single," Pete said. "The times I've seen her there hasn't been anyone else around."

"We don't know that for sure. We really haven't seen her that often," countered Tony. "Her husband or boyfriend or whatever might go on business trips. And the time I was following her car there was a woman with her."

"That means we'll have to take turns watching the house at night to make sure she does live alone. We don't need to mess with her at home if there is some hulking dude living with her."

"We've got guns, if it comes to that. We'll get our questions answered one way or another and go from there."

"The problem is she's going to see our faces. She'll be able to identify us. And I'm not into wearing a mask. That's for bank robbers and people who don't want to get sick or are   sick."

"I think we'll need some sort of disguise. She's seen us before. Especially since you went to the cat house. What a meow that was." Tony chuckled.

"Not funny. I could have died. Having allergies is no fun."

"Maybe we should just snatch her when she's out walking a dog, or follow her car and when she gets out, do it then. Or what about if we both jump in her car when she stops? Put a gun to her head to scare her and make her drive somewhere."

"Then what? We question her, then kick her out of the car and we drive her car back to ours? I don't know if that makes any sense. You know, she might not have anything to do with the guy. Plus, wouldn't she need a partner? Do you think she could have moved the body by herself?" asked Tony.

"This whole thing is really starting to mess with my head. I know we didn't have any choice, but jeez, even my wife's been asking what's going on with me."

"You better shape up. I don't need a partner who can't stand a little heat," growled Tony menacingly.

After much discussion, they concluded that kidnapping her at home would be best. Maybe they could just do the questioning at the house and wouldn't even have to take her to some other location. But if her answers weren't satisfactory, well . . .

Chapter 20

Scottie and Missy went for their walk early in the morning. When Scottie brought Missy home, Bonita wanted her to stay and have a cup of coffee.

"I'd love to, but this is a super busy day for me. Still, we've got to get together and compare notes about the missing guy. How about later this week? Also, Harper wants us to see her puppy and her condo. She sounded really happy when she called."

"I know. She called me too. How about I check with her and see how her calendar looks and get back to you."

Charlie picked up Scottie at her home about midmorning.

"This should be a great day for sailing," Scottie said. "It's a little windy, but I don't think that should be a problem. I absolutely love getting out on the water. I've only been on this sightseeing cruise one other time, and it was a lot of fun. I hope you like it."

"Hey, if you're with me I know it'll be good."

Scottie was the one who suggested taking this boating trip. Charlie said he hadn't been on this particular boat before but was more than willing to give it a try. They'd been seeing each other just about every day since they met. She was concerned maybe they were seeing too much of each other but since each occasion was so enjoyable, she didn't mention it.

"This is my treat, Charlie. It was my suggestion. And you've paid for everything else we've done."

"But you made that fantastic dinner the other night. To me that was special."

"I'm glad you liked it. It definitely was better than the other one I made. Just thinking of it makes me cringe. I swear, the burnt casserole smell is still in the house." Scottie wrinkled her nose just thinking about it.

"You can't count the casserole episode. Having two FBI agents in your house is enough to make anyone a little distracted."

Scottie bought their tickets in the little gift shop at the marina, and they boarded the boat. Several other passengers were already on board and seated at tables.

"Would you like to sit downstairs or upstairs?" Scottie asked.

"From what I saw when we walked to the boat, the upstairs looked like it would give a great view. And there's a canopy over the top. How about we give it a try."

"It seems like the wind has picked up. Do you think it'll be okay to eat up there?" Scottie asked a little skeptically.

Charlie looked out the window. "Oh, it should be fine. There's a chop on the water, but it's not too bad. Let's get our food and go find a table upstairs."

They got in the short line to place their order. Scottie ordered a cheeseburger and fries. Charlie ordered a hamburger and fries. The cook explained drinks could be obtained either downstairs or upstairs. After getting their plates, they moved to the condiment station. Scottie neatly stacked her cheeseburger with a tomato slice and chopped lettuce. She covered the top half of the bun with a generous blob of mustard and doused the French fries with ketchup. Charlie did the same but also had a large portion of fried onions on his burger. They decided they'd get their drinks upstairs.

The boat was slowly moving out of the harbor. As Scottie and Charlie started up the stairs she remarked, "This boat is really starting to rock and roll. Could be an interesting lunch." By the time they got up the stairs the wind had picked up even more. Looking around for an empty table and seeing none, Charlie suggested, "Let's go to the bar in the front, get our drinks, and if a table hasn't been freed up by then we'll take our trays and go back downstairs. Somebody might decide it's too windy for them to stay here."

As they started to walk toward the bar, a sudden fierce gust blew and took the top half of Scottie's burger and whipped it across to the nearest table, where it landed mustard side down on a young man's white T-shirt. The top of Charlie's bun went over the side of the boat. Next went the chopped lettuce off of both their burgers. Then the tomatoes. Charlie's tomato came to rest on the top of a woman's sandal. At the same time all the ketchupy French fries flew off their plates, some coming to rest on other people's plates, some on other people. One woman screamed as she took a fry off her glasses.

The people sitting at the tables were having difficulties keeping their napkins, hats, and other loose items under control. Scottie glanced at Charlie and got the giggles. A few fried onions were stuck to his green polo shirt "I think we'd better forget the drinks and go back downstairs. It's pretty wild up here." Holding tightly to the railing and carrying their near-empty trays while being tossed from side to side, they made it down the stairs.

Reaching the first deck, they stood, looked at each other, then their plates, and burst out laughing. Both their plates contained only the bottom portion of the hamburger bun, the meat sitting forlornly on it and some ketchup smears.

"You know, Scottie, life is really an adventure with you. I'm having a great time. There's certainly never a dull moment. I wonder what will happen next."

Chapter 21

Tina and Lenny kept their motorcycles in Tina's barn. Tina's was a BMW and Lenny's a Soft Tail Harley. Lenny had brought his from Miami the week before, just for the rally. They drove over Tina's land where everything would be set up: the food and drink tents, body painting tent, the memorabilia tent, the port-a-potties, and an area where games would be played. In addition, they'd need to rope off a space where people could set up their own individual tents or park their motorhomes. Many of the attendees came for the day and went home at night. But others, who lived further away, would bring small tents, campers or motorhomes in addition to their bikes.

Attendees would enter the rally area on a separate dirt road leading to Tina's property. The entrance was barely noticeable from the county road, and that was the way Tina wanted it. During the rally a discrete wooden sign would be put up to remind everyone they had reached their destination.

Tina looked back in the direction of her house and said to Lenny, "Looks like we lucked out. I think it's raining hard back at the house. I hope those idiots are working on the project I gave them. Back to the rally. I've got the tents ordered. Ruben will get them the day before and see that they get set up. The port-a-potties will be brought in then too. The food will be delivered around eleven on Saturday morning, but we'll have the beer tent set up at eight. It'll be up to you to get your tent ready with whatever you're going to sell.

Anyone who comes Friday afternoon or evening is on their own. You brought the other adult beverages and put them in the one of the storage sheds, right? And I don't want to know about what else you're bringing."

Lenny grinned. "Hey, you're making marijuana treats for dogs. Don't go getting religious on me. You know what these rallies are like."

"Yeah, you're right. I did dye my hair and eyebrows black and got a nipple ring. I still think the pink and green hair I had last year was better. Oh well. About the products you sell . . . it's just that I don't want the law to come joining the party. That's always in the back of my mind."

"Stop worrying. You know everyone who comes to these keeps their mouth shut. So, they get a little crazy. Who's to know? And this a secluded area. There're always a few people who have trouble even finding this place. Do you think we've got enough room for the games? Maybe we should mark off more space just to be on the safe side. What'd you think?" Tina and Lennie walked around the area allotted for the games and the music. "I guess we could add a little more," said Tina. "Maybe push back the seating area. We don't want spectators getting run over by the bikes. If I recall, one of your bros almost did run over someone last year. Not good."

"It was close, but nothing really happened. Just a graze."

"By the way, I got the Bruisin' Biker Bitches Band to play on Saturday night."

"Great! I really like them."

Tina snorted. "You would. About all they wear is their guitars."

"Look who's talking. I remember what you *didn't* wear last year," retorted Lenny with a laugh. "I'll be here on Friday morning to make sure Ruben and Carlos are getting the tents and stuff organized. They're not exactly the most reliable pair."

"You're telling me. Are we done here? I wanna get back to the house and see what those butt heads have done. It looks like the rain stopped. Let's hope we have good weather next week. Are you bringing your motor home?"

"Nah, I don't think so. I'll stay in town."

"You sure you want to drive back and forth? Think about it."

"Will do. Let's go."

Back at the house, Lenny put the puppies he was taking to Miami in the van and took off. Tina didn't see Ruben and Carlos in the barn, so she went in the house. "I might have known you two would be slacking off. You must have gotten the panda dogs done, since you're in here drinking beer and watching TV."

The two men looked at each other and Carlos spoke up. "Well, it's like this. We were working hard, and everything was coming along okay, and then it started to rain. I mean really rain. So, we had to quit."

Ruben stayed quiet.

"What the hell does the rain have to do with it? Weren't you in the barn?" asked Tina.

"Actually, we set up under the oak tree. We thought working there would be better than in the barn. We figured you wouldn't want us to get any paint or dye on the floor. And how were we supposed to know it was going to rain?" said Ruben, a whine creeping into his voice.

"Oh, come on. Like you would be worried about getting paint on the floor of the barn. With all the crap that's on that floor. Gimme a break. I want to see these dogs you were working on." Tina regarded the guys suspiciously. "Let's go and show me what you did."

As they walked to the barn the excuses started.

"First of all, we couldn't find the dogs we had planned to use. You must have sent them to Miami."

"Yeah, and it took us a while to find new ones."

"And then we had to haul everything outside. That took a while."

"And the dogs were kinda nervous. Fortunately, since we're comfort dog trainers, we got them calmed down."

Tina rolled her eyes at that remark.

Carlos walked over to the two crates that held the panda-dogs-to-be. Tina peered into the crates. "Take them out. I want a good look at them."

Carlos opened the doors of both crates, and the puppies bounded out.

Ruben's dog still had residual amounts of black poster paint over much of its body from rolling around in the grass, especially the back leg. While the rain had washed some of the paint off, there was enough left to make the puppy look like a Rorschach ink test. Black dye circles surrounded the eyes of Carlos's dog like heavy-framed glasses.

Tina looked at the dogs and then the guys and thought, *I can't laugh. But those puppies are a hoot.* "Dammit, those dogs are a mess. What the hell did you do to them? Obviously, this simple project was too much for you. What kinda paint did you use?"

Carlos spoke up. "Ruben used poster paint and I used dye."

Still trying hard not to laugh Tina said, "Since panda dogs aren't in your future, I'll have to dock the cost of the supplies from your pay. Ruben, get the poster paint washed off that pup. What were you thinking, using poster paint? Never mind, just get it off. Carlos if you used dye it'll take some time to grow out. Maybe you could trim off some of the black. Just be careful of the eyes."

"Maybe you could use the paints and other stuff at the rally," Carlos suggested. "You know, for the body painting."

"Hmm, that's really not a bad idea. Somehow, we always seem to run out of body paint. Get the stuff together in a sack and bring it in the house. I'll add it to some of my other rally stuff, so I don't forget it."

"Then we don't have to pay for all those things then?" asked Carlos.

Sighing, Tina said sternly, "Not this time. But you'd better watch what you do. I don't want any more screw-ups." She gave them both "the look" and left.

———————————

"Boy, it's a good thing I spoke up about the body painting. At least we won't have money taken out of our checks," said a pleased Carlos.

"I was going to suggest that," Ruben countered.

"Sure, you were. You wouldn't even have noticed if it *did* come out of your check."

"We're going to have to haul those tables back into the barn," said Ruben. "Is the plastic sack still outside to put the paints in?"

"I doubt it. We'd need a new one anyway. All that crap has gotta be wet. Speaking of crap, you're going to have to clean off the table your dog shit on. And you'd better go find that brush you threw away. And you might as well get some dry rags while you're at it."

"What do you mean, 'while I'm at it'?"

"The rags outside will be wet, and we'll need some dry ones to wipe off the supplies and Tina's trunk or whatever it is. I think I know where I can get a sack."

"If we wait for a while the sun will dry everything off."

"Jeez, Ruben, this is not a big deal. You know, we didn't exactly finish making the panda dogs. If it hadn't been for the rain, my dog would have been a great panda, but I'm glad Tina gave up on that gig. We'd better get everything put away though, or she may change her mind about taking money out of our checks."

Ruben *glared* at Carlos and shuffled off to get the rags. Carlos couldn't find a sack, but did come across a cardboard box in which to put the paints, dyes, and brushes. When Ruben returned, he dried off the supplies and cleaned the table he'd used. There was a fair amount of black dye on the table. "Maybe I should have put some newspapers on the table. On the other hand, these tables were a mess to start with," he said. "Speaking of a mess, are you getting yours cleaned off?"

"Don't ask. It's good enough."

"I'm going to go find the damn brush I tossed."

It took Ruben a while to find the paintbrush. When he finally found it, he bent over and grabbed it. Unfortunately, the brush had landed in a fire ant hill. The leader of the ant family gave the signal and they all chomped down on Ruben's hand and wrist. "What the hell," screamed Ruben, throwing the paintbrush away again and trying to rub the ants off on his shorts. "I have to go to the house and get medicine on these bites. Those buggers really got me."

"Well, hurry up and get back out here. I need help with these tables. Here, take Tina's bowl in with you." Carlos handed over the bowl.

Ruben hustled his chunky body as fast as he could toward the house. He carried the big bowl in his left hand, still rubbing his ant-bitten right hand on his pants. In his haste to get to the house, he tripped on the stoop at the back door. The bowl flew out of his hand, landing with a crash on the cement.

Tina opened the door. Seeing Rueben's red, sweaty face and the remains of the bowl, she growled, "Now what have you done?"

"Tina, I'm in bad shape. Fire ants bit my hand and my wrist. I gotta put something on these bites. What do you have? This is really bad," moaned Rueben.

Tina ignored his whining. "Is that my best mixing bowl you broke? Why was it outside? It belonged to my great Aunt Hilda. I have only a few remembrances of my old relatives, and that was one of them. It's going to be—"

"Carlos is the one who took the bowl out," Ruben interrupted. "It wasn't me. It's his fault. We needed to wash the brushes in something. What can I put on my hand?"

Tina shook her head in disgust. "There's a broom in the barn. Get this mess cleaned up now. I don't know if I have any lotion for your hand, and if I do, I don't know if I'll give it to you." She slammed the door shut.

"What a nasty bitch," Ruben hissed to himself.

After cleaning up the broken shards of the bowl, Ruben hurried to the house. Tina was sitting in the kitchen, smoking, drinking beer, and working on her finances. There was a tube of hemorrhoid cream on the table.

"Help yourself," she said, pointing to the tube without looking up.

Ruben picked it up. "But this is for hemorrhoids. Like I told you, I've got ant bites," he complained.

"Suit yourself."

Figuring there was no point in talking to her, he picked up the tube and returned to Carlos. "I broke that damn bowl, and Tina is in a really shitty mood," he said. "This is what she gave me for my ant bites." He showed the tube to Carlos.

"Hemorrhoid cream! Did you tell her where the bites are?"

"Screw you. Have you ever heard of using this on bites? My hand is on fire."

"Maybe. I can't remember for sure. Give it a try. If nothing else, it could prevent you from getting hemorrhoids. Just smear it on. We better get all this put away." Carlos waved his hand toward the table, chest, and paint supplies. "If Tina's in a funk now, think how she'll be if she sees this stuff still out here. I suppose you told her I got the bowl from the house."

"Well, you did."

"Yeah, but you broke it."

Ruben smeared half a tube of the cream on his hand and wrist. "Let's wait a couple minutes to see if this works before we start hauling these tables."

"Okay, time's up. I think the first thing we should do is put Tina's chest over by the side of the house. I heard her tell

Lenny earlier she was going to the grocery store this afternoon. When she leaves, we can put it back inside. It doesn't look like the rain bothered it too much. If Tina was mad about me taking the bowl, she'd blow a gasket if she knew you took out this chest." Carlos added "Grab the other end."

Ruben had trouble keeping his right hand on the chest because of the excess cream. They had almost made it to the side of the house when Ruben's greasy hand slipped off and the chest landed with a thud on the ground, splitting the left front leg.

"Holy Mother of God, now you did it." Carlos stood, hands on his hips glaring at Ruben. "What the hell do we do now?"

"I couldn't help it. You knew I had a gimpy hand. We should have waited longer before we tried carrying this. It's not my fault. All we need to do is glue the front leg back together. It's no big deal."

"It is your fault. You put too much of that cream on your hand. And where are you getting the glue from? You got some in your back pocket?"

"Don't be a smart ass. There's probably some in the barn. I'll go look."

"We gotta get this to the side of the house." Carlos picked up the piece of broken leg and stuck it in his pocket. They carried the chest the rest of the way to the side of the house and set it down. Fortunately, the other three legs were sturdy enough to hold it up.

Ruben came back from the barn with a roll of black electrical tape. "I couldn't find any glue, but this'll work."

"Like she's not going to notice black tape on the leg."

"I thought about that. All we need to do is turn the chest, so the front is facing the wall. She won't even see the leg."

"That means the latch will be facing the wall too."

"So? Maybe we can get some glue later and fix the leg. And I noticed you got a little black dye on the top of the chest. I bet she notices that."

"It's just a small spot. Hardly noticeable." Carlos got the leg taped together and they left the chest sitting outside.

Chapter 22

Scottie and Charlie finished the chart of the various strange happenings they'd experienced, especially Scottie. Nothing in particular stood out.

Scottie studied the chart and frowned. "The only people I think I'd recognize again are the fat guy at the house where the dead man was and the one who came to my client's house where I was feeding the cats. And I haven't seen either of them again as far as I know. Fatso I couldn't miss so there must be at least four different guys. The one Piper briefly saw and the one you saw were different than the two guys I saw."

"I wouldn't be able to recognize the one who pushed you over," Charlie added. "About all I remember is he was medium height and slim, but that's it. And definitely a fast runner. Now, what about your clients? Any problems with them? Did someone's dog complain to their owner you took it for walks that were too short, or it didn't get to take plenty of sniffs along the way?"

Scottie laughed and gave Charlie a light punch in the arm. "I'll have you know my furry clients and their owners are quite satisfied with the way I treat them. No complaints in that department. By the way, Kevin called to see how I was doing, and he still didn't have any more info on the dead man. He says the case is still open, of course, but the FBI, and local police are keeping the investigation quiet. I'm seeing Bonita and Harper tomorrow for lunch, so maybe

Bonita heard some gossip from her neighbors. I think I told you about the puppy Harper bought and how it was so sick. Apparently, it's okay now, and it'll be fun to see him."

"Going back to the chart, Scottie, what about cars, SUVs, or vans? Did you see the same one several times? The only ones I saw when you were shoved down were the black van and the gray sedan. No way I could describe who was in them. The sedan was a Cadillac; not sure of the van make."

"There was a dark sedan that I saw a couple times. Once I even thought it was following me. It was when I was taking Harper and her dog to the vet, although Harper didn't really think it was following us. The other times it was parked down the street. Maybe I'm just getting paranoid. Usually, I'm not the type to sweat the small things but I must admit these incidents have me somewhat worried."

"Well, you should be. This is scary stuff, and I don't want anything to happen to you. Think I'll stick around and make sure you're safe." Charlie put his arms around her and gave her a fierce hug.

Scottie sighed and hugged him back. "I certainly love having you around. It's comforting to have someone who understands and believes the crazy threats and the rest. You know, it's been a while since that guy tried to kidnap Buster so maybe they're done with me."

"Let's hope so." Charlie said doubtfully.

Bonita picked up Scottie the next day and they drove to Harper's condo. When Scottie rang the doorbell, she immediately heard barking. Harper opened the door grinning.

"I'm sure you heard my watch dog. He such a character. Come in, ladies. You both look wonderful. Scottie, you are so lucky to have that curly hair. I'd trade it for my poker straight hair any time." She pushed her straight brown hair back over her shoulders.

"You have gorgeous hair. It's so long and thick."

Bonita looked at the two women. "Enough of hair talk. I want to see all of your condo. And I must say, it's hard to believe this is the same dog. I could barely look at him the last time I saw him, he was such a mess."

The little dog was bouncing around to each of them, his tail wagging in excitement. His recovery was obviously complete, and his happiness was evident.

"Oh, he's a healthy boy now. And he's great company. In the evening he'll sit next to me when I'm reading or watching TV. I named him Huey."

"I think it suits him," Scottie said as she picked up the puppy. "You are such a cutie." Huey put his paws around her neck, gave her a big lick on the cheek, and then squirmed to get down.

Harper showed them around her tidy condo, which was furnished with an eclectic assortment of furniture, paintings, and other items she had collected on her travels around the world. Following the tour of the condo they had a delicious lunch of shrimp salad, sliced tomatoes, flaky croissants, and white wine, with key lime pie for dessert.

"That was a totally wonderful lunch. I'm stuffed," Scottie said, pushing her chair back from the table. "You've done a great job with the condo. There are so many interesting objects to look at. I could stay here all day."

"Well, you can some other time but not today. I have a plan for the three of us this afternoon. Actually, the four of us, because it involves Huey too." At the mention of his name, the puppy trotted over to Harper and sat beside her. "My neighbor across the hall, who also has a dog, found this cute shop that sells doggie clothes, treats, and all the rest. Oh, and the owner does psychic readings. Maybe we could do that too. What do you think?"

"I'm game," Bonita said with a laugh. "Maybe I'll find a dress for Missy. And I've never had a reading done. That might be fun."

Scottie checked the calendar on her phone. "I'm free this afternoon, so let's do it. I'm not sure about the reading, but I'd like to see the shop. Occasionally a client will ask about buying pet supplies somewhere other than the big chain stores. So, this place might be one I can recommend."

They drove in Bonita's car, Scottie in the front passenger seat and Harper and Huey in the back. The shop had a sign in the front yard advertising Pet Boutique and Psychic Readings.

"That's quite a combination of products and services," commented Scottie.

"I agree. I can't wait to check it out," said Bonita.

When they entered the shop, instead of a bell tinkling, a barking dog sounded. The proprietor was stocking the shelving unit with dog treats. She looked over and greeted her new customers.

"Hi ladies and cute puppy. Welcome to my shop. My name is Shonalee. What can I help you with?" asked the young woman.

The ladies introduced themselves and Huey.

Huey could smell the treats and was straining on his leash to check them out.

"I guess I'm going to have to buy some of those munchies. They must be really good," said Harper.

Shonalee laughed. "I haven't tried them, but dogs seem to enjoy them. Would you like the large size bag or the small?"

"The small would be fine for now. I'll see how he likes them." Harper smiled fondly down at Huey, whose tail was wagging wildly. "He's excited about them already."

"Please have a look around."

Scottie strolled around the boutique. One wall had a mural depicting dogs of all sizes and breeds shown in a parklike setting. The dark blue painted cement floor was decorated with a smattering of white paw prints. The doggie dresses, sweaters, and rain slickers hung on racks in the corner. Another rack held rain boots, socks, hats, scarfs, and boating goggles. The other side of the room carried a variety of leashes, halters, collars, bowls, crates, and toys. And of course, the yummy treats.

While Harper was buying the treats for Huey, Bonita and Scottie browsed through little doggie dresses for Missy. "She's really not a girly girl. But this might work. What do you think?" Bonita held out a green and yellow plaid sundress.

"When would you have her wear it? I don't think I've seen her in a dress before. Does she like having clothes on?" asked Scottie.

"She did have a dress when she was a puppy, but she outgrew it. I gave it away. If I recall, she didn't seem to mind wearing it. I'd only have her wear it for special occasions."

"Then I think you should get it. I can't wait to see how she looks in it. This shop has a nice selection of products. The clothes are unique." Scottie continued examining the clothes on the rack. "Here's another dress that might look good on her." The dress was orange with small white polka dots.

"That is cute, but I think I'll just buy one to make sure she'll be okay wearing it. I want to ask about the readings. I wonder how long they take."

"If it doesn't take too long, I think you should do it now. I'm not interested, though. I might not like what I hear. My life has been rather spooky lately," said Scottie with a troubled frown.

Bonita scrutinized Scottie's face. "I really hope there aren't any more strange episodes. Nothing happened recently, did it? Actually, I know you're going to be fine. You can handle anything."

"No, all's good with me. I was going to ask if you've got any news about the missing FBI agent. I hoped maybe someone in your neighborhood had info about him."

"Nope, haven't heard a thing. Hey, let's not talk about the bad things. We're here to have fun."

Scottie grinned. "You're absolutely right. Let's find out about the readings."

Bonita bought the dress for Missy, and then asked Shonalee about the readings. "Could I have one now? Where do you do them?"

Shonalee was more than happy to talk about the readings and how she was decorating the reading room. "Come with me, ladies. I'll show you the room," she said proudly as she led them to the reading room. "Ta Da." She waved her arm around the room. "I'm in the process of decorating it. It's been such fun. What do you think?"

"You've certainly made it cozy," Scottie said.

"I thought the light lavender walls and the dark blue ceiling gave the room a rather ethereal vibe. And I had little star lights put in the ceiling," Shonalee said. "A friend of mine was going to throw out this table, so I took it and painted it purple. It has two small drawers in it, which are handy."

There were two stuffed chairs in addition to chairs in front of and behind the purple table, which held a clear acrylic lamp with a purple shade. On the other side of the room stood a lighted glass shelving unit containing crystals, aromatherapy candles and necklaces with astrological symbols which, of course, were for sale.

"I still want to make a few tweaks here and there. But here I am going on about this room, and you want to know about the readings. So sorry, ladies."

Shonalee invited the women to sit down. She settled behind the table, and Bonita sat in front. Scottie and Harper sat in the stuffed chairs. They had left little Huey in the Pet Boutique, where he had fallen asleep on the floor. Harper had unhooked his leash, since he was sound asleep. For little boy dogs, shopping was a tiring ordeal.

"I have to explain I only do readings by appointment. Unless my assistant is here to help in the Boutique, I can't do readings. It wouldn't be fair to my clients if I had to interrupt the reading to assist someone in there. I make appointments on Tuesday and Thursday afternoons from one to four and on Wednesday evening from five to seven. The readings take about an hour. Astrology readings using a birth chart is my preference, but I can also do a three-card tarot reading, looking at the past, present, and future. Do you have a preference?" Shonalee asked Bonita.

"I've never had either one, so it would be up to you."

"If you want the astrology reading, I'll need your birth date, and time of birth. Do you have that info?"

"I have my birth date, of course, and I guess I probably can find the time somewhere at home," said Bonita looking toward the open doorway to the boutique. "Good heavens," she exclaimed, "what is he doing? Harper, go look at your dog."

Huey was a very happy camper. His short nap had given him the energy to check out his surroundings. It didn't take long to sniff out the shelving unit with the treats. He had managed to snatch a large bag off the shelf and tear it open, and it appeared he'd devoured more than half the contents.

By the time the visitors walked to the doorway, Huey was running in circles, then leaping in the air, racing around the room, and stopping to munch another treat.

"Huey, what are you doing? Have you gone berserk?" shouted Harper.

Hearing his name, the pup ran over to Harper, leapt into her arms, and then wanted to be put down. He saw Scottie and jumped into her arms and then down.

"He certainly has a lot of energy," said Shonalee.

"Really, I've never seen him like this. He's racing around like he's on amphetamines," said Harper with concern. "Listen, Shonalee, I'll pay for the bag he grabbed. I had no idea he could jump that high. Ladies I think we should leave before he tears the place apart." Harper swept up Huey and snapped his leash back on as he was trying to pull a package of doggie socks off the rack.

"No, you're definitely not paying for that bag of treats. I'll just put what's left in another bag and you can take it with you." Shonalee picked up the remainder of the treats, bagged them, and gave them to Scottie to hold. "You might want to put the treats in the trunk, so he doesn't smell them," Shonalee suggested.

Bonita eyed the puppy and shook her head. "I just hope he doesn't get sick in my car."

"Jeez, I hadn't even thought of that. Let's go in case he does get sick." Harper was out the door with a rambunctious Huey. Bonita told Shonalee she would call her later to set up an appointment for her reading.

Harper set Huey down to pee before getting in the back seat of the car, while Scottie and Bonita put the packages in the trunk. They hadn't traveled more than a half mile when Harper announced Huey was sound asleep. The three women all breathed a sigh of relief.

The puppy slept snuggled next to Harper all the way home. When they arrived at the condo, Scottie helped by carrying Harper's bags of treats, and Harper carried the sleeping puppy. Bonita waited in the car for Scottie.

When Scottie got back in the car, she turned to Bonita "Huey was still sound asleep. Harper put him in his bed. I hope he's going to be okay. Who knows what was in those munchies."

———————

As soon as her customers left, an upset Shonalee called Tina to tell her what had happened with the dog and the treats. The little guy must have eaten more than half a bag. Not good. She hadn't been about to mention the marijuana to the ladies.

Tina was totally unconcerned. "Well, what did you expect if the dumb dog eats so many? Wasn't the owner keeping an eye on him? Don't worry about it. It's not your fault. I haven't given any to the dogs here yet. I'll give them a try tomorrow. Gotta go, lots to do."

Shonalee looked down at her phone. "That was a big help, Tina," she said out loud to no one. "I'm beginning to wonder about you as a business partner." She planned to tell her new friend about what the puppy did when he picked her up to go out to dinner, but of course, not what made the treats special. She turned her thoughts toward what she could do to make this guy think she was special!

Chapter 23

"But Tina, me and Carlos really should go to the rally," Ruben said. "We gotta make sure that the tents don't have a problem and who knows what else. We'd be a big help. Think of all we did at the last rally,"

"Holy crap, I prefer not to think about what you did. How could I forget during the ax-throwing contest, when you almost chopped that freakin' girl's arm off? Did you forget about that? You're just lucky she didn't sue the pants off you. No, you and Carlos are taking the pooches to Miami. I don't want to hear any more about it." Tina lit another cigarette and blew a smoke ring.

Carlos shrugged. "I'm glad we're going to Miami. I get to see my sister and her family again. It must be four or five months since I've seen them. The kids have probably grown a lot."

Ruben had a sullen, pouty look on his face. "Oh sure, easy for you to say. Your sister likes you. She hates me. And those kids are always all over me, pawing me with their sticky, grubby little hands."

"Maybe the problem is your eating and drinking everything. You don't stop from the minute you get there. And for whatever reason, the kids like you. You should be glad somebody does."

"I can't help it if I eat a lot at her house. At least she's a good cook."

Tina flared up at that. "And what's that supposed to mean? You don't like my cooking? You can stay in Miami if you'd rather eat her cooking."

"No, Tina, yours is okay. She just makes different kinds of food. Mexican, I guess." At Tina's it was just mac and cheese, pizza, sandwiches, chips, wings, and more sandwiches.

"Whatever. You two can leave right after everything is set up on Friday, and be sure you get back Sunday night. Monday you take the tents back to town. Also, here's a bag of the treats Shonalee and I made. I want the two of you to give a couple of treats to some of the puppies. Take them out of their crates first. You each do one dog at a time. Watch them about ten to fifteen minutes to see how they act. Do you think you can handle that?"

"Like duh," said Ruben, bag of treats in hand as he went out the door, with Carlos following behind.

"You know, when Shonalee and Tina were baking these, they smelled pretty good. Have you tried one?" asked Ruben, shaking the bag.

"God no, it's dog food. I suppose you ate one."

"Not yet, but I'm thinking about it. How bad could they be? Take a whiff." Ruben opened the bag of treats and handed it over to Carlos.

"You're right, they don't smell bad. A little like peanut butter."

Ruben had a smug look on his face. "Guess what, I know a couple of the ingredients that went into making them."

"Big deal. Like what?"

"Peanut butter and weed. Bet you didn't know that. I'm going to give one a try." Ruben popped a treat in his mouth. "Really crunchy, a little hard, but quite tasty. Try one." He passed the bag over to Carlos.

"Couldn't hurt, I suppose." Carlos chewed the hard treat. "Not too bad, but I think they'd go down better with a beer."

"Good idea. I'll go get a six-pack."

"You'd better not let Tina see you or there'll be hell to pay. I don't know, maybe . . ."

"Stop worrying. Tina just went to town. She told me she had to pick up some stuff. I saw her leave, so I know she won't be back for a while."

"I didn't see her go."

"Well, she did. I'm going to get the beer." Ruben left Carlos sitting on the edge of the chaise lounge on the deck, holding the bag of dog treats.

Ruben decided it was too hot outside for him, so he called Carlos to come in the house.

An hour and a half later the two men were sprawled out in recliners, sound asleep with the TV blaring. Six empty beer cans and an empty bag of doggie treats sat on the coffee table.

Chapter 24

Tony and Pete were sitting outside at a picnic table, having a hot dog and beer lunch at Venice's north jetty. They'd put a "Closed for Lunch" sign on the door of their pawn shop and left. They also sold guns and ammo at their facility, but didn't advertise that part of the business. The guns, ammo, and collection of knives were mostly bought by customers through word of mouth.

"We shouldn't use my car when staking out the dog walker," said Tony, licking the mustard off his fingers. "If she hasn't already noticed my car, she probably would soon. We'll use yours or your wife's."

"No way can we use my wife's. She'd have a hissy fit. That's her baby. I'm surprised she lets me ride in it. You have to admit it's a cool ride though. Plus, it's pretty noticeable."

"Yeah, I guess you're right. A red Porsche is hard to miss. It'll have to be your SUV. But you don't have tinted windows, do you?" asked Tony.

Pete watched a fishing boat speed up to leave the jetty. "There's some tint, but not much. But with medium blue color my totally blah vehicle should be good. And she hasn't seen it before."

"One of us has to do a trip to her neighborhood tonight. We have to know the lay of the land, so to speak, by next week. The rally's this weekend, and I have a feeling in my gut we'd better get the info we want soon, or we could be in trouble. We can't put this off any longer."

"I can't do it tonight," answered Pete. "We've got friends from up north coming to dinner. Maybe you could do a run by her house. See if there's a car in the driveway and if it stays all night." He scrunched up his hot dog wrapper, threw it in the trash can, and stood admiring the boats cruising along. "Hell, it's too nice to go back to the store. Being on a boat fishing would be much better."

"I agree, but we have work to do at the store. Let's go." They walked to Tony's car as he continued talking. "Listen, if you can't help with the stakeout tonight, what about tomorrow night? I'm not driving my car in her area again. We're going to have to use your car."

"I think if she's home and there's nobody at her house tomorrow night, we should go in and get what info we can. Let's just get it done. What do you think?" asked Pete. "I'm really getting tired of this whole business, and Doreen is getting suspicious. She's been asking all kinds of questions. She probably thinks I'm having an affair."

"So, what are you telling her? You'd better not tell her our problem. Why don't you tell her you are having an affair? I could even back you up." Tony laughed.

"Yeah right. You're a big help. That's all I need. No thanks, I've got enough trouble now. How about I pick you up about eight tomorrow night? It shouldn't take long."

Back at the shop, Tony snapped his fingers. "Hey, I just got an idea. Why don't we pretend we're FBI guys asking her about the dead agent? This could be a clean approach. I'm bringing my gun anyway in case the plan goes south. I'm sure they all carry guns. Why didn't I think of this before?" Tony nodded, quite pleased with coming up with a new plan.

Pete shook his head negatively. "Wait a minute! No way am I waltzing into her house pretending to be an FBI agent. She'd probably want to see badges and who knows what else. And she'd probably want us to leave ID cards with names and phone numbers. And what questions would we ask? She probably doesn't even know he was an FBI agent. Another thing, the ones I've seen on TV are usually dressed in dark suits, white shirts, and ties. If my wife hadn't thought I was having an affair before, and she sees me leaving the house all dressed up . . . I'd be dead meat." Pete scowled and chewed on a fingernail.

Tony narrowed his eyes in thought. "Let's think about it. I still think it's a possible way to go. I bet we could get fake badges in the toy department at Walmart or Target. We'd just flash them really fast. I guess we couldn't wear sunglasses if we go at night. But maybe one of us could get a pair of regular glasses to look a little different. It's probably too late to get wigs."

"It won't work. Don't forget she's already seen me. You'd have to do it by yourself. Plus, I think it's best to wait until after the rally. I want to enjoy it, and I know Doreen is really looking forward to it. Just scouting out the neighborhood using my car is okay, but let's wait 'til next week to go in her house. I mean you going in her house as an FBI guy, not me," Pete added.

"I don't like it, but I see where you're coming from." Tony opened a large carton containing small boxes of ammo. He unlocked a display case in which he stacked a dozen of the small boxes. "No matter how you look at it, we're going to get this matter taken care of."

Chapter 25

Wearing a slight frown, Scottie paced around her lanai while speaking on her phone with Piper. "You know, I usually just walk small dogs. Rarely do I let them have a sleepover. And you said this one was a bit bigger than most of my furry clients."

"But this is an emergency," explained Piper. "The dog belongs to Jack's brother and his wife. And it's a very friendly dog. You'd like him. Besides, it's only two nights. Tomorrow night, and one night next week. Their regular dog sitter isn't available the two nights. Pl-l-e-e-a-a-s-s-e-e," she begged.

"Well, why don't you take care of him?" asked Scottie. "Since he already knows you, it should be a piece of cake."

"Oh no, I couldn't possibly. My calendar is totally full. And you're so wonderful with dogs and cats. You're absolutely the best," Piper gushed.

"Piper, you're laying it on a little thick. As long as it's only two nights. And don't ask again. No sleepovers and no big dogs. Okay?"

"I promise. I wouldn't ask now, but they're desperate and I wanted to help. Would it be okay if I bring him over about three tomorrow?"

"If you have to. Be sure you bring the leash, the food, a crate if he sleeps in one, any special toy, the works. Ask his owners what he's going to need," instructed Scottie.

"Will do. See you tomorrow aft."

How did I let her talk me into this job? thought Scottie. *But I guess she'd do the same for me. It's probably why we're good friends.*

The next afternoon, as Scottie looked out her front window, Piper drove into her driveway with her convertible top down. Sitting in the passenger seat, surveying the neighborhood, as if he owned it, was a German Shepherd. Piper clipped on his leash, and ran around to his side of the car, opened the door, and he jumped out.

"All right, Mr. B, do your business. Scottie is rather fussy, so you're going to have to really behave. I'll introduce you to her, bring your belongings in, and then I'm leaving. But I'll come and get you tomorrow. Do you understand?" she asked as she walked the dog over to a small shrub, which he promptly watered down. "Good boy. Let's go meet Scottie."

Scottie already had the door open, about to object, as in walked Piper and Mr. B.

Piper took off his leash and handed it to Scottie. Mr. B looked at Scottie, his intelligent dark eyes checking her out.

"Piper, you said he was a bit bigger than the dogs I usually have as a customer, but he's huge. I don't know if this is going to work. He looks rather fierce." Mr. B glanced around the room, swaggered over to a blue planter which housed a variety of succulents, lifted his leg, and peed. Most of the pee ran down the side of the pot and onto the wood floor.

"This isn't going to work, Piper. He's going to mark my entire house as his territory. And he's probably vicious." Scottie went to get paper toweling and a cleaning solution to wipe the floor and the planter.

"Mr. B, bad dog," said Piper. "Take that grin off your face. You do not potty in the house. Potty out. Scottie, I swear he's grinning. You can't stay if you're bad. He really is a pussy cat. Oops, wrong type of critter. Really, he won't be a problem, will you, Mr. B?" Mr. B wagged his tail. "I'm going to get his gear out of the car." Piper left quickly before Scottie had a chance to change her mind.

After cleaning up Mr. B's mess, Scottie decided she better get acquainted with her houseguest. "Okay, Mr. B, come see me," coaxed Scottie, extending her open hand. Mr. B slowly walked over to her. "Sit," said Scottie. Mr. B sat, and Scottie scratched him behind the ears. "First of all, potty out. I'm going to show you the back door and where you're going to do your business. We're going to get along fine, aren't we? And it's just for tonight and one night next week. So, you get to go home tomorrow and see your family. Thank God."

Piper hauled in a huge fluffy dog bed and a big tote with the rest of his belongings. Mr. B immediately stuck his nose in the tote, smelling his food.

"Oh no you don't," said Scottie, taking the tote. "You get your dinner later. Piper, did you ask what time he usually eats?" Piper was eyeing herself in the mirror by the front door as she put fresh lipstick on. "No, but maybe they added it to the note in the bag. They were going to put phone numbers on it, and there's a pill he takes, but I'm not sure when. Listen, I gotta go. You're the best." Piper gave Scottie a quick hug and hurried out the door.

Scottie rolled her eyes. "It's just you and me now, kiddo. I'm going to check your bag. Let's hope they put in a toy or two." Scottie pulled out the dog food and put it on the top of the refrigerator, Mr. B carefully watching her actions. She rummaged around until she found the note. It had all the information she needed. There were some rawhide chews in the bag, which Mr. B immediately wanted, in addition to a squeaky duck toy. Scottie gave him a chew stick and said, "I'm going to put your bowls in the laundry." Mr. B. was contentedly chewing the rawhide stick.

Later, after taking Mr. B for an evening walk, Scottie wanted some quiet time watching TV. She put Mr. B's bed next to her chair, but he wanted to sit in her lap. "If you weren't so big, I'd let you. Off. Go in your bed." Scottie pushed him to the floor. Ignoring his bed, he went to the sofa and sprawled out. "If you are going to camp out on my sofa then I'm going to have to put a blanket on it." After some pushing and shoving, she got the blanket under him.

Later, before going to bed, they made a quick trip outside, and Scottie put Mr. B's bed in her bedroom. "This is it, Mr. B, it's time to go to sleep. I know you slept all evening, but you could've watched TV with me. It actually was a pretty good movie. No wandering around the house. To be on the safe side, I'll close the bedroom door." Mr. B gave a small woof.

About 1:30 am Scottie was semi-wakened from a sound sleep by the sound of snoring. "You're snoring," she mumbled. The snoring continued. She and Charlie had become "friends with benefits," but he never snored when they slept together. Suddenly wide awake, she cautiously moved her hand over to the other side of the bed.

Fur. And dog breath.

Scottie turned on the nightstand light. Mr. B, his head on the pillow, was sound asleep right next to her. All he needed was a granny night cap and he'd look like the wolf from *Little Red Riding Hood*.

Do I dare wake him up and get him off the bed? she wondered. "Mr. B," she whispered. Nothing. "Mr. B," she said louder. He opened his eyes and looked at her and yawned. "You have to go sleep in your own bed. Off." She gave him a small push. Nothing. A harder push. A small growl. "That was rude. Get off."

Reluctantly he jumped off. "Go in your bed. Here, it looks very comfy." She fluffed up the bed. He just watched her. "Well, I'm going back to sleep."

The next morning when she got up, Mr. B was sleeping on her bed but at the foot end. "You are something else. I wonder if this is what you do at home. Let's go rustle up your breakfast." Mr. B led the way to the kitchen, tail wagging.

Chapter 26

Finally, rally time. Tina was beyond excited. "Lenny, I'm glad you got here early enough so we can check out the tents and make sure we've got everything. I've been so busy. I touched up the roots of my hair using part of the black hair dye from the panda project." Her pasty white skin made a sharp contrast to the black hair and eyebrows. In addition to the paints and other dye left over, she had also bought some regular body paint. It barely occurred to her that the black fabric dye, the black hair dye, and the poster paint wouldn't be the best mediums for body painting. "And my nipple ring doesn't hurt much anymore."

Lenny looked away, grimacing. "TMI."

He had shown up mid-morning on Friday to help Tina check to make sure everything was ready for the crowd. It wouldn't be a super large rally, maybe just a couple hundred people, with motor homes campers, and tents.

Some would start showing up in the afternoon, although the festivities wouldn't begin until the next day. In addition to the port-a-potties, bleachers, and band platform being put in place, Carlos and Ruben had set up the tents. Only one had collapsed and had to be set up again. It was the food tent, which would have been a disaster if the food and people were in it. Tina had Lenny check the other tents to make sure they were securely put together and wouldn't collapse.

She called over to Carlos and Ruben. "Hey, you two. I want you out of here. Take the puppies I pointed out and head to Miami. Be sure you're back Sunday night, because you have to take the tents back Monday morning. And there better not be any more speeding tickets."

"I still think we should stay in case you need help," groused Ruben.

"Forget it. Hit the road. I don't need your help." replied Tina.

"What if I promise not to get in the ax-throwing contest?"

"You heard what I said. Beat it." Tina had about all she could take of his whining.

"We're leaving," said Carlos. He gave Ruben a push on his back, and they left.

———————————

Scottie was at Charlie's house, enjoying the view of the intracoastal waterway from the deck of his house. He was getting them some after-dinner coffee with a splash of Bailey's chocolate-cherry liqueur.

"How does your calendar look tomorrow?" he asked as he put the coffee mugs on the table.

"In the morning I have one client I'll be taking for a walk. It shouldn't take too long. And it's early. Why?"

"I have a neighbor who lives a few doors down from me who's a motorcycle buff. He says there's a rally he's going to tomorrow and he thinks we might enjoy it. Have you ever been to one?"

"No, never. Have you? I imagine they're really noisy?"

"I went to one years ago, during my college days. I really don't remember much about it. There was a lot of drinking going on. The rallies today have probably changed a lot since then. It might be fun. Are you up for a new experience? I did ask my neighbor if there was any problem if we joined him, and he said we'd have to pay the entrance fee when we got there but otherwise no problem. Apparently, people usually register online and get a packet with information about the various events and music."

Scottie chuckled. "I'm always willing to experience new things. Somehow, I have a feeling this could be most interesting. Do we have to have a motorcycle? That wouldn't be my preferred way to travel."

"Since we don't have one, my car will have to do. I understand there'll be games and food and some bands. How about I pick you up about one-thirty? It'll take us a while to get there. And I'm to call for directions when we're in the vicinity of the place. He said it's kind of hard to find."

"What is the proper attire for a rally? I'd hate to be dressed inappropriately."

"Nothing fancy, that's for sure. It'll be fairly warm, so think cool and comfortable. T-shirt, light-weight jeans, shorts, that sort of stuff."

"I've got bug spray and sunblock I can bring. A hat probably would be a good idea. What about chairs. Do we bring our own?"

"I'm not sure about that. I'll throw a couple in the trunk."

Shonalee found Lenny shortly after she arrived at the rally. He was straddling his bike, talking with some scantily clad women who obviously wanted to get to know him better. A black headband held back his longish dark hair. He wore tight blue jeans and a black T-shirt. Shonalee felt overdressed compared to many of the other woman she observed. Her yellow capris, yellow flowered blouse, and big floppy yellow hat definitely set her apart.

"Hi Lenny, this is really, quite a … I don't know what to say." Shonalee, eyes wide open, took in the sights and sounds of the people and activities.

"Jump on, girl. I'll tour you around." He patted the passenger seat on his Harley. "See you later, ladies," he told his disappointed adoring fans.

"O – k – a – y, if you promise not to go too fast."

Lenny just grinned. He was in his glory. The noise from the motorcycles, the scantily clad women, the raucous laughter, the various smoke and food smells. It didn't get any better. "I'm sure glad you made it, Shonalee. You're going to have a helluva good time. We'll have to get you a beer or maybe something else. Lots of different kinds of smokes around here too. Whatever you want."

"Maybe later." Shonalee was more concerned about hanging on, as she watched the people and the multitude of colors and types of motorcycles. "I see there's even a tent where you can buy things. What do they sell? You went by too fast. I couldn't get a good look."

"Later. First of all, I want you to meet a couple of my biking buddies. They should be over by the beer tent." As they made their way to the beer tent, Shonalee suddenly spotted a coffin being pulled by a motorcycle. In it were three women. All had paint on the upper half of their body, and from what she could tell, were just wearing thongs. "OMG," Shonalee exclaimed. "Is that Tina in the back? Turn around. I've gotta see this. It's unbelievable. I've got to take a picture."

Sure enough, there was Tina, black hair waving in the wind. "Tina," yelled Shonalee.

Hearing her name, Tina turned, saw Shonalee and called for the driver to stop. "Hey, cuz, what do you think of my ride? Say hello to my coffin cronies." The other women grinned and said Hi.

Shonalee got off the motorcycle and walked over to the coffin. She could hardly believe her eyes. She wasn't even sure what to say. She couldn't imagine in her wildest dreams going totally bare breasted in public, even though her new boobies were something to behold. "Wow, you gals certainly got painted. I love the bright colors." The group barely fit in the coffin. Tina, being a big girl, sat in the back, her boob with the nipple ring squished against the back of the woman in front of her. "See ya later." Off they went.

"Come on, let's go," Lenny told Shonalee. "More to see." They continued driving around, and then Shonalee spotted Scottie. "Oh, stop. I see someone I know. She came into my shop."

A little perturbed at having to stop again, Lenny pulled over to the side, and Shonalee hopped off and greeted Scottie. "Hi, remember me? I own the doggie boutique. I wondered how the puppy was after eating all those treats."

"Sure, I remember you. Shonalee, isn't it? The puppy is fine. He did sleep for hours, though. Are you a motorcycle enthusiast? This is my first time at a rally. And I'd like you to meet my friend Charlie."

"Hi, Charlie," answered Shonalee, giving him the once over. "My friend is over there on the bike." She pointed to Lenny, who was impatiently waiting for her. "This is my first rally too. You can probably tell by the way I'm dressed." Shonalee looked approvingly at Scottie, who fit right in with her blue jeans and light blue T-shirt, a cowgirl hat on her curls. "I haven't lived in Florida very long. I probably wouldn't have come but my cousin owns this property, and I thought it would be fun. She really didn't want me to come. I'm not sure why. Are you enjoying yourselves?"

"So far we are. I don't know what they're cooking over there, but the smells are wonderful. It's making me hungry. How about you, Charlie? Shonalee, your friend over there looks like he's anxious for you to get back. I'll tell Harper you asked about Huey."

"Thanks. Tell her to come back to the boutique and get some more treats for him. Great to see you again and nice meeting you, Charlie." Shonalee hurried over to Lenny. She had a feeling he wasn't a very patient man.

"It's about time. No more stops. I want to check the stage where the next band is going to play. The last group had some issues with the power." Shonalee barely had time to get on the bike before they took off.

While Lenny spoke to the guys working on the power, Shonalee wandered off to watch the people involved in the ax-throwing contest. "That looks like it could be really dangerous. I think I'll step back a little," she mentioned to a guy standing next to her.

"Nah, not really. It helps to have a little practice. There was an idiot last year, though, who almost chopped a girl's arm off. But that was unusual. You gonna give it a try?"

"Me? No way. They'd be talking about me next year as the woman who almost chopped something off of somebody." They both chuckled. Shonalee walked back just in time as Lenny was ready to leave.

"Lenny, I want to look at the things for sale in the tent we went by. There might be something I want to buy."

"Okay, I'll drop you off. I've got to find my buddy Pete anyway. There's going to be a scavenger hunt in a little while. How about we do that?"

Shonalee loved games, so that sounded great to her. "I'd love it. See you in a bit." She browsed in the tent with all the items for sale. "You certainly have a variety of things here," she remarked to the woman in charge of sales." There were T-shirts, keychains, do-rags, head bands, tattoo sleeves, mugs, beer cozies, wallet chains, stretch bracelets, skull caps, and whips. "I think I'll take this bracelet. I don't think most of the other items would work for me." She slipped on the multicolored beaded bracelet and left the tent, watching the bikers go by while she waited for Lenny to return.

Suddenly a guy with a long black beard partially matted with what looked like barbeque sauce was standing right next to her. His leather vest barely covered his not-so-clean tank top. Both arms were totally tattooed. A potent beer and garlic breath, along with a strong body odor, almost made Shonalee do a projectile vomit.

"Excuse me, I have to find my friend." Shonalee started to move away from him, but he moved along with her.

"Listen sweet thing, me and you should get to know each other. I got a camper over in the parking lot where we could get acquainted." He grinned at her, showing a definite lack of dental hygiene.

"Get away from me, you, you creep, or I'll call—"

"Who you gonna call? The—" He didn't have a chance to finish his sentence. A robust woman, taller than he was, gave him a swift right to the head, knocking him to the ground. "I told you, no messing around. One of these times my trigger finger is gonna get too itchy." She gave him the stink eye and walked away, her wallet chain banging against her ample blue jean butt.

"That's my honey. Ain't she something? I better go catch up to her or she'll be pissed at me all day." Hitching up his pants and rubbing his jaw, he wandered off in the crowd looking for his "honey."

Shonalee was so relieved when Lenny showed up, she practically threw herself at him. "OMG you wouldn't believe this weird guy who tried to put the make on me. He was so gross, I thought I was going to throw up."

Lenny just shrugged. "Oh, I'm sure he was harmless. Don't worry about it. Everyone's here to have a good time. I finally see my partner Pete over there. Let's go before he takes off." He led Shonalee to a big man wearing a short sleeve, button-down shirt and a red cap.

"Hey, Pete. How are sales? Tony's managing the tent I assume. Did your wife come? Pete, this is Tina's cousin Shonalee."

"Hey." He barely looked at Shonalee. Pete was scanning the crowd of people, obviously distracted. A short time before when he was in the food tent, he was sure he recognized the dog walker woman. He hadn't had a chance to tell Tony, and he couldn't mention it to Lenny with this Shonalee woman next to him.

"Sales are good. Wifey's here somewhere with her girlfriends. They're planning to go on the scavenger hunt. See you later."

Pete could feel his heart racing. Maybe he and Tony could pull her aside somehow and question her. But it looked like she had a guy with her. And what if she recognized him and called the cops? But why would she do that? He'd just harassed her a little. He'd talk to Tony about it.

Chapter 27

Scottie and Charlie used the chairs they'd brought and found a safe place to eat the meal they got from the food tent. It was out of the way of the motorcycle traffic and a great location for people-watching.

"These pulled pork sandwiches are super good. I'm actually going to eat the whole thing," said Scottie wiping her fingers on her napkin.

"The baked beans aren't bad either. I'm not too fond of the cole slaw though. Too much vinegar. Look at that bike." Charlie pointed at an intricately painted motorcycle in a red, white, and blue motif. "Some of these bikes are really outstanding. That one doesn't need the Confederate flag though." They continued watching the parade of bikes going by.

"I love the one with all the Egyptian markings. And look how long that one is. Some of them must be awfully expensive. And the tattoos. I've never seen so many in my life." Scottie continued to be fascinated by everything she was seeing. "Did you see the woman with the leather vest? She was right next to me in the food line. I didn't want to point her out because I figured she'd notice. All she had on top was the vest, which laced up so you could see part of the Harley eagle tattooed across her breasts. I hate to think of what that will look like when she gets older. And look at the woman on the back of that bike. Fishnet stockings, a garter belt, a thong, and an almost bikini top."

"Sorry I missed that. Check out the one over there."

"Where? Oh, I think I see what you're referring to." Scottie's eyes went round as saucers. Sitting on the back of a bike was a gal with a painted upper body, wearing a thong and chaps.

"I hope she doesn't get burnt buns."

Charlie laughed. "That's a good one. I have a feeling she won't realize it until later if she does. What about the guy with the horns, you know, the Viking helmet and the bushy brown beard? It's a good thing he's got a big bike, because his girlfriend isn't little."

"That's for sure. They both look like they're nine months pregnant. And what's with the Freddy Krueger mask on her? I don't think most women would wear that."

"Maybe she's not a she."

"Well, it's got breasts. Who knows?"

"After seeing some of these people, I definitely feel a little overdressed, but that's okay. Should we check the activities? I saw a poster board back there with the times. There's also info on the various bands and when they're playing."

They put the chairs in the car and moseyed over to the board.

"This is one band I'd like to see and hear." Charlie pointed to The Bruisin' Biker Bitches Band. "Too bad they don't start playing until ten tonight."

"I'm sure they'd be wonderful," Scottie said sarcastically, rolling her eyes.

"Now you don't know. They might really be good."

"That's true. I shouldn't have said that." Then, for a moment, Scottie stopped talking and just stared. "Uh, oh. I think I see the guy who came to the house where I was feeding the cats. He's over there by the neon green bike. I can't be sure because of the sunglasses and hat, but there's definitely something about him . . . is he looking this way?" Scottie turned away and whispered to Charlie to look.

"There's just a woman standing near the bike. He must have left from there. What were you thinking about saying to him? Any idea?"

"I have no idea, but if he's the one who's been harassing me, I'd like to find out why. Maybe this would be a good place to approach him, you know, with all these people around. What do you think?"

"I guess it wouldn't hurt. If you spot him again let me know, because I didn't see him, so I don't know what he looks like."

"That's the problem. He looks like half the guys here. Jeans, shirt, hat, sunglasses. But I'm going to watch for him. What about this frozen T-shirt contest? Let's see what that's all about."

Scottie and Charlie wandered off hand in hand.

While Shonalee was busy taking in the sights and sounds, Lenny spotted another friend, in the midst of several guys who were sitting on their bikes.

"I wanna see a guy over there. I think you'll find him interesting. He's quite a character."

Shonalee wasn't paying attention to the location they were headed. Suddenly they were standing in front of a towering man with a ruddy face and squinty blue eyes, holding a live twelve-foot Burmese python draped across his shoulders.

"Is—is that real?" she stuttered. Blanching, she stepped back several paces.

Lenny just smiled and said, "Shonalee this is my friend Snake Slither and his reptilian friend, Lola. Snake found Lola when he was on one of those python hunts. Of course, she wasn't as lengthy a girl as she is now." Lenny and Snake shook hands while the snake slowly moved its head in the direction of Shonalee. Its beady black eyes stared at her, and its tongue darted out. She gave a movie-loud scream and jumped back even further.

"Get that fracking thing away from me. Lenny, will you give me a ride to my car? I'm leaving."

"Now what's the matter?" Her white face, wild eyes, and quivering body pretty much said it all. Fainting was a good possibility. "Oh, all right. See you later, Snake. Gotta take this one to her car because I think she's afraid of your friend."

"Oh, Lola's a good girl. And she's already had lunch. She might be thinking about dinner though. Just kidding."

On the way to her car, Shonalee shakily asked Lenny, "What is that guy's real name? I can't believe he was actually wearing that horrible creature on his neck. He must be crazy. I bet Snake's favorite song is 'Twistin' the Night Away.'"

"His last name really is Slither, and he's always liked snakes, so that's why everyone calls him Snake. His real name is Howard. He makes decent money having people take pictures with him and Lola."

"In my opinion, that snake would be much better as a pair of boots. I'm sorry I panicked, but snakes and spiders just freak me out. When you see Tina, tell her I left. Thanks for inviting me, Lenny, and showing me around. It's been a real eye opener."

"Are you sure you don't wanna stay? There's going to be a lot more going on. Some terrific bands. And you haven't even eaten yet."

"No thanks. I've got some plans for later today. And I think there are some ladies here looking forward to spending time with you." Shonalee quickly got into her car. Motorcycle rallies were never going to be on her list of things to do. Going out with older men with lots of money suited her much better. But there was something about Lenny. He had a certain charisma. It was obvious the women at the rally knew him well. Best to stay away from that man.

Tina wasn't happy. The black body paint on her smeared when she was on the coffin ride. If she hadn't been squished in the back with her boobies pushed into the woman in front of her, it wouldn't have happened. It turned out the artist had used poster paint. Between Tina's sweat and the humidity, any semblance of a design was totally destroyed.

"I'm gonna have to get some water and see if I can get the rest of this black paint off," she told her girlfriend. "I didn't know those idiots put the poster paint in with the regular body paint. I'm talking about Ruben and Carlos. The guys who work for me." Tina explained to her coffin buddies.

Using a bottle of water, she and her girlfriend tried to wipe off the black paint. It only smeared more. Also, her nipple ring was starting to hurt, and the whole area around it was getting red.

"Do you think I should have gotten a real gold ring instead of the one I got from the Dollar Store?" she asked her friend.

"Well, it doesn't look good. Boy, this water has just made the paint even more of a mess. Your back looks like you've been rolling around in a coal bin. I think you be better off putting on a T-shirt, especially if you're going to get in the boxing ring tonight. You could buy one of those neat ones. Like one that says 'Bad Ass Chick.' Or I saw another cute one that said 'Big Tough Titties.'"

"Yeah, I guess you're right. It just pisses me off that those dick weeds would put the poster paint with the body paint. I thought I was looking pretty foxy before this mess. Thank God I didn't get the full body paint. Did you see the women from Daytona with the full body paint? They look freakin' awesome. And I'm not boxing tonight. There was too much commotion last year, just because I broke that guy's jaw. He was such a wuss."

Tina glanced down at her at her large breasts which were starting to point south, and shook her head, then left to buy a T-shirt. The rest of the day had to go better. Definitely a real gold booby ring was in her future. One good thing, the earnings from the rally she would split with Lenny come to a sizable chunk of money. And Lenny and Shonalee seemed to be getting along well. Hopefully not too well, because that could be trouble.

———————————

"Have you seen the guy you mentioned? The one who came to the house when you were cat-sitting." asked Charlie.

"No. I keep looking around, but haven't seen him. I'd like to stop in the tent and get one of those tattoo sleeves. Maybe I can fool Piper into thinking I actually got my whole arm tattooed. I told her I was coming to this rally and I might get a tattoo. Have you seen anyone doing them here?"

"There was a tent we passed by that was doing them."

"Guess I missed it. Well, I wouldn't actually get one. I'm sure Piper doesn't know about tattoo sleeves."

"You're probably right. You know, I haven't seen my neighbor yet."

"Charlie, look over to your right. Is that couple doing what I think they're doing?"

"Yup, they're whipping each other. And laughing. If they do whipping with all these people watching, I wonder what they do when they're alone."

"I don't even want to think about it. They even have red marks on their arms and legs. I don't believe the marks are real welts, but jeez, who would do that? Then to be laughing. Maybe they're high on something or drunk."

"Could be. I noticed they were selling whips with the other stuff. I wonder how big a seller they are."

"Well, I'm sure not buying one. And you'd better not be either. I do want to get that tattoo sleeve though."

"How about we get your sleeve and then take off. This is about all I fun I can take."

"I totally agree."

Scottie and Charlie walked hand in hand through the crowd to the tent selling the rally merchandise. She bought the sleeve, and they headed for the car.

The band was getting louder as well as the crowd. The motorcycles made their own noise. A potpourri of smells wafted through the air. Food, beer, sweat, fuel, and smoke. There was a sense of urgency. This was the place to be yourself and party hard. And it wouldn't last long.

Chapter 28

While the games, eating, drinking, and music were being enjoyed by the crowd at the rally, the tent selling the motorcycle memorabilia was still doing a good business. But the tent behind the tent was selling other things, mainly guns, but also some knives: tactical folding knives, Bowie-fixed blade knives, and various other types. Lenny had brought most of the guns from Miami and stored them in Tina's storage unit, while Pete and Tony also brought some from their pawn shop. The guns from Miami were shipped in from South America. There were no serial numbers on those. Some had the numbers ground off or were ghost guns. There was no way to tell where they'd came from. Pete and Tony's guns were legal as far as they knew, although occasionally Tony would slip in a few he knew to be questionable. The knives also came from their shop.

"Tony, I think I saw her," said an excited Pete.

"Saw who? I'm glad you finally showed up. I'm starving, so I'm going to get something to eat. You're in charge. Lenny should be back before too long. We've been doing really well. I'll tell you about it when I get back." Tony plopped on his hat and started to leave.

"Don't you want to hear who I think I saw?"

"No, not now. Later. Like I said, I'm hungry." Shaking his head, Tony left Pete to man the tent.

Pete felt his world was swirling out of control. He found talking to Tony getting more and more difficult, especially if it concerned the dog walker. Going to scare her at the house with the cats was dumb. But how was he to know there were cats there? They spoiled everything. Damn allergies! Now she knew what he looked like, and he hadn't even had a chance to find out what she knew. Thinking about it gave him headaches and stomach problems. Plus, the wife insisted on coming, but now she wanted to spend all her time with her girlfriends doing who knows what. Just as he was lamenting his woes, a woman in extremely short blue jean shorts and an orange bikini top came up to him.

"So, this is where you're selling the guns? I want to buy one, and I want a pink one with rhinestones. Or maybe an orange one. Those are my favorite colors." She swished her black hair over her shoulder. Her hair was long, trailing way down her back, with numerous vibrant orange stripes like a tiger. Her makeup was Goth. Black lips and lots of black eye makeup. She looked more ready for Halloween than a motorcycle rally.

The guns were in locked cases. There were pistols: Glocks, Berettas, and Sig Sauers. Another case had rifles and shotguns, some decked out with lights, lasers, and/or scopes. Then there were the semiautomatic rifles and automatic guns, the latter being illegal. One item not for sale was the ammunition. It was much too dangerous at a rally. If you wanted danger, the ax-throwing contest, the boxing, the whipping, not to mention some of the other activities, could be dangerous enough.

"I hate to tell you, but we just have what you see. No pink or orange. But maybe one of the pistols we have would work for you." Pete caught the smell of her hand-rolled "cigarette" and wondered how many she'd already smoked. The Goth look was repulsive to him.

"I don't know. They look like the kind guys use. I want a girly one. Although I guess those MF19s, or whatever they're called, are pretty amazing, but probably too big for me." She hopped around and gave a loud honking laugh. A guy looking in another gun case glanced at her and shook his head, as if to say, "Bimbo."

"Have you used a gun before?" asked Pete. Maybe encouraging her wasn't a good idea.

"Just once. I was about five or six. My brother had a BB gun and I wanted to use it, but he wouldn't let me. Said I was too young. So, one day when he wasn't in his room, I took it and was going to go outside and try to shoot something. I don't know what. Just as I was about to go out the door, in he walks, and I was so startled I somehow pulled the trigger. Shot him in the eye." Another loud honking laugh erupted from her.

"That's not funny. Was he able to see from that eye afterwards?"

"Not very well. My folks were really pissed. But I think that shows I could probably be a good shooter. Didn't even try, and I shot his eye. Do you have any beer here? Now I'm thirsty. Or some chips?" She took one last drag from her joint.

"Nope, you'll have to go to the food tent." No way was she going to get a beer from the cooler behind him. He could hardly stand to look at her.

"I guess. Maybe I'll come back later. I have to give some thought to those ugly guns." More loud honking laughter and she was gone.

Lenny showed up an hour later. "This rally is really rocking. There are some wild characters out there. I think even more than last year."

"I think so too. Always are some real weirdos," agreed Pete. "Can you take over now? I really should go find Doreen. Haven't seen her all day."

"You both staying the night?" asked Lenny, sipping on a beer.

"Nah, I brought the camper for me. We both stayed in it last year, and she hated it. Too small and she didn't like the noise going on all night. She came with some friends this year. That way she can go home with them tonight and get some peace and quiet."

"Probably a smart move. I'm riding to town tonight too, but I'll be back early in the morning. Is Tony staying with you in the camper?"

"He did ride here with me, but he's got friends from out of town who have one of those mega-motor homes and I think that's where he's staying tonight. Can't blame him. Definitely a much better deal than the camper."

While Pete wandered around trying to find his wife as well as the dog-walking woman, Tony stood in the back of the crowd, listening to the band. The bluegrass music was just what he needed. He ran through his plan, comforted by the feel of the knife he had slipped into his boot. Pete wasn't the worst partner he'd ever had, but he always found something to worry about. Recently it had been his health, then his wife, stuff in the shop, the weather, and now this goddam dog-walking woman. He wouldn't get off it. Killing the FBI guy hadn't been the best idea, but they didn't have a choice. And if Pete hadn't insisted on harassing the woman, she wouldn't be an issue now. Once Pete got his mind set, there was no way to get him to change it. Well, there was one way, and it would be permanent.

Tony spotted Pete walking away from his wife and her girlfriends. Judging by the grouchy look on his face and the slouched shoulders, it hadn't been a pleasant conversation.

"Hey, Pete. Where are you going? Do you have any of that good bourbon in your camper? I could sure use a shot. What's with Doreen? You seem bent out of shape."

"I am. I told her I didn't know what time I'd be home tomorrow, but she said it didn't matter because she was going to Marco Island for a couple of days with her girlfriends. She's got some time off from work. I guess they're all chipping in to pay for a suite. Christ, she's never home. But boy, if I'm not home when she thinks I should be . . ."

"I hear you. Been down that road. After three divorces, believe me, being single is the way to go. Come on, let's get that drink so you can forget about your marital bliss." Tony laughed and slapped Pete on the back.

The plan was going better than expected. With Pete's wife going to Marco Island, she wouldn't even know he hadn't made it home. At least for a while. He'd tell Lenny he'd seen an extremely soused Pete staggering off toward the woods. Lenny wouldn't like it because he'd have more work to do. Too bad. But it was all going to work out.

Chapter 29

Tina was in a good mood. The rally had been a success. Several people told her how great it was, and they wanted her to be sure to have another one soon. Of course, they didn't have to do the planning and the clean-up. But the money they'd taken in made it worth doing. If only she could go back to bed and sleep for a couple of days. But that wasn't going to happen. Work, work, work.

First things first. She called Carlos and Ruben. "Hey, Rube. Where are you guys?" she asked as she puffed on her cigarette.

"We just left Miami. Lots of traffic like always. Carlos's sister woke us up super early. Tina, did you tell her to get us out of bed at the crack of dawn? It was a nasty thing to do. But then she did fix us breakfast burritos. That woman can cook."

"No comment. You want nasty, wait until you see the mess that you two have to clean up on the rally grounds. Some people can be such slobs."

Ruben looked over at Carlos sitting beside him in the passenger seat and rolled his eyes. "We can hardly wait," Carlos said facetiously, rubbing his blurry eyes. The folks at the rally weren't the only ones who'd partied hearty.

"Get here ASAP. But no speeding tickets."

"We'll get there when we get there," smart-mouthed Ruben as he ended the call. Easy to say and do when Tina was miles away.

"Open up one of those tacos your sister sent with us," he ordered.

"No way," Carlos said, "we just had breakfast. They're for lunch. You eat too much. Carmen was cooking the whole time we were there."

"Hey, I had to keep my strength up since your nephews kept wanting me to play with them all the time. They couldn't let me alone for one minute. Had to have their grubby little hands on me constantly. And I even had to babysit while you all went out to have a good time."

"Come on, you enjoyed it."

"Actually, they are cute little kids and fun to be with. At least for a little while. So, give me a taco."

"Okay, Ruben, but remember, this is your lunch." Carlos reached back in the van, opened the cooler with the tacos, and unwrapped one for Ruben. He didn't tell him about the taco chips, a container of salsa, and the beer that was also in the cooler. He'd want them too.

When Ruben and Carlos arrived at the rally site, crews were taking away the port-a-potties, bleachers, tables, bandstand, and miscellaneous other paraphernalia. Tina spotted them as soon as they arrived.

"Why'd you hang up on me?" she growled, glaring at Ruben.

"Connection wasn't good in that area. I could hardly hear you."

"Like I'm supposed to believe that. You two get those tents down and take them back to town. When you get back here, I want you to clean up the camping area. I did a brief walk-around, and it's a freaking mess. You'll need the box of big garbage bags I left near the truck. And I suggest you wear gloves. Lenny took the sign down by the road and he's been helping direct traffic for the vendors. He's packing up his van now, although he doesn't have much to take back to Miami. He's leaving his bike in the barn so don't touch it.

"How was the rally?" Carlos asked.

"Sales were good overall. The guys who have the pawn shop sold most of their stuff too. I didn't get a chance to talk to the couple selling the memorabilia, but from what I could tell they did all right. How was your trip?"

Ruben yawned and then Carlos did the same.

"Our trip . . ." started Carlos.

"You'll have to tell me later," Tina snapped. "Go get the tents down. I'm going back to the house. I have some paperwork to do. I'll take my bike."

Ruben and Carlos slowly walked away, and Carlos whispered, "Why did she ask about our trip if she didn't want to know about it?"

"That's Tina. It's all about her. Like why do we care about what happened at the rally, since she didn't want us to be there? And I gather Lenny isn't going to help us with the tents. What a crappy job. I'm going to get a taco from the van while you get started. I'll be right back." Ruben pretended he didn't hear Carlos' profane comment.

They eventually managed to get the tents taken apart and loaded into Tina's pickup truck. It was a one-ton white Ford truck with red flame detailing. She'd bought it from a farmer who owned a large citrus orchard. It had been his son's, but the kid went off to college, so of course he wanted a cooler vehicle to drive around campus. Ruben and Carlos usually drove the van, but on occasion they did get to drive the truck which they preferred.

When they returned from delivering the tents to the rental shop, Carlos was hungry. He'd been thinking about his sister's tacos all the way back from town. She definitely knew how to cook.

"Time for lunch. I'm getting the tacos out of the cooler. My sister put in a bunch. She even put in a couple for Tina. Do you want one? I saw she also put in some beer."

Ruben shuffled his feet, glanced over to the truck, and mumbled, "Nah, I'm good. I'm going over to the camping area to start on the clean-up. I'll take the garbage bags with me."

Carlos couldn't believe his ears. Ruben not eating and actually offering to do some work! Either he was taken over by aliens or he had done something he shouldn't have. It turned out to be the latter. When Carlos opened the cooler, the words emitting from his mouth turned the air blue. The cooler contained two empty beer bottles, an empty dish that had held salsa, a wad of empty wrappers, a few broken taco chips, and two unopened beers. That was it. He might have known. He should have put a lock on the cooler. Or on Ruben's mouth. Tina was going to hear about this. He jumped into the truck and took off for the house.

"Tina, that shitty Ruben ate everything," tattled Carlos.

"What are you talking about?" asked Tina as she was slapping bologna on some white bread.

"My sister made tacos for the three of us, plus she packed taco chips, salsa, and beer. Slimeball ate it all. Only thing left were two beers and some crumbs."

"I think Ruben will just explode one of these days. Well, here you go." Tina handed Carlos the bologna sandwich. "I don't cook like your sister, but I'm not bad."

Carlos opened up the sandwich. Two slices of bologna. That was it, no butter or mustard. "Uh, is there any cheese I could add to this?"

"Don't know, Mr. Fussy. Check the fridge. Also, bring me the little jar of garlic."

"What are you going do with that?" asked Carlos.

"Put it on my sandwich. What did you think I was going to do? Put it up my nose?"

There was some yellow American cheese, but the package had been left open, so it was dried out. Better than nothing. Carlos took out the cheese, mustard, and garlic.

After doctoring up their sandwiches, Tina and Carlos sat at her kitchen table. Tina had thrown a bag of Cheetos on the table. They had to push aside the ashtrays and the beer cans so they could set their plates down.

"I'm gonna get a Coke," said Carlos. "You want one?"

"Nah, get me a beer. I think I'm still in rally mode. You know I never tried diced garlic on a sandwich before. One of my friends suggested it. She said it's really good and healthy for you. I like it." Tina munched on her bologna and garlic sandwich. "You should try it."

"Jeez, I can certainly smell it. You'll definitely be safe from vampires. I hope you don't have a date tonight."

"Don't know why you say that. Any garlic smell will be gone by tonight anyway."

He doesn't need to know whether I have a date or not thought Tina. *And, actually, I do. It's been a while. Rallies are good places to hook-up. Now what the hell's his name. Oh, I know. Elmo. Makes me think of Sesame Street. He seemed nice. Maybe a little rough around the edges. Hope he changes his clothes and takes a bath.*

Carlos got up from the table and took his plate and glass to the sink. "I'd better get back and help what's his name clean up, although he really doesn't deserve any help." Anything to get away from the garlic smell. She must have put half the contents of the jar on her sandwich. "See you later, Tina."

"See you tomorrow. I won't be home tonight." Tina gave a little smirk and patted the Bantu knots on her head.

As Carlos was on his way back to the rally site to help Ruben with the clean-up, his cellphone rang. An agitated, nearly hysterical Ruben was on the line. "You gotta get here right away. There's a . . . there's a guy here, and I think he's dead. No, I know he's dead. I didn't do it. Why did I have to be the one to find him? Hurry up. Don't tell Tina." Click.

Ruben was hot. His face was the color of a cooked shrimp, and he was sweating profusely, his tank top totally wet. How could this happen to him? Finding another body. Maybe it would be best to just take off and pretend he'd never seen him. Carlos would be really freaked out. He'd better get his butt here soon. Since they were the last ones here, they'd probably get the blame.

"Ruben, where are you?" Carlos called. "I'm not going hunting for you and your so-called dead guy. I can't believe you really found another body."

He found Ruben sitting on a big log with his head back and his eyes closed. Carlos walked up to him and kicked his foot, jarring him alert.

"Christ, you don't need to be so sneaky," yelled a startled Ruben. "It's about time you showed up. I've been working my ass off. First, I want to show you the body I found. We've got to decide what to do."

"What do you mean, 'we'? You're the one who found him. If there really is a body."

"Oh, there's a body, all right. Come on, I'll show you. I tell you; this guy did not have a good time at the rally."

Ruben led the way into the trees toward the back of the camping area. Partially leaning against a live oak tree was the body of a man who, without a doubt, was deceased. His head sagged downward toward his chest. It appeared that his throat had been slit. Blowfly larva crawled around the neck. Dried blood covered the front of his shirt and the ground next to him.

"See, I told you," said Ruben. "I didn't go close to him. I didn't want to destroy the evidence. They always complain about that on those detective shows. What do you think? Should we just pretend we never saw him?"

Carlos shook his head and backed away. "Well, you're right he's definitely dead. I dunno about pretending we haven't seen him. Maybe people would think we did it when he is found. Do you think other people saw him? He's kinda out of the way. I guess there could have been tents this far back. When we cleaned up last year, were the tents this far back?"

"I can't remember. The only reason I walked back here was the beer cans. It was like someone wanted to see how far they could throw them. Does he look familiar to you?"

"Jeez, Ruben, one glance at him was enough. I'd rather not look again." Carlos headed in the opposite direction, his face ashen. "Who does he look like?"

"I think one of the guys from the rally last year. It's hard to say for sure. You know, with his head tilted. Tina's gonna be pissed when she finds out he's on her property. She'll probably blame us, and we'll get fired. And the cops will come and find the puppy mill and the marijuana."

"Don't call it a puppy mill. It's a puppy farm. And I'm not sure about the weed. I didn't see any."

"Don't forget about the dog treats."

"She could have bought the weed from someone else."

"Tina's got money but she's cheap. I bet she has a patch somewhere. I'm hot. Let's go sit in the truck and decide what to do with you know who." Ruben mopped his brow with the bottom of his tank top.

"We're gonna have to think this through. This is serious shit. I still can't believe it, another body. We don't want the cops finding out what we did with the other dead guy or that we were living in that house when we shouldn't have been."

Chapter 30

Tony unlocked the door to the pawn shop. He strolled in and gazed around. It was going to be different without Pete, that was for sure. He'd actually done him a favor. At least Pete wouldn't have to always be worried about whatever. He wouldn't have his wife always nagging at him. Yep, it should work out fine. Might have to get a new partner though. See how it goes.

He ran a check list in his mind. Need to call Pete's wife at home, leave a message on the phone. 'Where's Pete?' It's good she's not home. Pete's cellphone was turned off and somehow got dropped in a port-a-potty. Don't need to worry about that one. The gun sales were good. Knife sales not so good. One had to be cleaned off a lot. Hope it sells soon. Be good to have that one gone. It'll all work out. Wonder if Pete was right about the dog-walking woman? Maybe she could be a potential problem. Have to think about that one and possibly take some action. Tie up all the loose ends. Seems one thing leads to another.

Scottie and Charlie were having Piper and Jack over for a dinner of fresh grouper. Scottie made potato salad and a strawberry pie. After she set the table in the lanai, she'd gone into the bedroom to put on the tattoo sleeve she'd bought at the rally. She'd bought two sleeves but decided she'd only wear one. Two was a bit much. The white sundress would make the sleeve definitely stand out. The fabric was a lightweight nylon with a circus motif. She slipped it on and viewed herself in the mirror. Wow. The shoulder to wrist sleeve looked like the real thing. Her only jewelry was a white pearl ring and gold hoop earrings.

"Charlie, what do you think?" Scottie stood in front of him, waiting for a comment on the tattoo sleeve. Men often didn't notice the things you hoped they would.

"Think about what? Just kidding. That sleeve is pretty amazing but it's just not you. I'm glad it isn't real. It'll be interesting to see what Piper says."

"I told her I got it and that it hurt like hell and took all day. She couldn't believe I'd do such a crazy thing. I said she should have it done, but she claimed she'd stick to her only tattoo being permanent eyeliner."

When Piper and Jack arrived, Scottie was in the lanai putting a vase of pink roses on the table. Piper spotted Scottie outside and turned to Jack. "OMG, I can't believe she did it. Look at her arm. I'm going to have a major chat with that woman. Who knows what she's planning to do next?"

"Oh, leave her alone. It might be a neat design. Let's go check it out."

"Scottie Shelton, I want to see that arm of yours. You do realize that in two more days you're going to be tired of that tattoo and you'll have to wear long-sleeved clothes the rest of your life."

Scottie was totally enjoying herself. This was working out better than she hoped. "Oh, come on, Piper. You're just jealous. I know you want one." She gave Jack a wink and saw him grinning.

"I saw that wink. What's going on with you two?" asked a puzzled Piper. "Charlie, do you know what they're up to?"

"No idea," an amused Charlie answered.

"I guess I'd better fess up. Jack what do you think?"

Piper peered closely at Scottie's arm. "That's not a real tattoo. I can't believe you faked me out like that. I didn't know there was such a thing. I'm feeling better now. You had me worried." She gave Scottie a quick hug clearly relieved that her friend hadn't done something she would later regret.

During dinner Scottie and Charlie told their guests about what they'd heard and seen at the rally. Scottie even had some pictures she had taken with her phone.

"I have to tell you about this one woman I saw," she said. "It was unbelievable. I don't think you saw her, Charlie. You had gone to get us some extra napkins because eating the food was kind of sloppy. This gal had absolutely no clothing on. It was all paint. She was painted to look like she had on frayed blue jean shorts and a dark pink tank top. I have to admit, it was very well done. I mean, I took a second look, and the only reason I did was because some guys sitting near me made comments about how good she looked without clothes."

"How come you didn't tell me about her? I should have checked her out. I didn't see a picture of her on your phone either," a disappointed Charlie commented with a chuckle.

Grinning, Jack said, "I agree. You should've told him about her, or at least taken a picture."

"You guys. Neither of you are old enough to see anything like that. Piper, can you imagine yourself going around with just body paint? Not anything I would do. But then there were a lot of goings on that I wouldn't get involved in. Still, we had a good time, and it sure seemed like everyone else did too. You really should go to one sometime."

Piper looked doubtful. "Maybe. We'll see. Changing the subject. Have you had any more unusual activity at your house or strange things happening to you?"

"You mean besides Mr. B?"

"I wasn't referring to Mr. B, who by the way, is still planning to spend one more night with you. I meant the people trying to scare you or worse."

"No, thank goodness. But I think I saw the guy who might be messing with me at the rally. Unfortunately, I never got to speak to him. He melted into the crowd before I had a chance. It might not have even been him. There were lots of guys wearing T-shirts or tanks and jeans, but this guy had on a short-sleeve button-down shirt. There weren't too many dressed like that. Hopefully, that's the last of the creepy episodes. It's been a while since I've been harassed."

Chapter 31

Carlos and Ruben were faced with a huge dilemma. What to do with the body, if anything.

"I think we should just leave him there. It's none of our business. Pretend we never saw him." Ruben tried to turn the air conditioning up in the truck, but it was already as high as it would go.

"Problem is we did see him. And we're the last ones here. For sure we'd get blamed. We'd have to hire a lawyer, and you know how expensive that could be."

"How about we tell Tina what we found? After all, he's on her property. Let her take care of him. It's really her problem."

Carlos gave a big sigh. "You really think that's a good idea? You know Tina. She'd probably fire us and say we brought the body from Miami or something crazy like that."

"That's stupid. Why'd we do that? We didn't even know the guy."

"I'm not saying we'd ever do that, numbnuts. Get serious."

They sat there quietly in the truck, each trying to come up with a suitable solution until a snore emanated from Ruben.

"What the . . . are you sleeping?" Carlos gave him a fierce nudge in the shoulder.

"Huh? Why'd you do that? I was trying to think."

"Oh really. And what's your plan?" asked Carlos, knowing full well he probably didn't have one.

"I think we should do what we did to the other one. You know."

Carlos looked at Ruben in amazement. "Wow, you *were* thinking about our situation. So, you get your ideas when you're asleep?" he said sarcastically.

"Asleep or awake. I'm good. What do you think? It worked the last time."

"We were in a major hurry that time. Just dumped him in the river, clothes and all."

"Whatever. At least that one wasn't covered in blood like this one. I think there might be a river not too far from here. A branch of the Myakka or something. Maybe that would work. But, you know, I don't even like looking at the bloody mess."

"We can just roll him in a tarp, stick him in the back of the truck, and away we go."

"Except we don't have a tarp. And Tina's going to get suspicious if we say we want to use the truck. For sure she'd ask why. And we can't put him in the truck the way he is."

"What do you mean? You want to give him a bath first?"

"Shape up, Ruben. I'm saying we can't go riding around with a body in the back of the truck uncovered."

"I guess. Maybe a garbage bag? There's some we didn't use. And toss him off at the dump with the other garbage bags."

"It'd take more than one bag, and I bet they'd notice the smell at the dump after a while. Then they'd trace him back here."

"For someone we didn't even know he's sure causing us a lot of trouble," groused Ruben, lighting up a smoke. He took a deep drag and held it, then chuckled and said, "This will help me get more good ideas."

"Get rid of that thing right now. You're not the best thinker when you're high. Where'd you get it from, anyway?"

"Found a little pouch with a few joints. One of the campers probably lost it."

"Well, this is not the time to zonk out. We don't have a lot of time to get the job done."

"Okay, okay. You're such a buzz kill." He took another hit, then threw the rest out the window.

"This is what we'll do. You go take his clothes off, and I'll get the bags and then join you."

"We didn't take the clothes off the other guy. And why am 'I' taking his clothes off? It's 'we' are going take the clothes off."

"You have to take off the clothes because like I told you, I can't stand to look at him. We can put the shirt, pants, and shoes in different trash bags from the rally. We don't want them showing up on the shore where they could be recognized. If you remember, we were in such a hurry with the other body we didn't have time to undress the guy. I wonder why he was never found. At least we never heard anything about him."

"Which is fine with me. He probably got eaten up by some critter. Well, you can take the pants off. That way you don't have to look at his head and neck. You make me do all the dirty work. I wonder if he has a wallet or a cellphone on him. Whoever did him in probably took them."

"If there is a wallet and there are credit cards, we're not using them. Got that? We can take the cash, but that's it. And we're not using the cellphone. We could be tracked down. Let's get going." Carlos felt like his heart was beating as fast as hummingbird wings. Way too much stress.

Ruben grabbed some garbage bags, and they went back to where the body was propped against the tree. Carlos averted his eyes from the upper part of the body. Getting the shirt off was going to be really icky. Ruben didn't appear to have any qualms about it.

"I'm going to wait till you have the shirt off before I take off the pants. We're going to leave his underwear on, right?"

"Christ, Carlos, I don't care, leave them on unless there's gold or jewels in them. He probably thought he had jewels in them. Get it?" Ruben cracked up, obviously a little stoned now. Then he switched gears and cursed. "The blood has dried all over the shirt so it's hard opening the buttons. Plus, he keeps falling over. Come here and hold him up."

Carlos shook his head. "Just let him fall over. It'll be easier that way, or can't you bend over that far to take the shirt off?"

"Of course I can bend over that far."

Carlos braved a peek as Ruben let the body go. It fell sideways, causing the head to turn to the side and almost become detached. Carlos gagged. Hopefully, the head wouldn't come off. Ruben bent over, lost his balance, and wound up sitting on the outstretched arm of the corpse.

"Holy shit. I'm on his arm. Come and help me," he yelled.

"Just move your ass off his arm and you can work on the shirt right where you are," suggested Carlos.

"You gotta come and help now. Before the fire ants know I'm here. You know what they do to me. I got two buttons open. Maybe I can rip it open."

"No, don't do that. The buttons will fly all over and we'll never find them."

"Then get over here. This ain't easy. This guy's not helping at all."

Carlos glanced down at Ruben sitting on the ground next to the body. It'd take a forklift to get them both up.

He knelt down on the other side of the body and pulled the shirt out of the pants while looking away from the body. Just by feel he managed to get the three bottom buttons open.

"I'm going pull his pants off now," Carlos announced. "I can't believe I'm saying that. Guess I better take his shoe off first. Did you get the rest of the buttons?"

"Yeah, and you've got to help me roll him over so we can get the shirt off all the way. I got it started, but I can't get any leverage."

"Let me finish getting the pants off first."

"No, the shirt has to come off now. I'm sure the ants are getting ready to attack any second. I can't stay here sitting on the ground. He's smelly and there are maggots on his neck." Ruben's face was getting redder and redder, the panic in his voice clearly evident.

"Oh, all right. You're right about the smell. Is it you or the dead guy? Here, take my hands. Jeez, your hands are dirty and sweaty." Carlos wrinkled his face in disgust as he tried to pull Ruben up.

"In case you didn't notice, I've been working on the bloody part of the job. You're going to have to pull harder than that." Ruben hadn't budged an inch from the ground.

"I don't think this is going to work. You're too heavy. I'll probably dislocate a shoulder or get a hernia. Maybe I should just call someone."

"Oh, like 911? You know we can't call anyone. Now, just put some back muscle into it. I'm not fat, I'm big-boned. On the count of three, lift me up. One, two, three."

Holding Ruben's hands, Carlos pulled as hard as he could to get Ruben into almost a standing position. Unfortunately, Ruben, teetered forward, not quite balanced on his feet, knocking Carlos to the ground and falling on top of him.

"Ooof." Carlos had the wind knocked out of him. "Get the hell off of me. You're gonna kill me. You must weigh two tons. And you stink."

With a grunt and great effort Ruben managed to roll his body off of Carlos. Carlos quickly jumped up and away from Ruben.

"It's your fault I fell. You should have made sure I was totally standing. And you don't smell so good yourself," a miffed Ruben complained, sitting on the ground. "Now what am I supposed to do?"

Carlos considered his coworker and shook his head. "I know one thing; I'm not going to try to get you up. I probably have not only a hernia and a dislocated shoulder but broken ribs. Maybe you could scoot over to that tree and try holding on to it and work your way up."

"I'm not a dog. I don't scoot," said an exasperated Ruben. He managed to maneuver himself onto his knees and crawl the short distance to the tree Carlos pointed out. "I'm going to need knee surgery. You should have cleared the sticks and the other crap I had to crawl over. My knees are probably all bloody." With much swearing and grunting he managed to grab the tree, get off his knees and slowly make it to a standing position.

"Now what? I need something to drink," said a huffing and puffing Ruben.

Ignoring Ruben's latest demand, Carlos started to take off the shoe of the dead man. "Just go ahead and see if you can get his arms out of the shirt."

"Okay, but I'm gonna need help getting him in a sitting position. I'm glad he wasn't wearing a T-shirt. Let's hope the head doesn't come off."

Carlos squelched the urge to retch. "You had to say that. I got his shoe off. Let me get the pants off before we get him sitting up. This is so much worse than the last time. The other one was neat and tidy. This guy is a bloody mess." After much tugging the pants finally slid free.

"Don't forget to get the wallet," Ruben said. "I could use some extra money."

"It's 'we' could use some extra money." Carlos checked all the pockets. Nothing. "No wallet or anything else. Must have been a robbery," he declared.

"Just our luck. Okay, let's get his arms out of this shirt. Then we can get him in the bags. You're going to have to help me get him sitting up. I can't do it by myself."

"Can't you do anything? I took the shoes and his pants off. You only have the shirt to work on."

"Get over here and stop being such a wuss."

Carlos folded up the pants and placed the shoe on top. His stomach churning, he turned to Ruben and the body.

"This better be quick. This is really getting to me. Okay, you take one shoulder and I'll take the other. We should be able to hoist him up against the tree. But I'm not going to look at him."

"Whatever. I'll pull up this shoulder, since I'm closest to it." Ruben put both hands on the shoulder and pulled it upward.

Carlos grasped the other shoulder while looking in the opposite direction. With simultaneous grunts they got the body into a partial sitting position. The head now dangled toward Ruben.

"Rube, don't you have one of those super-duper knives with all the gizmos on it? I bet there're some scissors on it."

"I think it's in the truck, in the glove box. Why don't you go get it? You know, that might work. We could just cut the shirt near the collar and down the back and it would be easy to get his arms through the sleeves."

Sure enough, scissors were a part of the knife. Carlos handed them to Ruben. "Here you go. Let me know when you're done the cutting the shirt, and I'll pull the arm through the shirt on my side."

It actually worked. They managed to get the shirt off.

"Okay, let's bag 'em and 'tag em. Isn't that what they say on TV shows?" asked Carlos.

"Yep, that's it, or maybe it's the other way. Tell you what, knowing how sensitive you are and what a tender tummy you have, I'll bag the top half and you can do the bottom," Ruben said sarcastically.

Carlos again pretended he didn't hear the comment and quickly shoved the body into the garbage bag up to the waist. Ruben did the same on the top half, carefully making sure the head was still attached. They tied the bags together and tied another around the middle of the body. Between the two of them they managed to load the body in the front part of the truck bed. They then divided up the clothes and the shoes and shoved them into different bags of rally trash.

"How could there be so much trash?" grumbled Ruben as he threw the last bag in the back of the truck.

"It just tells you there was a lot of eating and drinking and who knows what else going on. I guess we'll have to go to the dump first to get rid of the garbage and then go to the river . . ."

"But won't someone at the dump see what's left in the truck and wonder about it?"

"For once you're right. We'll have to dump the body off first and then the garbage," Carlos said. He narrowed his eyes at the mound of trash obscuring the body in the truck bed.

"How the hell we gonna do that? We put him in first, and now the trash bags are piled up in front of him. I gotta cool off." Ruben's face was beet red. He yanked open the door of the truck, climbed in, and turned up the air conditioning.

Carlos joined him. The air conditioning felt wonderful. "The way I see it, we have two options. One, we take all the trash bags out first, then move the body to the front and reload the trash in the back. Or option two, you climb over the trash and then haul the body over it so he's right in front. We just grab the body and throw it in the river, minus the bags he's in, of course. And then we go to the dump and get rid of all that garbage."

"You come up with the stupidest ideas. Did your mother drop you on your head when you were a baby or what?" Ruben looked at his partner and shook his head.

"Okay, smartass, what's your plan? We'd better do something damn quick. Things are getting pretty smelly in the back of this truck, and Tina's gonna be wondering where we are."

"All right, how about this?" Ruben had a rather smug look on his face.

Chapter 32

Tony was quite pleased with himself. Things were going well. Pete's wife, Doreen, had called him when she arrived home Monday night, saying she hadn't been able to get hold of her husband. Plus, the camper wasn't at home. It was usually parked next to the side of the house when not in use. She had sounded concerned but not panicked. Yet.

Tony calmly reassured her everything was fine. He said the last time he'd seen Pete was Saturday night at the rally. He informed her they had drinks in the camper and then he'd left to see friends. Pete had coyly mentioned he was seeing someone later in the camper. Nothing to worry about. Pete had been drinking a lot. Probably nothing happened. Obviously, Tony didn't tell her he'd left a dead, bloody Pete slouched against a tree. After that he'd driven the camper to town and parked it on the street near the beach with the key in it. Easy pickings.

After leaving the camper, Tony had found walking the approximately two miles to his house quite therapeutic. A great way to clear the mind and think about the future. It was late and, except for an occasional break in the clouds and the periodic streetlight, quite dark. He carried his duffle bag, which was mostly empty. He'd changed his clothes in the camper after dispatching his partner. He'd even thought to bring an extra pair of shoes. Just in case. He'd dumped his soiled clothing in the trash at the rally, along with the sanitizer wipes he used to clean his hands.

At home the next morning he'd driven his car down the street where he'd left the camper; it was no longer there. He congratulated himself for the clever thinking on the way to get rid of the camper. There would be more fingerprints in addition to his and Pete's on the steering wheel.

Doreen called the pawn shop the next day, and Tony said that Pete hadn't shown up for work. Now she was beginning to panic.

"Where the hell do you think he is? I think I'd better call the cops. He's never done anything like this before."

In a calm, soothing voice, Tony said, "I'm sure he'll show up. I'd wait before calling the cops. I think there's a time limit before they do anything. You know he's been acting kinda uptight lately. Has he been that way at home? Sort of moody? He hasn't been himself, but he didn't tell me about any problems, and I didn't want to pry. Is everything okay at home?"

"Now that you mention it, he has been acting rather strangely. Like something is bothering him, but he hasn't said what. I even asked him several times. I know he didn't like me going with the girls to Marco Island, but hell, he does his stuff, and I don't say much. Besides, he was acting weird before the Marco trip. What do you think I should do?"

"Have you called your friends? Maybe they've heard from him. Or what about his mom? It seems like he talks to her quite a bit. Is he worried about her?"

"I did call his mom. I didn't want to get her too excited because she has a heart condition, so I just asked if she'd heard about the rally we went to. She hadn't heard from him either. Same with the friends I called. Something is definitely wrong." Doreen began sniffling.

Tony did some quick thinking. He had to calm her down. No cops this soon. "Listen, if neither of us has heard from him by tonight when I close up the shop, how about I pick you up and we go to dinner and figure out what to do?"

"I guess," she said doubtfully. "I gotta get to work. I told them I'd be a little late. Call me later this afternoon."

"Definitely. Now stop worrying. Everything will be fine. I'll call afer I leave work." Keeping tabs on her was the best thing to do. Besides, she wasn't bad looking. And he didn't have to be concerned about Pete getting jealous. Hell, maybe he could even get her to work at the shop. He checked out the knives in the glass case and smiled.

Strolling to the front window of the shop, Tony turned his thoughts to the dog walker. What was Pete going to tell him about her? Maybe he should have listened.

Couldn't have been much. Pete was just such a paranoid dick. Although the dog walker could be a problem, and something did need to be done. The quick hang-up calls he'd made to her on a burner phone were probably stupid. Maybe a drive by the house. Late at night so she wouldn't see the car. Just to see if the friend stayed over. Pretending to be an FBI agent might be the way to get some info about what she knew. Might be a dumb idea, but it wasn't going away.

Tony called Doreen after he got home from work. He gave his best impression of concern. She definitely was getting more upset. There was some minor weeping as she explained she'd had no news from or about Pete.

Tony swirled the ice around in his glass of scotch. "There's got to be a logical explanation about where he is. The fact he took off in the camper . . . well, I hate to say it, but it doesn't look good."

"You think he's been having an affair and took off with some woman?" Doreen asked.

"Listen, I'm gonna come and see you. I'll be there in a half an hour. Pete was my best buddy for a long time. I don't want you to worry about him by yourself. He means a lot to both of us," he lied smoothly.

"Okay, you're right. See you soon. It helps to have someone who understands how you feel when your life has been turned upside down."

Chapter 33

"Well, hi there," Scottie said. "It's great to hear from you. It seems like it's been ages since we've talked."

Bonita gave a small chuckle. "I know. Out-of-town company has been keeping me busy. Two different groups. Fortunately, they were easy to entertain. I only cooked a couple of meals, and the rest of the time we ate out. Plus, they even took Missy out for walks. What have you been doing?"

"Missy, do you have to?" she said to the dog. "She insists on sitting in my lap. I think she recognizes your voice."

"Of course, she does. We're good walking friends. Hi, Missy," Scottie called over the phone. "Bonita, did I tell you Charlie and I went to a motorcycle rally? What a hoot."

"No, you didn't. Tell me about it. That doesn't sound like your kind of thing."

"It really isn't, but we had a good time." Scottie went on to tell Bonita the highlights of their adventure. She had her friend in fits of hysterical laughter with some of her descriptions.

"I did hear there was a rally not too far from here, but only because a gal in my book club was talking to a friend of a friend who said there was a couple who had gone to a rally and the wife hasn't seen her husband since. Do you think it could be the same one you went to?"

"Maybe. This one wasn't too far from here. I wouldn't think a lot of rallies would be held at the same time in the same area. It wasn't a big one though. From what I've been told, quite small compared to rallies in South Dakota or California, or even Daytona Beach. Maybe her husband just ran off with some dingbat. I'm sure there were all sorts of mood enhancers being smoked, injected, and drunk. People can do crazy things under the influence."

"You're right there. And who knows if I really got the story correct. It was at least third-hand info."

"Stories do tend to be embellished after a while. But I have to tell you that I thought I saw one of the guys at the rally who's been harassing me. I only saw him briefly, and Charlie didn't see him at all. Of course, he wouldn't recognize him anyway. It was probably my imagination, but there was just something about him. Although I have to say, nothing has happened to me for a while." A few hang-up calls weren't worth mentioning.

"You're usually good at recognizing people. But as long as you're not bothered again, I wouldn't worry about it. I haven't heard anything about the missing guy, and the FBI agents haven't been around here asking questions. At least not that I know of. That situation was so weird."

"You got that right. They're probably still working on the case, but we just don't know about it. I haven't had a chance to ask Kevin if he's heard anything."

"The reason I called was to ask you and Charlie to dinner one night this week," said Bonita.

"Sounds great. Unfortunately, this is one of those weeks. Charlie's going to Miami for a couple of days to give lectures at the medical school, and Mr. B is going to spend some time with me. You know the dog I mean. He's even staying overnight again. I don't know why I let Piper talk me into these things. He's such a huge dog. Not my type at all, although he is very handsome and affectionate. How about next week? I'll check with Charlie to see when he's free and call you back."

"Works for me. Have fun with Mr. B. Talk to you later."

Scottie made a mental checklist of chores around the house that she'd been putting off for some time. Straightening out her clothes closet, organizing her shoes, washing the glass tables on the lanai. Some ironing to do. Surely ironing must be some sort of sin in Florida. The list was endless, and she knew she'd have to take Mr. B. for a long walk and wouldn't have time to do many chores with him at her house. She set to work. Putting on her ear buds and listening to some fun Latin music made the work not so mundane.

That night, after fixing herself a grilled cheese and bacon sandwich and a cup of tomato soup, she sat alone at the kitchen table. It was relaxing to be alone occasionally, but she did miss Charlie. He was kind, considerate, and they laughed a lot. They'd grown so comfortable with one another. She hadn't been seeing her friends as often since she met Charlie, but she knew they were there if she needed them and vice versa. And of course, Kevin. It was time to call her nephew and catch up with him. No weird people, dead bodies or bizarre happenings need enter her peaceful life. She knew that's not the way life always treats you. But for now, life was good.

Chapter 34

After Ruben and Carlos finally got the cargo in the back of the truck organized, they attempted to use a map app on their phones to find the river where they planned to dump the body.

"Jesus H. Christ, this stupid phone doesn't work right," complained Ruben.

"Oh really. I'm shocked. I think I finally found the river. Take a look." Carlos handed his phone over to his partner and pointed to the map. "See, we're here. If we turn left out of here and drive along until we get to this—"

"Just give me directions. I don't want to look at that damn phone. Let's get this done." Ruben started up the truck, spun the tires, and they were on their way.

"Okay, okay. Just cool your jets. I don't think it's too far away."

After about a half an hour, Carlos was shifting in his seat. "Uh, I think we must have missed the turnoff."

"What do you mean? Aren't you paying attention to the freaking map?"

"Of course I'm looking at the map. If you weren't driving so bloody fast we wouldn't have missed it. Turn around and drive slower."

Ruben gave Carlos the stink eye and turned the truck around. After about fifteen minutes they found the turn off, and drove on a dirt road to a secluded spot along the river, and stopped.

Ruben opened the tailgate on the truck and ordered Carlos to take one end of the body.

"Which end is the feet? That's what I want."

"Here, take this." Ruben pointed to the garbage bag that held the feet. He grabbed the other end, determining from a telltale lump that the head was no longer attached. It had moved further down the sack. The trip in the truck apparently was too much for it. He didn't say anything to Carlos. It was going to be tricky getting the body out of the bags and into the river without Carlos seeing the headless traveler.

They hauled the body to the edge of the river. They both stood admiring the river a moment. It flowed along slowly, gurgling quietly, the trees along both sides framing it beautifully.

"I kinda like this river," said Carlos. "I think it'd be fun to kayak on it or something. Do people swim in here?"

Ruben stepped back a few paces, not answering the question. "Do you see what I see on the bank over there?"

"Holy Mother of God, it's huge. I don't think I've ever seen a gator that big." Carlos turned his shocked face to Ruben. "Come on, hurry up before that big boy decides we're his next meal instead of our bag buddy here. That answers my question about swimming in the river."

They quickly untied the bag that was tied around the middle of the body and had started to pull the other bags off when Ruben told Carlos to pull his bag all the way off and go back to start the truck. He knew Carlos would freak out seeing the head roll out.

"Are you going to be able to push him in the water by yourself?"

"Yeah, I think so. Go on. We gotta get out of here." As soon as Carlos started back to the truck, Ruben pulled the other bag off the body, and the head rolled into the river. Bending over to push the body out as far as he could, he almost found himself in the river as well. On glancing up he noticed the gator quietly slipping into the water. Holy shit. It was heading toward him.

Ruben grabbed the garbage bags and headed for the truck. He wasn't a runner, but he definitely was a fast waddler. When he got to the truck, he threw the bags in the back, yanked open the door, hopped in, slammed the door shut, and heaved several deep breaths.

"What's the matter with you?" asked Carlos. "The ants after you again? Did you get him into the water?"

"Not ants. That damn gator slid into the water and started swimming right toward me. You should have seen his beady little eyes aiming at me. I just escaped the jaws of death."

"You would have made a great happy meal for him. Hopefully he'll be satisfied with the snack we left him." Carlos laughed nervously. He started the truck down the road.

"I don't appreciate that remark you made about me," Ruben said as he mopped his face with the bottom of his filthy shirt. "I could have been killed by that gator. A lot you would have cared." Ruben turned an offended face toward the side window. You know who your friends are when they think you'd make a good gator meal."

"Oh, stop whining. It would never have gotten you, but at least it'll find the body. We'd better get the garbage to the dump. Tina's gonna wonder where the hell we've been. We should have been back to her place ages ago."

"Whatever," Ruben mumbled, feeling stressed out, hungry, thirsty, dirty, and abused. "Happy gator meal, my ass."

———————————

Tina's date had not gone well. He looked a hell of a lot better at the rally when she was drunk. When he picked her up at her house, she wasn't sure he'd even changed his clothes since the rally. The jeans looked like they could stand up with no one in them, except the weight of the gigantic belt buckle would take them down. Without the cowboy hat, the combover of the four brown hairs was not impressive, nor was the missing incisor.

Having told her he was taking her out for an evening of great dining and dancing, Tina had dressed accordingly. She wore a sleeveless, low-cut, blue and white striped dress. The stripes somewhat blended in with her various body rolls. Big blue and white plastic earrings and white super high-heels completed her ensemble. She was disappointed when he opened the car door of his early model Hyundai to find the passenger seat full of fast-food containers and soda cans.

"And where am I supposed to sit?" she growled at him.

"Oh, sorry about that." He pushed the trash on the floor.

"No way am I going to put my feet in that shit," Tina said.

"You're a bit of a prima donna, aren't you? But you're a real woman." He threw the wrappers and cans into the back seat.

"What's that supposed to mean? Real woman."

"I like women with a little heft to 'em."

"That's insulting. I not sure I want to go to dinner with you."

"Aw, come on. I'm just kidding. We'll have a blast."

The dining venue turned out to be Bubba's Bistro. The menu was rather esoteric, featuring mostly a variety of unusual sandwiches and burgers. Her date ordered a liver and onion sandwich, and she ordered the tongue and cream cheese wrap. A pitcher of house IPA beer washed down the food perfectly. As for the dancing, the music was just the country tunes coming over the bar speakers, and the dance floor was the size of a napkin. They attempted one dance, but his halitosis and the fact he stomped on her big toe put an end to that. The only positive thing she found about the dining experience was she could say she had been there. On the way back to Tina's house his nonstop discourse of his job as a flag man on a road construction job put her to sleep.

When they did arrive at her house, she quickly said good-night and got out of the car before he could ask to see her again or spend the night with her.

It wasn't just the disappointing date that put her in a bad mood. The latest litter of puppies hadn't done well. Two little ones had died. And the sale of puppies had been going down. One of the best retail pet shops had discontinued selling puppies and kittens. That hurt. Then there was always that post-rally let down, which didn't help. All that planning and excitement and then it was over. Plus, more doggie treats needed to be made, and Shonalee was always too busy with her shop and her new boyfriend to come and help. No way would she ask Carlos or Ruben to go anywhere near the treats. All in all, she was nursing a case of grouchiness and self-pity.

And in walked Carlos and Ruben, hours late and looking and smelling like they'd never bathed.

"What shit hole have you been wallowing in?" she shouted. "Jeez, you stink, and you're bloody late. Go hose off outside." Tina held her nose and waved her arms to shoo them out.

"I'm not gonna hose off outside. Besides my clean clothes are in here," whined Ruben.

"Just give us a bag we can put the dirty clothes in, and we'll take a shower in the house," suggested Carlos.

"You two drive me crazy. Why do I put up with you?" Tina picked up her pack of cigarettes and lit one. She really needed a different type of smoke. She scrounged around under the sink and found a bag for them to put their clothes in. "And you'd better clean that shower when you're done so it shines like the sun. Dimwits."

"You got it, Tina. Thanks," said Carlos. He scurried off before she could change her mind, leaving Ruben standing in the kitchen.

"Can I have a beer, Tina? I'm really thirsty," Ruben said, meekly shuffling his feet.

"Take one and drink it outside, stink-bomb." Tina shook her head in disgust while she opened the kitchen windows and then turned the ceiling fan on high, trying to get rid of the foul odors the men carried in with them. Cigarette smells were never an issue.

After the guys showered (with Ruben complaining he had to clean both his and Carlos's dirt out of the shower) and put on clean clothes, they asked Tina if there was anything to eat. They were starving.

"Eat whatever you can find in the fridge," she offered, knowing there wasn't much.

Congealed mac and cheese, three slimy hotdogs, and a bottle of pickled herring. But there was beer, so it wasn't all bad.

"You got any crackers?" asked Carlos.

"Check the right-hand cupboard by the stove. I think there might be some there," suggested Tina.

Carlos found the crackers and took the bottle of pickled herring.

"What am I supposed to eat? Do you think these hotdogs are any good?" Ruben took the hotdogs out of the open package, and they slipped out of his hands to the floor. They definitely were slimy. "You got any buns, Tina?"

"Just rinse 'em off and warm 'em up. No buns." Tina could care less. The little bit of leftover food from the rally was long gone, and she hadn't been in the mood to go to the grocery store.

After eating their not-so-gourmet meal, washed down by a couple of beers, the guys eyed each other and then looked at Tina expectantly, as if wondering what she had in store for them.

Tina debated whether this was a good time to tell the guys what she was thinking would be her next project. Maybe not yet. While there were still a few dogs in the barn, maybe the guys could train a couple of comfort dogs to take to Shonalee. She'd been so impressed by how quickly the first ones sold she'd been asking for more. The woman who bought the female puppy actually worked part time for Shonalee now, and even brought the dog to work with her. By gradually selling off the dogs Tina planned to get out of the dog business.

"So, guys, Shonalee would like a couple more comfort dogs. For some reason she thought the two you trained were great. I can't imagine why. Anyway, after you get all the critters and their crates taken care of, pick out two dogs that would make good puppies to take to Shonalee. And put some real effort into it this time. She may have thought you did a good job, but I know better."

Ruben looked plaintively at Tina, totally ignoring what she'd just said, and asked, "When are you going grocery shopping? I need to keep my strength up. I think I'm feeling a little faint." He leaned back in his chair, closing his eyes and letting his arms go slack at his sides. It didn't work.

Tina snorted at that comment. "Ruben, you could go a week without eating. You've got plenty of fat to keep you going. But if you must know, I'm going to the grocery store first thing in the morning."

"We'll start on the barn right after we've had breakfast then," said Carlos.

Tina just shook her head. These guys were something else. It would be interesting to see what they thought about her next project.

Chapter 35

After getting all the chores done on her to-do list, Scottie sat on the chaise lounge in the lanai with a glass of iced tea, enjoying that feeling of satisfaction, knowing she'd accomplished what she set out to do. She checked the calendar on her phone for upcoming commitments. The next item was Mr. B. visiting. Oh boy! He'd better behave, or else. Or else what? But he really could be quite sweet. Charlie would be back later in the week. Two dogs to walk before he got back, in addition to Mr. B.

Perhaps she could squeeze in a lunch one day with the girls. And maybe she could talk Piper into a couple hours of shopping. Piper was a shopping maven. She knew everything about everything when it came to shopping, and her stamina was phenomenal. It was always a fun time. She couldn't let thoughts of strange hang-up calls in the night ruin what should be a pleasant week. She needed to forget about them; but easier said than done.

The doorbell rang. Scottie looked through the peephole in the front door. She now made a point of checking who was at the door after having her recent experiences. This time it was Piper and Mr. B.

"Hi, you two. Come on in. Piper, I like your jacket. Is it new?" asked Scottie. She then turned her attention to Mr. B, who casually sauntered over to the large flowerpot in the corner, lifted his leg, and peed on it. This was the same pot he had watered the last time he visited. At least the plant hadn't died.

"Mr. B," yelled Piper. "Why did you do that? You are a bad dog. Scottie, I'm so sorry. He just did his business before we came in. Let me clean up his mess. I know where your cleaning stuff is."

Scottie stood, hands on hips, glaring at the German shepherd, who was now sitting remorsefully in front of her, sad eyes, his tail gently wagging. "I'm not sure I'm going to let you stay with me if you can't behave. I thought we were going to be friends. One more episode like that and you're out of here." Mr. B walked closer to her and gave her a quick lick on the hand, as if to say "We can still be friends."

After Piper returned with the cleaning supplies and cleaned up the mess, she said. "Oh Scottie, I do apologize. I thought he was supposed to be well behaved. At least it's just this one last visit."

"Right. No more big dogs and no sleepovers. I don't think I told you that the last time he was here, he insisted on sleeping in my bed."

Piper chuckled. "Since Charlie isn't here, it's nice to have someone."

"Let me tell you, it's not the same."

Mr. B paid close attention to the two women talking, as if he knew he was the topic of conversation.

"I hate to clean and run but, I think I'll leave before he does anything else." Piper picked up her purse and looked at Scottie. "You two going to be okay?"

"We'll be fine. Won't we, Mr. B?" He stood up and gave a weak "Woof." She followed Piper to the door. "You're going to pick him up tomorrow, right? I was thinking maybe we could do some shopping later in the week."

"Sounds good, and yes I am going to pick him up tomorrow, probably around noon."

Once Piper left, Scottie decided a long walk would do her and Mr. B good. She and Charlie had been enjoying the good life, and she felt the great dinners and drinks were starting to show. You can only do that for so long. Mr. B, on the other hand, looked quite slim and trim as he strutted beside Scottie.

"Mr. B, you really amaze me. How can you possibly leave your calling card on so many things? You must have really tanked up before you got to my house."

He just gave her an innocent look and went back to reading the pee-mail left by some other dogs.

When they got back to Scottie's house, Mr. B followed her around like a furry shadow from room to room. "Do you think I'm going to leave you all by yourself? We're stuck with each other until tomorrow afternoon when Piper comes to get you. So just relax. Take a nap. See? Your bed is over there. I'll put a chew stick in it, and you'll be all set."

Surprisingly it worked. Mr. B plopped down in his big fluffy bed, propped the chew stick between his paws, and appeared to be perfectly content chewing away.

They both took a nap in the afternoon. Scottie hadn't been sleeping well. The hang-up calls in the night did bother her. Strange dreams and waking up frequently, almost as if expecting the phone to ring, frayed her normal sound sleep patterns. She hoped Mr. B remembered he wasn't allowed to sleep on her bed next to her.

Chapter 36

Tony picked up Pete's wife at her house. Doreen's green patterned blouse and green pants showed off her slim figure. Tony thought she was quite attractive. They'd never been close, even though he'd seen her frequently over the years. Pete was always nearby and didn't want her talking with other guys. Sometimes it was annoying, having him hovering next to her so she barely said a word.

Tony had spruced up his appearance wearing a crisp long sleeve white shirt and dark pants. The doorbell hadn't even finished ringing when Doreen opened it and pulled him into the house.

"Oh, I'm so glad you're here," she whispered, quietly shutting the door, and giving him a big hug.

"Why are you whispering?" asked Tony, whispering himself and unwrapping her arms from around his torso.

"I didn't want the neighbors to hear. They're really nosy, and of course they don't know about Pete," she replied in her normal voice. "Maybe I should have met you at the restaurant instead of you coming here."

"They weren't outside, and even if they were, big deal. As far as they know I'm coming here to see Pete."

"But then they'll see the two of us leaving together."

"If you're that worried about it, then drive your own car," said an exasperated Tony. He noted her puckered brow and sad eyes. Just what he needed, another problem to take care of. She might have a point though. Separate cars would probably be best. That way they could say they accidently happened to go to the same restaurant.

He got to the restaurant first and took a table in the horse-shoe shaped bar that featured stools and high-top tables. Lots of dark wood gave it a cozy atmosphere. She walked in shortly after, and strolled casually up to his table for two, and made a point of saying how nice it was to run into him. And of course, he invited her to sit at his table.

It didn't take them long to realize that sitting in a crowded bar wasn't the best place to discuss the topic of a missing husband. Too many people sitting too close. Oh well, too late to move. Tony flagged down the waitress and ordered two beers.

"Have you heard from anyone?" asked Tony, bending across the table so he didn't have to raise his voice. "I haven't. But then I don't always have my phone with me. But no voicemail messages or texts."

"I haven't heard anything either. I did give—" Doreen abruptly stopped talking as the waitress put the cocktail napkins and beers on the table. "I did give his mother a call though. It might have been a mistake. I mean, she just lost it. Said the police need to be notified right away and on and on. What do you think? Maybe that's what needs to be done. I still can't believe he'd just—you know what. Plus, that vehicle is really small for two people, if that's the case. And what about clothes and stuff? He probably doesn't have much with him."

"How much does he need? If he does have someone with him, they may not be wearing clothes that much anyway." Seeing the aghast expression on her face he realized he'd said the wrong thing. "Just kidding."

"That was a horrible thing to say. How could you? What do you know that you haven't told me? Who is she? What will my friends think? What do I tell his mother?" Her voice had risen considerably, and the couple sitting at the next table was watching them.

Tony was beginning to see his mistake. Not only should they not have sat in the bar, but it would also have been best to go outside, far away from other people. He hadn't realized how loud she could get.

Doreen flagged down the waitress and ordered a pitcher of beer. Tony remembered Pete had mentioned her drinking demons. He decided they'd better order something to eat right away. Maybe if her mouth was full, she wouldn't be talking. He needed to do the talking.

"Why don't we order now?" he suggested.

"So soon? Well, I guess so. Can I see your dinner menu?" Doreen asked the waitress. "I really don't feel like bar food tonight."

The waitress caught the roll of Tony's eyes and smiled sweetly. "I'll get you the menu and your pitcher of beer."

Doreen ordered a wedge salad, shrimp scampi with rice, broccoli, and chocolate cake for dessert. Tony ordered a hot dog and fries.

"You're certainly a girl who likes her food," commented Tony, watching her scarf down the food between big gulps of beer. What did Pete see in her? Although he had to admit she wasn't bad looking. Long, light brown hair with gold highlights, blue eyes, glasses, and a figure that was worth at least a second glance.

"Hey, this situation is giving me the munchies," she said. "Plus, you're paying. I just don't know what to do. Maybe the police could put a notice out about the camper. I could say it was stolen and not mention anything about Pete. If they find the camper, then they'd find Pete and whoever is with him. What do you think of that?"

Tony frowned. "Let's not mention any names. Your idea's not bad, but I still think we should wait a bit. Are you working tomorrow?" He knew she only worked part time at a bank. If he could get her to come and work at the shop, he could keep an eye on her, plus he could use some help.

"Nope, not tomorrow. Maybe I'll go see his mom. Try to calm her down. I don't want her calling the cops before I do. She'd never believe he'd run off with some other woman."

"Why don't you just give her a call? Don't mention anything about another woman and let her know you'll handle everything. It'd be great if you could come and give me a hand at the shop tomorrow. Quite a few items have come in, and there hasn't been time to get them displayed. You know, with just me taking care of it all."

"Hey, it's not my job," Doreen said. "I can't help it if your partner doesn't show up."

"I understand that. Don't forget my partner, as half owner of the store, has to do half the work. Since he's not available, I thought you could fill in until he shows up. You might actually enjoy it. And having a good-looking woman working in the shop would be great."

He immediately wondered if this was a mistake. She might be more of a pain in the ass than any help. But it would be good to be able to keep an eye on her, if only part time.

"I guess I could try it. On my days off, I sleep later, so I won't be able to get there until ten-ish."

"Getting there at ten would work. Glad we ran into each other and had a chance to catch up," said Tony in a voice loud enough to be heard by anyone bothering to listen. "I've got stuff to do, so I'm going to take off." He motioned to the waitress for the bill.

"But we haven't finished the pitcher," complained Doreen.

"No more for me. Don't forget you have to drive yourself home. And you're working tomorrow." *Maybe she'll finish the rest of the pitcher and have an accident on the way home. That would take care of one problem.*

Tony grabbed his dark suit jacket from the back seat of his car and put it on. He'd seen the way FBI guys on TV shows dressed. He'd decided he was going to go with Pete's idea of pretending to be an FBI agent. Why not? Just ask a few questions and leave. What could the woman possibly know? Damn Pete for doing all that harassing. She probably would have forgotten about everything she may have seen or heard if it hadn't been for that. Doing the recent hang-up calls was a mistake on his part. It was almost as if Pete was haunting and taunting him to do this ridiculous crap. He could picture him grinning. He shook his head to get the image to fall out.

Driving slowing to her house, Tony tried out names he could use when he introduced himself. Maybe something like Hank Hammer or Stan Steele. It had to be macho sounding. He settled on Max Diablo. Tony wasn't sure what Diablo meant, but there was a nice ring to it. As for what questions to ask, he'd figure that out when he saw her.

When he reached the street where Scottie lived, he drove past her house. Lights on, no car in the driveway. Good sign there were no guests. He parked his car around the corner from her house.

He patted his breast pocket to make sure the fake ID he'd bought in the toy department was there. He knew it was really phony-looking, but he planned to just flash it.

He retrieved his gun from the glove box and put it in the pocket of his suit coat. After thinking about it he decided he really didn't need it, so he put it back in the glove box. From what he remembered; she wasn't that big. He could handle whatever she might do. This should be a piece of cake.

Chapter 37

Scottie spread a blanket over the sofa, thinking that her large, furry visitor might want to join her. Preparing to watch something on Netflix, she put her glass of white wine and a small dish of popcorn on the end table. Mr. B was watching her every move from his bed on the floor. The moment she sat down he trotted over, jumped up on the sofa, and plopped down with his head on her lap, waiting for a kernel of popcorn to fall. Scottie found what she thought would be an interesting movie to watch. They were both contentedly enjoying the evening when the doorbell rang.

Scottie pushed Mr. B's head off her lap, put the movie on pause, and went to the door. Watching out of the peep-hole, she saw a man she didn't recognize. "Who is it?" she asked.

"Agent Diablo with the FBI. I've come to ask you some questions," replied Tony. He wished he had a more authoritative voice.

"May I see some ID?" asked Scottie. She wondered who would have the name of Devil? Really weird. She would have changed it if were hers. Mr. B stood right next to her sensing a change in her.

"Of course." The man whipped out an identification badge and quickly closed it. Scottie didn't get a good look at it, but then her porch light wasn't exactly the brightest.

"I've already spoken to the other agents. I gave them all my information," she said. "Have you checked with them?"

The man appeared momentarily taken aback. Then he said "Of course I've spoken with the others. I just have a few follow-up questions. It won't take long. And I can tell you what we've learned so far."

That last comment got her. Scottie's curiosity was aroused. "Well, okay, if it doesn't take long."

She opened the door, he walked in, and froze at the sight of the huge German shepherd. Scottie noticed the dog was alert and didn't appear friendly.

"Have a chair," she offered. There was something about him that was different than the other agents. What? The shoes for one thing. Light tan loafers with a dark suit. And he didn't look like he was in good shape. The other agents were lean and obviously fit. She was beginning to feel this one could just be mean. She sat on the sofa across from him, with Mr. B sitting on the floor right beside her, eyeing the stranger.

"What questions do you have for me that weren't already asked?" Scottie asked. "You did read the file with my replies, right?

"Ah well, I didn't get the complete file. That's why I thought you could go over what you told the other agent."

Agent? Didn't he know there were two? Scottie was definitely getting some bad vibes from the guy. "Why don't you tell me what you've learned so far? Maybe it'll jog my memory." She noticed Agent Diablo was either tapping his foot on the floor or rubbing his hand back and forth on the arm of the chair. What was he so nervous about? Mr. B nudged even closer to her, so he was leaning into her leg.

"You know, I could really use a glass of water, would you mind?" the agent casually asked. "I've been talking so much today, I'm really dry. Then I can tell you what we've discovered."

"I guess so. Wait here. I'll be right back," said Scottie. Something definitely was wrong. She could feel it. The hair on her neck was prickling. Of course, her cellphone had to be in the bedroom, and she didn't have a land line. Maybe get a knife while she was in the kitchen. But she would look rather silly, walking back into the great room with a glass of water in one hand and a knife in the other. And although she was suspicious of him, what if he actually was a real agent? Could it be she was just paranoid?

Scottie casually walked to the kitchen with Mr. B following her. And the agent following him. Why was he coming into the kitchen? She had told him to wait. Did he have a gun? What if he grabbed a knife? *Act cool. Try to remember what was taught in the personal safety class taken about a year ago. Pressure points in the neck. Going limp. The nose, eyes. What else?*

"Do you take ice in your water, Agent Diablo?" asked Scottie. She thought he could probably hear her knees shaking.

"Sure, why not," he replied. He was walking close behind her now.

Scottie reached into the cupboard and took out a tall drinking glass. She could sense he was right behind her and smell gross beer breath. This definitely was no FBI agent. In her peripheral vision she could see Mr. B with his hackles up. Maybe he could help.

"I'll get your ice," Scottie said as she turned around and saw his big hands were about to go around her neck. In what seemed like slow motion to her, she swung the glass into the agent's nose. Amazingly the only thing that broke was his nose.

"You bitch. You broke my nose. You'll pay for that." In a flash he pushed her against the counter and his hands went around her neck. Blood was gushing from his nose.

Scottie pushed against his chest to no avail. She tried to get his hands off of her neck. Scratching his hands, her feet kicked at his legs. It was getting harder to breathe. Panic was starting to set in. She could feel herself getting light-headed.

That's when Mr. B flew into action.

Chapter 38

Mr. B could sense the fear in Scottie. The nasty human was doing bad things to her. It was up to him to take care of this. He couldn't let anything happen to his friend. After all, she did take him for walks, feed him, including extra treats, and let him sleep on her bed.

Because Tony's arms were up and his hands were around Scottie's neck, Mr. B went for his arm. He leaped up and clamped his sharp teeth into Tony's arm, tearing through his jacket, shirt, the flesh, and a vein. An expanse of fabric from the jacket and the shirt hung down. An excruciating howl emitted from the bad man. His arms went down, and he released his hands from Scottie's neck.

"Get this beast away from me," he yelled, drawing a foot back to give Mr. B a fierce kick. Mr. B continued to hold on as blood dripped from Tony's arm.

"I wouldn't do that. He's part of a K-9 patrol. You know what they can do," Scottie lied as she slipped away from his reach. She didn't know if Mr. B was trained to do more than "sit" and "stay."

The guy's face was the color of old mashed potatoes. "Just get him off of me. I'm going to bleed out."

Scottie didn't need that. "Okay, I'll call him off. First you put your phone, your badge, whatever it is, your wallet, and if you have a gun or a knife, that too, or any other kind of weapon on the counter. When Mr. B releases you, walk over to this chair and sit down. And I wouldn't move after that if I were you."

The assailant slowly took out his wallet and the fake badge from his pocket and put them on the counter.

"And your phone," said Scottie. "I know you have one."

He added his phone to the other things on the counter.

She moved a chair from the dining table near the kitchen and away from any other furniture. Definitely not on a rug. Blood on her rug wasn't going to happen. She just had to figure out what was best to say to the dog.

Scottie bent down and quietly said, "Mr. B, sweetie, come here. It's okay. You're a good boy."

Mr. B looked at her to make sure he really should let go of the bad human's arm. He finally did.

"You gotta call 911. I'm bleeding really bad." The guy collapsed into the chair Scottie indicated, holding his hand over his bleeding arm. His nose continued to bleed also, dripping blood down his chin and onto his white shirt. What a mess.

"Here, mop up your nose." Scottie dumped a couple of paper towels in his lap. "Mr. B come

here." The dog walked over to her with a quizzical look on his face as if to say, now what? "Sit. Stay."

She pointed to the fake agent, and Mr. B sat right in front of him, his hackles up again and a low growl in his throat. "That order applies to both of you," Scottie said, glaring at the guy. "You know what will happen if you move. It won't be just your arm the next time." She ran to the bedroom to get her phone.

Diablo shifted a bit in the chair. "Mr. B nice doggie," he murmured. Mr. B's growl got a little louder; he wasn't having any of that soft talk from him.

Scottie called a real agent, all the while watching the intruder. The fake one looked rather comical. Part of the paper toweling was stuffed up his nose, the rest hanging down his chest. He continued to hold his hand over the bite that kept bleeding. He made a point of not looking at the dog. He glowered at Scottie with malice, as if imagining ways he could get his hands around her neck again.

With a hoarse, shaky voice, she said, "Agent Myers, this is Scottie Shelton. I'm the one who wound up having a burnt dinner because you were questioning me. Well, I've got a guy sitting in my house right now claiming to be an FBI agent. Says his name is Agent Diablo. He attempted to choke me to death, but he was bitten on his arm by the dog I'm taking care of. I'm not sure how bad the bite is, but he's really bleeding. If you could get here right away or send someone, I'd really appreciate it."

"We don't have anyone named Diablo working on the case, and certainly not anyone who would strangle you. You're not making this up are you?" questioned Agent Myers.

"Sir," said an exasperated Scottie, "The guy tried to kill me. Please get someone here immediately!" Scottie gave him her address, hoping he wrote it down correctly. Next, she called Kevin.

"This is your Auntie calling. Could you come over right away?" She explained the situation. "I've already called the FBI, but I thought maybe you could get here quicker. And maybe bring an ambulance before the guy bleeds all over my kitchen floor."

Diablo took his hand off his bleeding arm long enough to give her the finger. In doing so the torn fabric from his jacket and shirt he had been pressing over the wound fell, causing blood to drip on the floor. The paper towels hanging from his nose were extremely bloody by now. "I need more paper towels," he mumbled. And softly, as if he hoped she couldn't hear, "Bitch."

"I heard that. I wouldn't try to get smart with me, considering your situation. Impersonating an FBI agent and attempted murder are activities that are really frowned upon." Scottie put her phone in the back pocket of her jeans and then pulled off some more paper toweling and tossed it on the floor near Diablo so he could pick it up. He was quite a sight! The FBI guy and Kevin had better get here soon. Might be a good idea to get a butcher knife in case the guy tried something. Although so far Mr. B seemed to be taking good care of him. The dog's talented nose was twitching as he smelled the blood dripping from the intruder.

Scottie side-stepped into the kitchen, watching Diablo the entire time. No way was she going to turn her back on him. Her sore throat was a definite reminder of what he could do to her. Mr. B, seeing her going to the kitchen apparently thought maybe treats were involved and started to follow her, leaving the assailant alone.

The guy stood unsteadily, snatched his phone and wallet off the counter, and staggered toward the door.

"Don't you dare leave this house," Scottie ordered. "Get back to that chair immediately." She grabbed a butcher knife from the drawer and waved it in his direction. "And I mean now." No way was he going to escape. Not with help on the way. God, her throat was sore. Yelling didn't help. Sensing how upset she was, Mr. B started growling again and moved toward the intruder.

"Don't you dare let him near me," muttered the guy through the paper towel hanging from his nose. "He'll kill me." He moved backward, hoping to get far away from the dog.

"That's what you were going to do to me, so sit down like I said. You're not going anywhere. Moving around will just make you bleed more. You probably will bleed out if you do." Scottie had no idea if that was true, but what the hell. She pointed the knife toward the chair. "But first put that phone and wallet back on the counter."

The guy wavered, looking pallid and weak, whether it was from lack of blood or the shitty situation he was in. He put the phone and wallet on the counter and then wobbled to the chair and plunked down. "I need more paper towels." He threw the wet ones on the floor.

Scottie got him more toweling. He really didn't look good. He'd better not die on her watch. Surely the wound wasn't that bad. She wanted to know why he wanted to kill her. What had she done to deserve all the nasty stuff? She pulled out a chair and sat a healthy distance away from him, with the knife on her lap. Mr. B padded to his water bowl, slurped up some water, picked up his chew stick, then spread out on the floor next to her.

It was quiet. Nothing was being said. There was just the steady soft hum of the refrigerator and Mr. B. working on his chew stick. Diablo's eyes were closed. Scottie's eyes were wide open. Something was going to happen. One way or another.

"Hey, Diablo. Why did you come to my house pretending to be an FBI agent? And you actually tried to kill me. Why? You're the one who's been messing with me, aren't you? What's it all about? I deserve some answers."

No answer. Scottie was getting anxious. Why hadn't Kevin shown up yet, or the FBI guys? Her assailant was just sitting still with his eyes closed. Maybe he was asleep or unconscious. All of a sudden, the phone in her back pocket chimed.

Chapter 39

Tony kept his eyes closed. He felt lousy, and he definitely wasn't going to give her any information. Besides, he needed to concentrate on what to say when the law showed up. He could tell them she's a nutcase, how he was afraid for his life. Maybe he could say she came after him with the knife, broke his nose with a glass, and then made the dog bite him. And how he just accidently come to the wrong house, and she lured him in. No, it would be better if he left before the cops showed up. Get in his car and drive to Doreen's. She could fix him up. That's what he was going to do. But how? He'd have to be fast. No more wimping around. What's the worst that could happen? The dog kills him, or she stabs him with the knife.

Then the broad's phone rang. He watched through half closed eyes. This was his chance. She was distracted. The dog wasn't paying attention to him either. He slowly stood up. So far so good.

"Hi, Charlie. I'm so glad you called," said Scottie. "I've been having quite an evening." She paused.

"OMG he's trying to get away. I gotta go." Scottie shoved her phone in her pocket. Still holding the knife, she ran out the front door after Tony. "Hey, you, stop right there!"

Tony continued down the sidewalk. He was running as if his life depended on it. Which it did. If he could just get around the corner and to his car. Thank God he hadn't put his car key on the counter with his phone and wallet. That was bad enough. The cops would definitely have his name and everything else.

Scottie was racing down the sidewalk after Diablo as a police car with a flashing bubble light pulled up along beside her. "That's him!" she shouted. "Stop him!"

Christ, if only he could get to his car. He rounded the corner. Wow! Maybe he was in luck. Apparently, there was a party going on in the neighborhood. His car was tucked in between two other vehicles. All the parking spots on the street were full. He jumped into his car and ducked down. A couple of cars went by, and then the one with the flashing light. He waited a minute and then sat up. No more traffic coming his way, and he couldn't see the cars that had cruised by. He maneuvered his car out of the parking spot, sped off and headed for Doreen's house.

When Scottie got back to her house Agent Myers was walking up to her door. Loud barking was coming from inside the house. Mr. B did not like suddenly finding himself alone.

"Agent Myers, good to see you again," said Scottie, shaking hands with him.

"How about we go inside, and you can tell me what is going on."

"You'd better let me go in first and get Mr. B calmed down. He doesn't know you, so no telling what he'd do." She opened the door and quickly closed it before an agitated Mr. B seeing the stranger, tried to sneak out. He continued to look at her and bark as if to say, "Why'd you leave me? I wanted to go too."

Scottie headed for the kitchen. "How about a treat, Mr. B?" That got his attention. "Sit." She gave him another chew stick. "Good boy. Now go in your bed." She indicated the fluffy bed near the sofa, and amazingly he plopped down in it.

"Okay, I think it's safe to come in," Scottie told Agent Myers standing outside the door. When he walked in, Mr. B gave a low growl, started to get up, and then looked at Scottie.

"No, Mr. B, good man. Down." He settled back in his bed to work on his treat.

"I can see why you had me wait outside. You've got yourself one big dog," exclaimed Agent Myers. "You didn't have him the last time I was here."

"Oh, he's not mine. I'm dog-sitting and only for tonight. And thank goodness he's here. I'd be dead if he wasn't." After they were seated Scottie started to tell him about the events of the evening when Kevin walked in. Mr. B, sensing he wasn't a problem stayed in his bed.

"You've probably met my nephew Kevin Shelton," she said to the FBI agent. "Kevin saw me running after the guy who tried to choke me, so he drove around the corner to see if he could catch him. Did you see him?"

"Unfortunately, there's some kinda party going on around the corner. Street full of cars. I didn't see anyone walking or running on the sidewalk or street," responded Kevin. "And since I don't know what he drives, I couldn't tell if one of the cars was his. Your neck looks red, and your voice is huskier than usual. He really did attack you."

Scottie gingerly felt her neck and twisted her head left and right. "I think I'll be fine, but my throat really hurts." Suddenly excited, she said, "I just thought of something. There had to be two guys harassing me. I don't think I ever saw the one who was here tonight. He definitely didn't come to the house where I was taking care of the cats."

"Can you give us a description of him?" asked Agent Myers. "And are there things that he handled besides your neck?" There was a slight smile on his face.

Scottie pondered a minute. "I'd say he was a medium-build, white guy. Paunchy. I'm not sure about the eyes. Slicked back brown hair, like you'd see in old movies, and he was starting to grow a mustache. And as for something he touched, you're going to be impressed. His wallet, phone, and fake ID are on the counter."

The men gaped at her. Agent Myers immediately went to the counter, and saw the three items, but didn't touch them. "I am impressed. Why the hell did he leave them here? We don't usually see items like that left by a would-be killer. Do you have some tongs and some baggies I can put them in? I didn't bring an evidence bag." He took photos with his phone of the items.

Scottie got him the tongs and several plastic bags. "Let's just say Mr. B and I were very persuasive."

Agent Myers noticed the bloody paper towels and the drinking glass still on the floor. "That's his blood, I assume." After taking more photos he collected those too.

"He claimed I broke his nose when I hit it with the glass. I'm not sure about that, but it sure bled a lot, and then Mr. B tore into his arm and wouldn't let go. That's when I told him to empty his pockets."

"That's my Auntie Scottie. You don't mess with her," said Kevin, grinning.

"One thing I didn't think of at the time, he probably had a key to his car that he didn't give me. I'm sure he's long gone."

"He won't get far since we have these." Agent Myers held up the baggies.

Chapter 40

Tony knew he was in bad shape, both mentally and physically. His head ached, and his nose, although it pretty much stopped bleeding, throbbed, and his arm was in excruciating pain. Probably infected. No telling what that dog had been licking and eating.

Hopefully Doreen would be home and alone. His appearance left a lot to be desired. Torn, bloody clothes and a smashed -up nose. Enough to scare anybody. No wallet, no phone. Dumb, dumb. He needed a stiff drink.

Pulling up to Doreen's house, he was happy to see the lights on and there wasn't a car in the driveway. He started to take off his jacket but decided against it. If he pulled it together across his chest, it might cover up some of his bloody white shirt. He pulled the visor down in the car to look into the mirror and quickly closed it. Worse than he imagined.

Doreen called out when Tony rang the doorbell ring. "Who is it?"

"It's me, Tony. I gotta see you."

"Okay, okay. Give me a minute." She opened the door wearing a silky black robe over a black nightgown. "Oh my God. What the hell happened to you?"

"Don't even go there," said Tony as he pushed his way into the house. "Just a bit of a problem, and I need your help. A vicious dog attacked me. He bit my arm really bad. Do you have some stuff you can put on it? Some antiseptic and some kind of bandage?"

"Uh, I guess so. And what happened to your face? Your nose looks funny. Did the dog do that too? Why didn't you go to Urgent Care?"

"It was a big dog. You're the first one I thought of. So, can you fix me up?" Tony was getting a little perturbed. He hadn't come to be quizzed, but to get some help.

"Let's go to the bathroom and I'll see what I have we can put on that bite. And you really look like you need a shower." Doreen sashayed in front of him to the bathroom.

"I guess I do. Do you think I could borrow one of Pete's T-shirts? How about I take a shower and then you can patch me up? I could sure use a drink too."

"You're getting a little bossy, you know. Don't get any blood on my towels and clean the shower when you're done. I'll see if I can find a T-shirt big enough to fit you." She went off muttering, "I'm not running an Urgent Care/Bar here. Be just my luck if Pete shows up and finds Tony in the shower. Though if he's run off with some bimbo it would serve him right."

Tony peeled off his clothes and got in the shower. Everything hurt. Doreen opened the bathroom door a crack and threw in a black T-shirt. "Here's the shirt. Might be a little tight."

A short time later Tony found Doreen in the kitchen about to refresh her drink. "I sure could use one of those."

"Help yourself," replied Doreen. "The glasses are in there." She pointed to the cabinet near him. The T-shirt was having a hard time covering his hairy belly. He held a wad of toilet paper over his bleeding arm.

"Your arm is in awful shape. You really should get some stitches. Let's get a bandage on it. I don't want that blood dripping all over my house. How did you have a run in with this dog?"

"It's a long story. I don't want to get into it now." No way was he going to tell her what happened. Going to the dog-walker's house was the stupidest thing he had ever done. What was he thinking? Now he needed to get Doreen involved in his new plans. He hoped she'd be receptive. Might have to do some real smooth talking and get her to have a couple more drinks.

They went back to the bathroom, where Doreen grabbed the first aid supplies from under the sink. She put some antiseptic on the wound, some gauze over it, and taped it down.

"Doreen, I appreciate you doctoring me up. You're doing a terrific job. I think you missed your calling. You don't happen to have any pain pills, do you?"

"Tony, you're lucky I have these few medical supplies. We usually pack a small medical kit when we go on trips, but it's in the camper. I have some over-the-counter pills that will help a little. I think you should go home now and see your doctor tomorrow. You don't want to get an infection." She obviously didn't want him lingering here at her house. It seemed strange he would come to see her with a medical emergency anyway.

"Doreen, listen, I've been thinking. This deal with the dog biting me—well, the dog got the worst end of it. Now the owner is after me. He was yelling it was a show dog I killed and how expensive it was."

"You killed it?" asked a shocked Doreen.

"Well, it was me or the dog. Anyway, I was wondering if maybe the two of us could get out of town for a few days. Take your car and put mine in your garage. We're both stressed out about Pete, and now me with this dog thing. It would do us good. And I really like being with you. You're such good company and foxy looking too."

Doreen gave him a skeptical frown. "Tony, we both have jobs. You can't just run away from the shop, and I work at the bank tomorrow. Plus, what if Pete comes home and finds me gone and your car in the garage?"

"Aw, come on, Doreen. A fun getaway is what we need. We could leave a note for Pete saying we've gone to look for him. What do you say?" He tried his best to make pleading "puppy dog eyes." "How about I refresh our drinks?" Without waiting for an answer, he went to the kitchen and poured them both a hefty shot. He wasn't going to say anything about having no money, credit cards, or phone until they were well on their way. This had to work.

"Tony, does the dog owner know where you live? Is that why you want to get out of town? Why don't you try to work something out with him? Maybe offer to buy him a new dog. You're obviously not telling me everything," Doreen said as she reluctantly accepted the large refill.

They both sat on the sofa, sipping their drinks. Thinking.

Finally, Doreen spoke up. Maybe the scotch was getting to her. "You might be right. Getting out of town for a few days could be a good thing. Now, we're not having an affair. It would be purely platonic. Got that? And we'd have to leave a note for Pete. I don't understand why his phone isn't working."

"Absolutely, no hanky-panky." Tony noticed she was slurring her words a bit and her black silky robe had partly opened up. Instead of leaving in the morning, maybe they should leave tonight. She might change her mind in the morning.

"Why don't you go and pack a bag? Throw in a few things, and we can leave tonight. Obviously, I don't have anything to pack." Tony chuckled, trying to keep the conversation light.

"My small suitcase is high up on the shelf in the bedroom closet. You'll have to get it down for me. This is such short notice. I usually start packing a week ahead of time when I go out of town. I'll probably forget all kinds of stuff."

"Well, we're not going to be gone long. Don't worry about it." Hovering in the bedroom, Tony watched as she took out shorts, capris, tops, undies, nightgown, and robe, and spread them on the bed. Then to his amazement, she put many of the items back where they came from and took out other clothes. Women. Who could figure them out?

"Tony, will you make sure the front and back doors are locked, and the sliders? We'll leave from the garage. I've got to get my makeup and special shampoo and some other things."

Shortly after that they were cruising down the interstate highway in Doreen's red Porsche convertible and Tony's car was parked in her garage.

"This is some car," commented Tony. "I didn't know they pay so well at the bank."

"Oh yeah, they pay really awesome wages," said Doreen. Tony knew she was lying because Pete had told him she had inherited a good sum of money from her grandmother. Tony was lying too—sort of.

He wasn't going to tell her he didn't have his drivers' license with him. He had convinced her she'd had too much to drink so he should drive. He was loving it. The top was down on the car, even though Doreen claimed her hair would be a total mess. It wasn't long before Doreen's eyes were closed, and her chin was resting on her chest. The muffled snore indicated a sound asleep.

Tony spotted a Walmart, took the next exit, and made his way back to it. When he stopped Doreen suddenly woke up. "What are we doing here?"

"I need to pick up a few clothes. As you know, I don't have anything with me. You don't want to hang with me looking like this."

"Well, you do have a point. But I'm gonna wait here in the car."

He couldn't remember if he had told her about not having his wallet or phone. "Uh, remember I told you I don't have my wallet or my phone with me? So obviously I don't have my credit card. If you don't mind, we could use your card and I'll pay you back. So, I think you'd better come with me in case they ask about my using your card."

"Oh brother, you're getting to be a real pain in the ass. Put the top up on the car," she ordered.

Tony picked out two pairs of shorts, a pair of long pants, underwear, and three T-shirts. Spotting some rubber sandals, he added them to the cart, and using her card Doreen paid for it all.

After they were back in the car, Doreen said, "And I'll have the receipt, please," as she held out her hand. "You can pay me when we get back. Is this how you expected this whole adventure to go? Everything going on my card? Some getaway pal you turned out to be."

"C'mon, Doreen. You know I'm good for it. And it's not my fault," whined Tony. "I was only thinking of you when I suggested going away."

"Yeah, r-i-g-h-t. Well, I'm keeping track of all the receipts, so don't think you're going to stick me with the bills."

"Believe me, I wouldn't think of it. What kinda guy do you take me for?"

Chapter 41

The FBI guy left after obtaining as much information from Scottie as possible. Scottie made him promise to keep her informed. Kevin stayed behind, wanting to visit with his aunt and make sure she was going to be okay.

"You sure had an exciting evening," he said. "It's a good thing you called the FBI guy you spoke to before. They should be able to get all the info they need about your attacker from his phone and wallet to track him down. I still can't believe he just put them on the counter."

"I think he got scared when he saw all the blood, and then of course Mr. B wasn't letting go of his arm. That scared him too. I'm trying not to think what would have happened if the dog wasn't here." Scottie felt a little shaky, now that the adrenaline rush was dissipating. Someone actually wanting to kill her. Unbelievable.

"Auntie, how about I get you a glass of wine? You look like you could use it." Kevin took a bottle of white wine from the chiller and poured her a glass.

"That's great, thanks, Kev. Have one yourself. Or if you prefer, I think there's some beer in the fridge."

"Maybe I should stay the night. In case he comes back. Although if he's bleeding a lot that's probably the last thing he'd want to do. Plus, the way you and your friend took care of him, I don't think he'd chance it. That's the kind of dog you want on your side." He smiled at Mr. B, who had dozed off, half his body in his bed and half on the floor.

"Saving damsels in distress apparently zonks you out," said Scottie. "I'll be fine. Sorry if I interrupted you from something when I called."

"I was just watching a game on TV. I'm recording it, so no problem. I'm glad you called. I wish I'd been able to catch the guy getting into his car if that's what he did. I'll be checking with Agent Myers later to find out what information he's discovered."

"Why don't you take off and finish watching your game. The excitement is over for tonight, and all's well. The FBI has his info, so they'll catch him."

"If you're sure you'll be okay," said Kevin hesitantly.

"Absolutely, you go. I insist. Besides, I have to call Charlie, and you don't want to hear all that mushy stuff." Scottie grinned.

"I'm out of here." He kissed her on the cheek and was out the door.

Scottie and Charlie had a long phone call, with her telling him about the fake FBI guy and what had happened. It concluded with the mushy stuff.

Later she took Mr. B for his nightly walk in the neighborhood. Mr. B was a good listener. At least Scottie thought he was since he periodically glanced up at her. "You know, Mr. B, this has been one of the worst nights of my life. Never even in my wildest nightmares did I have someone trying to kill me. And I'll never forget that you saved me. You can come and pee on my flowerpot any time you want. I can't wait to tell Piper about you when she comes tomorrow to pick you up."

Chapter 42

Tony had been driving with one arm for the last ten miles, and that arm was getting about as sore as the one with the dog bite. The arm with the bite was oozing blood through the bandage Doreen had put on it. Doreen had fallen asleep again and was leaning on his shoulder. That didn't help either. He couldn't take any more. They'd gone far enough.

"Hey, sleepyhead, wake up. We're here," Tony said as he pulled into a parking lot.

"Huh, where are we?" asked a drowsy Doreen. She sat up and looked around. "Why'd we stop?"

"We're at a hotel in Fort Myers Beach. It's right on the water so it should be fun. Let's hope they have a room. We had to stop because my arm is killing me. And my other arm is really tired. Driving with one arm isn't easy."

"What the hell! You were driving my car with one arm? Are you some kind of idiot? We could have been killed," shrieked Doreen.

"Calm down. I kept everything under control. This will be a great place to have a little R and R. Come on let's go check in." Tony leaned over, gave her a quick peck on the cheek, and got out of the car.

Doreen slowly got out the car and glared at him. "This better be a great place, or we're gonna hit the road—and I'll be driving."

Fortunately, there was a room available, and Doreen made sure it had two queen-sized beds. She headed straight for the bar, where a rock and roll band and a boisterous crowd, lifted her spirits considerably. Having napped during the entire ride and sobered up somewhat, she was ready to party, already snapping her fingers and swaying to the music.

"Hey, Tony, let's stay for a while and listen to the band. They're really good. Maybe we could even dance a little."

"Aw, Doreen, I'm beat, and my arm is killing me. Plus, the bandage you put on is soaked. I need a new one. Maybe we could just go up to the room," he suggested.

Doreen scowled. "And here I thought this was gonna be a great getaway. Well, okay. Go get our bags and I'll meet you in the room."

"Could you come and help me? Your bag is kinda heavy, and—"

"I know. I know. You've only got one usable arm. I think I've heard that before."

Once in the room Tony asked meekly, "Do you think you could put a new bandage on my arm?"

"I don't have any medical supplies with me. And I'm not a nurse. Maybe they have some Band-aids at the desk downstairs."

"Doreen, you know I need more than Band-aids. What should we do? There must be something here we can use."

"Well, we can't tear a strip off of a sheet or the drapes to use for a bandage. They'd bill you a fortune for the damage."

Tony looked around the room, then went into the bathroom. He came out holding a hand towel. "What about this?"

"Maybe that would work. Except how would you keep it on your arm? Wait, I have an idea. I could loan you one of my scrunchies—you know, that I pull my hair back with."

Twenty minutes later Tony had his new towel bandage on, secured by a pink and purple striped scrunchy. He noticed she had a plain black scrunchy, but he figured he'd better not push his luck, or she might ask for the pink and purple one back.

The next morning after a so-so night's sleep they went down to have breakfast. They sat outside, both in a somewhat better mood. It was a lovely Florida morning, the sun sparkling on the water, people walking on the beach, and a few healthy types swimming laps back and forth along the shore.

"Boy, am I ready for a cup of coffee," said Doreen.

"Me too. And I'm hungry. By the way, you look great in that outfit," said Tony, admiring Doreen's black and white striped tank top and black shorts.

"Thanks." Before she could say more the waitress suddenly appeared to take their orders. She turned to Doreen, but Tony jumped right in to give his order first: banana pancakes with whipped cream, bacon, orange juice, coffee, and a blueberry muffin. Doreen rolled her eyes and ordered a fruit crepe and coffee.

It was while they were enjoying their breakfast that it happened. Doreen's phone rang, a cheery bird cheeping sound. She dug around in her purse and answered it. "Yup, that's me. Yes, my husband has a camper like that. Is he there? I'd like to give him a piece of my mind. What did you say?" And at the response she let out a scream of such volume that some of the guests sloshed coffee out of their cups as they were about to take a drink.

Chapter 43

Shonalee was excited. Not because of going to Tina's, but because she was planning a luncheon at her new friend's condo on Longboat Key. Since he was visiting his son in New Jersey, he gave her permission to use the condo as she liked. She knew he was quite smitten with her.

Shonalee pulled into Tina's yard, got out of the car, and stood still for a moment. What's different. No barking. That was it.

"Wow, Tina, it's so quiet in your yard. What's going on?" she worriedly asked as she gave her cousin a hug.

"Nothing's going on. Just got rid of the damn dogs. They were driving me crazy. I do have the two dogs for you that I promised. Ruben and Carlos are training them as we speak. They're cute and should be quick sales. I was so glad you finally said you'd come and help me make a batch of doggie treats. You said they sell pretty fast."

Shonalee grinned. "You won't believe it. I can't keep them in stock. That's why I keep bugging you for more. I know it's a pain in the butt to make them, but we're making some good money. The peanut butter ones seem to be the best sellers."

"Well, I bought a lot of cheap peanut butter, and my neighbor down the road—you met her I think, the one who raises turkeys— she gave me a bunch of turkey scraps when she did some butchering. I cooked them up so we can make a batch using that. I think we should have a glass of wine and some cheese and crackers before we start." Tina took a couple of wine glasses out of the cupboard and set them on the table, then filled both glasses to the top before Shonalee could answer.

Shonalee wrinkled her nose behind Tina's back. Shonalee didn't drink jug wine, but what choice did she have? Not only was Tina her cousin but also her business partner.

"Tina, no cheese, and crackers for me. I've been trying to keep my weight where it is. How about we just sip while we work? I have to get home at a decent time because I have a lot of planning to do. I'm staying at my friend's condo for a few days."

"Is this the guy with the fancy place on the Gulf?"

"Yes, and it's absolutely gorgeous. He's visiting his son up north right now."

"So, what's the planning you have to do? You doing something kinky while he's gone?"

Shonalee hesitated. She really hadn't planned to tell Tina about the luncheon she was having for the ladies. She mentally gave herself a couple of good swift kicks.

"I'm going to have a luncheon for some of the gals I've gotten to know fairly well. They're good customers. Well, actually one isn't a customer, but she's referred several people to the shop. I've done tarot-readings for a couple of them, plus they've bought dog outfits and lots of treats. It should be fun. I'm having it catered. I just need to finalize the menu, get the table set, and pick up the flowers. You know, stuff like that."

Tina lit up a cigarette, took a dramatic drag, and squinted as she blew smoke out. "I think I should come. After all, the comfort dogs come from here as well as the treats. And I haven't been invited to this condo yet." She gave Shonalee a "Don't you dare say no" look.

"But you don't know any of the women. It would probably be boring for you." Shonalee was furiously mixing the treat mixture in a bowl, trying to think of other reasons Tina might not want to come.

"That's no problem for me. I meet people easily, and I'm sure I won't be bored. Count me in when you're setting the table."

"Actually, it's just a customer appreciation luncheon," Shonalee said, trying one more attempt to discourage her from attending.

"Just what are you saying, missy? You don't want me to come." The air filled with smoke and a hefty dose of tension.

"Of course not. You can come if you want to. I wanted you to know who would be there and what it would be like," explained Shonalee as she slid a cookie sheet with treats into the oven.

"I'm glad that's settled then. I have a new dress that I've only worn once. I bought it for the date with the guy I met at the rally. Think that's what I'll wear."

Shonalee took a very tiny sip of her wine. "So how was that date? You never said anything about it."

"Oh, it was wonderful, Tina trilled. "Dinner and dancing–that sort of thing."

"So, are you going to go out with him again?" asked Shonalee.

"Probably not. It turned out he really wasn't my type. I think we should have quite a few bags of treats for you to take to the shop," said Tina, changing the subject.

"And it's a good thing, because my shelves are almost empty." They spent the rest of the afternoon baking and bagging the doggie treats. Tina saved a few bags for the two puppies Ruben and Carlos were supposed to be training. They were not the peanut butter treats. She had a feeling the puppies would never get to munch them if the guys knew there was peanut butter in them.

After Doreen's scream that almost broke the sound barrier, her eyes filled with tears as she listened to the caller. "Are you sure you have the right vehicle?" More listening. "Okay, I'll be home as soon as I can. I'm in Fort Myers now," she said with a catch in her voice. She dabbed at her eyes with a napkin and looked plaintively at Tony.

"What the hell happened? Is Pete, okay?"

"We've got to leave right away. Let's get our shit together, check out, and hit the road. I need to get home. I'll tell   you   when   we're   on   our   way."

Chapter 44

Shonalee was ready for her guests. She wore a pale-yellow dress with short sleeves and buttons down the front. Her hair was pulled back and fastened with a clip. She surveyed the table and smiled. The bowl of white roses looked beautiful with the dark blue placemats and the blue rimmed china she had found in the dining room china closet. The water glasses were full and the wine glasses ready for wine or iced tea. It was a sunny day, just a light breeze, perfect for eating out on the balcony. And of course, the view was spectacular. Her smile faded. Tina was coming. All she could do was hope for the best.

Shortly before noon her guests began arriving: Scottie, Bonita, Harper, Candy, and Piper. No Tina yet.

There were plenty of oohs and aahs as they admired the table setting and lovely view. Shonalee thought they all looked fabulous. Casually elegant. After a few introductions were made they all sat down. There was one empty chair. One of the catering staff asked each of them their wine or tea preference and returned with bottles of red and white wine. No one wanted tea. As she was pouring the wine, the door to the condo opened abruptly and Tina blew in.

She immediately noticed the women sitting at the table on the balcony and crossed the room, patting her black hair and trying to yank her tight blue and white horizontal striped dress into place. "Jesus H. Christ. It's impossible to get a parking spot around here. I had to park the damn pickup half a mile down the street." She wiped the sweat off her forehead with her arm and plunked herself down in the empty chair.

Cringing inwardly but smiling sweetly, Shonalee said "Ladies, I'd like you to meet Tina, my partner in procuring the yummy treats for your doggies, and she's also responsible for getting the comfort dogs trained. Tina, let me introduce you to everyone."

"And I'm also her cousin," Tina added loudly. She smiled at each of the women as Shonalee mentioned their names. After Shonalee finished with the introductions, the gal pouring the wine asked Tina what she would prefer. "I'd like a beer if you have it."

"Unfortunately, we're only serving wine and iced tea."

Tina hemmed and hawed and finally said, "I guess I'll have red wine. I'm really thirsty, though, so you'll probably have to fill my glass pretty often."

Shonalee spoke up. "Tina, we'll keep your water glass filled too." She glanced pointedly at the helper, who gave a small nod. There was always one.

Scottie happened to be seated at one end of the table, with Tina to her right. Scottie turned to Tina and commented, "You look awfully familiar. Have we met before? I recognize your hairstyle."

Tina shrugged. "They're called bantu knots."

Shonalee spoke up. "I know where you saw Tina. At the motorcycle rally."

"You were at the rally?" asked a shocked Tina. "Did you enjoy it?

"Yes, I did. It was the first one I ever went to. We had a lot of fun. Were you one of the women riding around on one of those fancy motorcycles? Some of them were just outstanding."

"I did some of that, but I was also one of the broads riding in the coffin. I had my body painted. Maybe that's where you saw me. I was kinda pissed because some of the paint got messed up. I wound up putting a T-shirt on."

Candy's mouth was hanging open. "What do you mean, you were riding in a coffin?"

"Yep, there were three of us squished in the coffin being pulled by a motorcycle. We were naked on top."

Piper was grinning. "Scottie told me about that."

"There were certainly a lot of different activities going on and items being sold," said Scottie.

Tina's eyebrows went up. She gulped down the rest of her wine and held out her glass for a refill. Just what else had this woman seen?

"Actually, I bought a tattoo sleeve from the booth selling all the different items," Scottie added. "Piper saw it."

"I did. Scottie totally faked me out. I was about to give her a lecture until I took a closer look and realized it was fabric."

Scottie chuckled. "I probably should have bought some other things, but I didn't."

.

Chapter 45

Tony and Doreen got checked out of the hotel and were headed back to her house. Doreen was driving, but not well. Tears were running down her face, blurring her vision. Also, her nose was running.

"Jeez, Doreen, I don't think you should be driving. You almost sideswiped that truck when you passed it. I think you should tell me what's going on. Does it have something to do with Pete?"

Doreen pulled off the highway and came to a stop in the parking lot of a rest stop. After mopping up her face and blowing her nose, she turned to Tony.

"You were right. Pete must have been having an affair," she said through muffled sobs. "That was the police on the phone earlier. They found the camper totally burned up. The license plate was sort of destroyed, but they could read enough of it to figure out who the camper belonged to. There were two bodies, but both were so badly burned, I—I can't talk about it. It's too horrible." More tears and nose blowing.

"My God, I can't believe it. You said the bodies were burned? How did that happen?"

"I said I don't want to talk about it. All I know is that the police said the camper rolled over and blew up."

"Doreen, I'm so sorry about Pete. It's a hell of a way to go." He absently patted her hand. There must have been guns and ammunition in the camper, and that's why it blew up. How hard would it be to identify the bodies? Might take a while, but seemed there was always a way, dental records, DNA, whatever. He'd be off the hook for a while. But then what if Pete's body was found in the woods near the rally grounds? Too much to think about. "Doreen, why don't I drive? I know this must be really hard for you, Pete running off with another woman like that. But I'm here for you, anything I can help you with."

"Thanks, Tony. I appreciate it. Maybe you should drive. My mind wouldn't be on the driving. I wonder who she was. Like, was it someone I know, like a friend or some woman at the rally? I just can't wrap my mind about Pete taking off like that. It doesn't seem like something he'd do. And you know what's really bad? I can't help but think 'Well, they deserved it.' But that's a nasty way to think."

They switched seats and got back on the road. "Tony, what about your arm? Can you use both arms? I wasn't even thinking about it. I don't want you driving my car if you can't use both arms."

"Hey, I'll be fine. No problem." He wasn't fine; the arm was extremely painful and oozing. But he wasn't going to tell Doreen that. Maybe he should go to Urgent Care, before some weird infection sets in and his arm needed to be cut off. He wanted to get his car out of Doreen's garage and go home. Too bad Doreen told the cops she was in Fort Myers. For sure she'd tell them he went with her. Now it was going to look like *they* were having an affair, which of course they weren't. He was going to have to tell Lenny about Pete. It would definitely be a phone call, not in person. Too dangerous. Lenny would not want any links to him and his business. Tony's life was spinning out of control. And he couldn't get rid of the image of Pete's grinning face.

They made it to Doreen's house in good time. Surprisingly, the traffic had been fairly light. Tony got his car out of her garage, and she put hers in.

"Boy, Doreen, I'm so sorry our little getaway turned out like this." They stood facing each other, neither sure what to say. "Are you gonna call his mom?" asked Tony.

"I don't know. I'll ask the cops if they've called her. Maybe I'll go over and see her. Except I don't know when the cops are coming here. I think I'll just go inside and cry for a while." Tears formed in her eyes.

"I'll haul your bag in and then head for home. Maybe you should call your girlfriends, see if they can come over."

"Mmm, I'll see. I'll add up the receipts and let you know how much this stupid trip cost. You can pay me next time I see you."

Tony carried her bag into the living room and left. Suddenly he remembered about not having his wallet or phone. How the hell was he going to call Lenny? Use a neighbor's phone? No, go and use the landline in the shop.

"Hey, Lenny, how you doing? It's Tony. I got some bad news to tell you. It's about Pete."

"What about Pete? I don't like the sounds of this," growled Lenny.

"Yeah, there's been an accident. I got this news from Doreen. She said the camper rolled over somewhere out in the country and blew up. The two people in it were also blown up. Sounded pretty bad."

"Who was with him if it wasn't Doreen?" asked Lenny.

"Beats me. He must have found some young chick."

"The cops are gonna be asking you a lot of questions. You two owned the pawn shop. And that means your gonna need to check your inventory to see if there are any questionable items there. I better get my stuff from Tina's and the few guns I have in your shop to be on the safe side. Of course, you remember about your mouth."

"My mouth?"

"Yeah, too much talking could close it forever." Click.

The conversation during the luncheon touched on a variety of topics, from the rally, dogs, travel, books, men, shopping, and more. Shonalee noticed the women all seemed to be enjoying the food. There were two different types of quiches, shrimp and veggie, and the spinach salad with strawberries and candied pecans was also a hit.

In the midst of this pleasantry, Tina was wondering just what Scottie had seen and heard at the rally. That could be a real problem. Then Tina's phone rang. Of course, her ring tone was barking dogs.

"If you'll excuse me ladies, I have to take this call. It may be important," she said, withdrawing to the privacy of the living room. Tina walked almost to the front door of the condo, listening to an upset Lenny on the phone. "Sorry to hear about Pete, Lenny. How's Doreen doing?"

"I have no idea. Haven't spoken to her. And don't plan to right now. I'm going to come to your place and empty the storage units. I suggest you get rid of anything you don't want the cops to see. Gotta go. See you soon."

Tina thought of her lovely plants she had so carefully tended. Maybe if she had Ruben and Carlos pull them up and put the pot in pots—but then where to put the pots? She'd have to tell the guys they were tomato plants, or they'd probably smoke them.

"Hey, Shonalee, something's come up, I gotta go home. Bring me my purse. It's hanging on the back of the chair," yelled Tina from the front door.

Shonalee got up from the table, frowning, grabbed Tina's purse, and excused herself.

"Tina, what's happened? Why do you have to leave? Don't you have the treats in the truck for the shop?"

"I'll have the guys get them to you. I've got another project they're going to be working on, and they'll have to come and get supplies."

Shonalee eyed Tina's worried face. Something was going on. "I hope nobody is hurt or sick."

"Oh no. Nothing like that." If you're dead, you're no longer sick or hurt. So that wasn't a lie, she figured. "Just some things I have to do to the property. Say goodbye to the girls for me." A door slam and she was gone.

Chapter 46

The first thing Tina did when she got home was look in the pole barn. She had ordered Ruben and Carlos to clean up the barn since most of the empty dog crates had been sold and to get the two puppies trained. The puppies were sound asleep, and she noticed that one of them had a lot of burrs. Where the hell had the dog been? Scanning the pole barn, she noticed the floor had been swept but not washed. Her motorcycle and Lenny's were parked in the far corner near the riding mower, and dog bowls had been stacked on one of the tables, along with a half-empty bag of dog food. Various farmyard tools were scattered around. Obviously, the guys hadn't worked too hard.

Tina shook her head in disgust. What no-good lazy louts. She left the barn and went into the house. "All right you dimwits, where are you?" she yelled, throwing her purse on the table.

"We're in here watching the news," Carlos responded as he quickly changed the TV channel.

"Well, turn it off and get in here."

Carlos and Ruben eyed each other and shrugged. Ruben shoved his empty chip bag and cookie wrappers under the sofa cushion but left the beer cans on the coffee table.

"Jeez, Tina, you're all dressed up," exclaimed Carlos clearly trying to butter her up a bit. It must have been some fancy shindig."

"It was, and I can't wait to get this dress off." Both men looked alarmed, as if afraid she would do it in the kitchen. She had taken off her shoes the moment she got in the house. Boots, flip-flops, shorts, capris, and T-shirts were more her style. "But before I do, we have to talk. Come sit at the table. You know we only have the two dogs left, the ones you're training. By the way, how's that going?

"Great. They're good dogs," said Ruben.

"Yup, good dogs," agreed Carlos.

Tina gave them the stink eye. She didn't believe a word they said. "Why is one of them covered in burrs?"

Ruben figured telling Tina the puppy got away from him, and he didn't feel like running after it wouldn't be a good thing. Puppies usually come back on their own. Wrong. Two hours had gone by and no dog. Ruben successfully talked Carlos into helping him look for it. They finally found the puppy sound asleep on the front porch of the house. It had obviously wandered all over, picking up burrs.

"I took the dog for a walk, and it rubbed up against a sticker bush," lied Ruben.

Carlos tried to hold back a snicker, and Tina rolled her eyes and said, "Well, have fun getting the burrs off. And the day after tomorrow I want you to show me just how well they've been trained. Plus, the barn still needs work. That floor needs a good wash."

"That's a really big floor to wash. It took forever just to sweep it," said Carlos.

"That's for sure," agreed Ruben. "What we need is a Zamboni mop. I could ride that around and have it done in no time."

Tina snorted and said, "In your dreams. The only Zamboni mop here will be powered by your arms, and I don't want to hear any whining. But listen, guys, I came up with a plan I think you'll really like. It's raising chickens and selling the eggs and sometimes the chickens. What do you think?"

"Chickens!" squeaked Carlos. Eating eggs and chicken, yes, but raising chickens? No way. "Why would you want to do a crazy thing like that?"

"I need a beer," said Ruben going over to the refrigerator. Sometimes it was best to just stay out of a conversation. One good thing about chickens at least no training would be involved.

Tina scowled at Carlos. "And just what's wrong with raising chickens?"

"Well, for one thing where would you put them? And what would you do with the eggs if you get any? And what were you thinking that Ruben and I would have to do?" Ruben could see Carlos was starting to get a little riled up. His knee was bouncing up and down.

"Calm down. We'll use part of the barn inside, and build an outside area connected to the barn where they can scratch around in the dirt. The storage sheds will be empty, so maybe they can be used somehow. I've got a couple of sources already lined up that said they would buy the eggs. Hey Ruben, are you listening?"

Ruben zoned out on his second beer stared out the window. "Huh. What?" he asked.

"I suggest you pay attention because I've got some projects for you two.

Carlos was in the barn, dozing on one of the worktables, his feet hanging over the end. He had bunched up some semi-clean rags to use as a pillow. The puppy he was supposed to be training sat in a crate totally bored. At the sound of voices near the barn, the dog started barking loudly, causing Carlos to jump up off the table and run out the side door of the barn and around the back.

"Holy shit, this is why Tina comes back here," Carlos whispered to himself. He gazed in amazement at the two long rows of marijuana plants. Carlos knew Tina got the weed from somewhere, but it never occurred to him to look behind the barn. Listening to snatches of voices coming from inside the barn, he determined Lenny was loading his motorcycle into his van. When Carlos finally heard no more sounds coming from inside the barn, he quietly opened the side door a crack to make sure no one was there. Empty. He headed back into the barn.

"Tina, you know this might be the end of having rallies on your property," commented Lenny, flicking his cigarette ash over the railing and into the yard. "According to Tony the explosion that blew up the camper was humongous. No telling what was in that camper besides the two people."

"What a horrible way to go. Do they know who was with him since it wasn't Doreen? Maybe someone he was screwing around with? I don't see why the cops would come to see me anyway."

Lenny sighed. "Don't forget the rally was apparently the last place anyone saw him. Never heard about him messing around with anyone. But he did say once that Doreen was always going places with her girlfriends."

"Changing the subject, you're right about the rallies. I think that was the last one. I'm going to either come up with some other businesses or sell the place, or at least part of it. I'm glad I got rid of the dogs, but I always enjoyed the rallies," said Tina with a worried face. She hoped to be signing a lucrative contract to sell most of her property, but she wasn't going to tell him about how much money she might make.

"Got any possible business in mind?" asked Lenny.

"A while back a guy contacted me about buying some of the land to put up a marijuana growing factory. You know, for medical purposes supposedly. The company is called Hi and Higher."

Lenny chuckled. "Perfect. Then you wouldn't have to grow your own. Just make it part of the deal. He gives you a certain amount free when you want it."

"That's not a bad idea. For now, I'm planning to raise chickens. Sell the eggs and some of the chickens. I'm going to sell them as 'Happy Chickens' and 'Happy Eggs'. It's going to be a small project to start with. Want to see how it goes." *Not sure I'll really raise chickens,* she thought. *But let 'em think I am. I'm starting to think maybe the only chicken will be on my plate.*

"Why happy?" asked Lenny. "And how do you know when a chicken is happy?"

"How the hell would I know?" said Tina, her face getting flushed. "Just living with me should make them happy." *What a bozo. I'm not going to tell him how I was going to make them happy.*

Lenny leaned forward in his chair getting in Tina's space, his black eyes boring into her face.

"Tina, I'm sure the Feds will be coming out to see you. I don't want you talking about Pete and Tony, and of course me. They don't need to know about the guns and knives or anything else. Got that?"

"Jeez Lenny, whaddya think I am, stupid?" asked Tina. "The two you need to worry about are Tony and Doreen. I'm sure one of them will blab. I still don't think anyone in law enforcement will come to see me."

Lenny sat back in his chair. "Well, Tony and Doreen better keep their mouths shut. I'm on my way to talk to them next. I left a message for Tony on his phone, so he knows I'm coming. Then I decided maybe I'd better go see Doreen too."

Chapter 47

Ruben was sitting with a zonked-out puppy on his lap. A few extra treats always put the dogs to sleep. Ruben had dragged a rickety beach chair from the barn and put it near the side of the house in the shade. It was a good place to pull the burrs from the dog's fur. Just around the corner from where he was sitting was the deck where Tina and Lenny were discussing the state of their business. Ruben heard everything. The Feds were coming. He couldn't wait to tell Carlos. They'd have to get away from Tina's place. Being questioned by the Feds wouldn't be good. Not that they'd really done anything. Just moved two bodies to different locations on the river. Big deal.

"Where have you been?" asked Carlos when Ruben entered the barn. "I got something to tell you."

"Well, I've got something to tell you. Really important info," retorted Ruben, huffing and puffing as he leaned the beach chair against the wall and put the puppy in its crate.

"Hey, my news is important too," said Carlos.

"Yeah, yeah. Whatever. Now listen," Ruben whispered, looking around to make sure they were alone. "I was sitting by the house around the corner from the deck. Tina and Lenny were on the deck talking. Lenny said the FBI would be coming here to talk to Tina. It's about some guy that got blown up in a truck or something. And he was last seen at the rally."

"What does that have to do with us?" asked a puzzled Carlos, munching on a dog treat that was from a bag that was supposed to go to Shonalee.

"Nothing maybe. But what about the you-know-what that we . . .?"

Carlos was silent. The Feds coming might be a problem. He looked at Ruben. Dirty tank top, not quite covering his belly. Cargo shorts just as dirty. Bald head glistening with sweat. Three-day growth of beard.

"Maybe we should go and stay with my sister for a while," suggested Carlos. "I really don't want the FBI questioning us. One of us just might slip up and say something dumb."

Ruben grabbed a couple of doggie treats from the bag. He gave one to Carlos's dog and kept one for himself. His own puppy was asleep.

"How long could we stay with your sister? And how would we get there? I'm sure as hell not walking to Miami. And you know Tina's not gonna say 'Go ahead and take the truck or van.' Guess we'll have to stay here and wing it if they start asking questions."

"The thing is we couldn't stay too long with Carmen. I know you like her cooking, but her place is just too small. She'd probably let us stay for a while. Maybe after we drop off the puppies with Shonalee we could just continue on to Miami."

Ruben shook his head. "Wouldn't work. Tina would have the cops after us in a flash for stealing her van."

"Why couldn't she have Lenny drive it back here?"

"Then how is he supposed to get back to Miami? He just put his motorcycle in his van. And I don't think he would want to come back here from what I heard."

Carlos ran his fingers through his hair. "How about this? We tell Tina that Carmen is sick, and she needs us to help with the kids and whatever. We'll get the van back to her as soon as possible."

"That might work. It's the part about getting the van back to her that could be a problem. How we gonna do that?" asked Ruben, dubious.

"Maybe you could drive the van back and I'll borrow Carmen's car, follow you to Tina's and take you back?"

Ruben snorted. "Isn't Tina gonna wonder how we could leave a sick Carmen with the kids running all over? Sounds like a dumb idea."

"Okay, smartass, what's your brilliant idea?" Carlos scoffed, and the puppy started barking as if to agree.

"Actually, I do have an idea. Remember the dude we had dinner with at Carmen's? An old, retired guy. What if we could get him to follow you to Tina's and drive you back?" suggested Ruben, feeling quite clever.

Carlos didn't say anything.

"Well?" said Ruben waiting for a response.

"Give Carmen a call and see what she says."

"She's your sister. You call her. I'm the one who came up with the idea," said Ruben, chomping down on another doggie treat.

"You are something else, you know," said Carlos. "If I call her you have to tell Tina the situation. And I don't want to hear any of your complaining."

"Complaining! You gotta be kidding. That's not my style. But just so I don't have to listen to your BS, I'll talk to her."

Chapter 48

Scottie was on the phone again, listening to scratchy elevator music while waiting to talk with Agent Myers. It was the fourth time she'd called. It was always the same. Either she was told to leave a message, or he had no further information about her case. Really annoying. She'd practically handed Diablo/Tony to them on a platter. Gave them his phone and wallet. How could they not have apprehended him by now?

"Hello, Agent Myers. This is Scottie Sheldon. You know what I'm calling about. Have you caught him?" she asked eagerly while pacing around the great room of her house.

"Not yet. But we have several—"

"You've got to be kidding. You don't have him yet! It shouldn't be that hard. There must be info on his phone that's a big help." Scottie rolled her eyes. "Maybe I should come with you on the search. I could borrow Mr. B, you know, the big dog. Have him sniff the wallet or whatever is in it."

"We appreciate your help and your offer, but we have everything under control, and we'll keep you up-to-date as we proceed with our investigation."

"Where did you say he works?" asked Scottie, knowing they had never told her where he worked.

"He's part owner of a pawn—hey, I don't believe we mentioned his occupation. Very sneaky on your part. Don't be getting any crazy ideas. Leave it to us."

Scottie was grinning. "Absolutely, you're the pros. But please call if you learn anything." After ending the call, she quickly searched the internet for information on local pawn shops. There were two in the area. *I need to check them out,* she thought. *Maybe I can look in the windows and if Diablo is there, I'll call Agent Lowell. Or I might have to go in the shop. If I do that, I'll need a disguise. Maybe the blonde wig I used at Halloween. That might work.*

Scottie dug around in her boxes of holiday paraphernalia until she found the wig. After putting on the long blonde wig, sunglasses, blue jeans, a navy tank top, and sneakers, she decided something else was needed. Aha! Jewelry. She put on four silver rings, large silver hoop earrings, and a silver bracelet She'd ask the pawn broker if they sold silver jewelry, explaining she was really into silver. Scottie was good to go. Time to see if blondes really have more fun and are good at catching nasty guys.

Tony bought a couple of burner phones. He wanted to keep in touch with Doreen to find out what she learned from the cops about Pete. He was rather surprised that no one had discovered Pete's body in the woods at the rally site. Maybe bobcats or panthers had carried the body away and devoured him. Driving out there to check would seem suspicious. He'd just stay home and pretend to be upset about the death of his wonderful partner. Out of respect he'd keep the shop closed for a while.

The first pawn shop Scottie checked out had a sign displayed in the front window saying Bart's Barber Shop was coming soon. Apparently there no longer was a pawn shop at this location. She then drove to the address of the other shop. The name of the shop was Tony and Pete's Pawn Shop. The only vehicle parked out front was a large white van. The dark tint on the windows prevented her from seeing if there was anyone inside.

"Guess, I'll just have to find out if he's here," she mumbled to herself as she got out of the car. As she started to walk to the shop a tall guy with lots of black hair got out of the van.

"Hey, you, the shop is closed," called the guy as he walked over to her. He gave her the once over. Not bad. He always liked blondes.

"Do you know what time it's supposed to open today?" asked Scottie. "Tony usually has it open by now." Sometimes improvising is necessary.

"Oh, so you know Tony. When did you see him last?"

"Not too long ago. We've done some business together." *Boy, have we done some "business."*

The guy eyed her suspiciously. "And what kind of business did you two do?" he asked taking a few steps closer to her, his black eyes boring into her.

Scottie wanted to take an equal number of steps back from him, but she held her ground. "Oh, I buy silver jewelry from him, as you can see." She held her hand out to show him her rings. "Pretty cool, huh?"

"Definitely. I hate to tell you this, but Tony isn't coming in today. You'll have to come back tomorrow or some other day."

"I'm really disappointed, but if you know for sure he won't be here, I guess I'll go. By the way, what's your name?" asked Scottie.

"Bob."

"Mine's Abby," she said. "Nice meeting you." She got into her car and backed up slowly so she could see the license plate on the van. Quickly repeating it to herself, she drove away. After rounding the corner Scottie pulled over to the side of the street and typed the license plate number in the note app on her phone.

I've got to get home and get this wig off. It's driving me crazy. I don't know how Dolly Parton does it. Then I'll call Agent Myer and give him the license plate number of the van.

I'll show him I'm on the case, thought Scottie. *That guy "Bob" was sending off bad vibes, and he obviously knew Tony.*

Chapter 49

Tina was in the living room in her recliner, reading one of her favorite tabloids, *Smears and Cheers*. She pretended not to notice when Ruben plopped down on the sofa. And he appeared to be clean, which usually meant he wanted something.

"Ah, Tina, I wanna ask you something, it's kinda important." Ruben's face was flushed with nerves.

"Really, I'm shocked," said Tina facetiously. "Now what do you want?"

"Well, it's like this. Carlos's sister Carmen is real sick. She might even need an operation. So, it looks like we gotta go take care of the kids and the house."

Tina thought about this. "How long is this mission of mercy supposed to last?"

"I don't know, Tina. It's hard to tell."

"After you drop the puppies off with Shonalee, you and Carlos are supposed to pick up supplies to get the barn ready for the chickens. And who's gonna take care of the chickens when they get here? And how are you two getting to Miami? Hitchhike? Have you even thought about it?"

"Of course, we have," he said indignantly. "What do you think—"

"Oh, don't get your feathers in a twist."

Ruben looked up in hopeful confusion.

After talking with Tina, Ruben returned to Carlos in the barn, ostensibly to work with the puppies. Ruben let them out of their crates, and the two little fur balls were roughhousing with each other.

"Okay, what's the word from Tina? Did she say we could use the van?" asked Carlos, pacing back and forth. "If we can't use the van, we're SOL."

"Stop that damn walking around. Get a chair and sit down. You're making me nervous," said an exasperated Ruben. "It's gonna work out okay. We can take the puppies to Shonalee and then go to Miami. She said since we won't be around to start on the chicken house or whatever it is, she'll put that off till we get back. It was my smooth talking that convinced her. How did it go with your sister?"

"Yeah, right, your smooth talking. I think it went pretty good with Carmen. She asked a lot of questions. I didn't tell our story about her being sick. I just said we want to come and help her out, you know, with the kids. That way she wouldn't have to pay for a babysitter. But she said you do eat a lot. We may have to pay her something because of that."

"She never said that."

"Yes, she did. You can ask her."

"What about the guy we need to help us get the van back to Tina?"

"That wasn't so easy. He's kind of a grouch. We have to pay for the gas, plus extra for the wear and tear on his car, plus buy him breakfast and lunch. But at least he'll drive to Tina's so we can get the van back to her. I'll be glad when all this crap is behind us." Looking rather glum, Carlos picked up the puppy he was supposed to have trained and went outside.

Ruben, sensing his buddy was feeling down, picked up the other puppy and followed Carlos outside.

"Listen up, bro," Ruben said in a cheery voice. "You like being in Miami. It's gonna be great. You know people there, and we'll be with your sister and the kids."

"And you like Carmen's cooking, and I think you actually like the kids."

Ruben didn't say anything. Letting go of the puppy, he stood watching the two little dogs running around and doing a lot of sniffing. "Guess we better try training these critters to do at least one thing. Come here, you fur face," he yelled at his puppy, who paid no attention to him.

"That went well," snickered Carlos. "You know you have to use treats to get them to come to you. Small treats, not the big ones that put 'em to sleep."

Ruben was about to make a smart-ass remark when he noticed Tina walking toward them. She had a bounce in her step, her boobs were straining to get out of her tight neon yellow tank top. Plus, there was a grin on her face. Not her usual demeanor when dealing with Carlos and Ruben.

"Hi guys, how's the training coming? asked Tina as she bent down to pick up the small dog that had trotted to her. Ruben and Carlos looked at each other. Tina holding a dog and letting it lick her face? Would wonders never cease!

"Well, they're not quite ready yet. But you have to consider how young they are," Carlos explained. "We've been working super hard trying to get them to learn the basics."

"Actually, it really doesn't matter if they're trained or not because tomorrow, you're taking them to Shonalee. She knows a woman who has a neighbor who will take one right away." Tina put the puppy on the ground and then pulled up the shoulder of her tank top to wipe her face.

"If we're taking the dogs to her tomorrow, we could continue on to Miami right after." suggested Carlos.

"Okay, but I want the van back right away, or else. And it better be clean and full of gas," cautioned Tina with a scowl.

"You know I said we would. We'll have it back the next day. Not to worry," said Ruben. Actually, they didn't know when the van would be returned. They needed to check with the grouchy old man to see when he'd be available.

"When you tell me not to worry, I worry," said Tina. "I do have a chore for you now. Come with me after you put the dogs in their crates. I'll show you what I want done."

They put the puppies in the crates and then followed Tina behind the barn. Tina pointed to the plants growing along the back of the barn. "See these plants here? I want them all pulled out and hauled over to this area." Tina indicated a sandy area well away from the barn where no trees or shrubs grew.

"Tina, I have to ask you. Are these plants what I think they are?" asked Carlos, looking totally innocent. "Why would you want them pulled up?"

"They're potato plants. I won't be needing them anymore," replied Tina.

Ruben snickered. "No way are those potato plants. I know potato plants, and those ain't potato plants. Why the hell would you want them yanked out? They look healthy. I'm sure they could be put to good use."

"All right you smart asses. This is what I want you to do. Dig a shallow pit in this area, and after you pull them up, put them in the wheelbarrow and dump them in the pit. Don't bury 'em—just dump 'em. And I mean all of them. Got that?"

"Sure, Tina. No problem-o," said Ruben as the three of them walked back to the barn.

"Dinner is at six sharp tonight. That means you're cleaned up and at the table," ordered Tina.

"Does that mean you're fixing something special?" Carlos asked hopefully. So far none of Tina's meals had been special.

"Guess you'll have to wait and see," Tina said smugly, tossing her long black hair over her shoulder as she walked to the house.

"Something special" would mean Tina would have to go to the grocery store, because there sure wasn't anything in Tina's kitchen that would qualify as "special." As soon as Tina was out of listening distance, Carlos nudged Ruben and said, "If she leaves the house, we have to put all our stuff in the van. We'll be leaving right from Shonalee's place tomorrow to go to Miami. I mean, we haven't told her we're not coming back here to stay. Be sure you don't slip up and say what our plans are."

"Me slip up? No way," exclaimed Ruben, a look of mock horror on his face.

Carlos ignored him. Suddenly he excitedly pointed as Tina was leaving in her truck. "Hey, there she goes. I bet she's going to the grocery store. Let's go pack up. I'm gonna dump all my stuff in those big black garbage bags and throw 'em in the van."

"Don't forget we have to have clean clothes on for dinner, so you'd better leave a few out. I wonder why she's getting so fussy. She expects a lot from us," complained Ruben.

"You got that right. Maybe she's got a new project she's working on."

"Nah, I think it's a guy. That's what she really needs. A good romp in the hay."

Chapter 50

Scottie drove home at a faster speed than she should have, but she wanted to call Agent Myers and give him the license number on the van. The first thing she did when she got home was to take off the wig. After running her fingers through her curly hair and breathing a sigh of relief, she called Agent Myers.

Of course, she had to leave a message. They never answered their phone. She gave the license plate number of the van at the pawn shop, but also information about the driver in the van. Scottie explained that "Bob," said Tony wouldn't be in the store until the next day.

Just as she was finishing the voicemail message, the doorbell rang. Scottie now made a point of always looking through the peephole before opening the door. She had learned her lesson. Seeing it was Charlie, she was more than happy to unlock the door to let him in.

"Oh Charlie, I'm so glad to see you," she exclaimed as she threw her arms around him.

"Okay, what have you done now?" Charlie laughed as he hugged her, a big smile on his face.

"Let's go sit in the lanai. I'll get us a cup of coffee and I'll tell you what's happened." As they sipped their coffee, Scottie told Charlie how she had checked out the pawn shops and about the van that was parked there.

"One thing I don't understand, Charlie. Why would this Bob guy be at the pawn shop if he knew Tony wasn't going to be there until tomorrow? Maybe he was going to break in. What do you think? He looked like he could be the type. And you know what? He looked familiar, but I can't think of where I've seen him before."

"If he was going to break in, I don't think he'd be parked in front of the shop. He'd be in the back. There must be another explanation."

"Could be he was just waiting for Tony to show up. Like maybe they had an appointment and Tony was late. Do you think we should go back and see if that's what's going on?"

"Nope, I think we should sit here, drink our coffee, and talk about us."

Tony was sitting in his gloomy living room, sipping scotch. It was a little early in the day for the scotch, but he needed it. He had drawn the drapes throughout the house. He didn't bother to clean up the take-out food boxes on the tables in the living room and the kitchen, despite the musty smell.

Weird thoughts were flying around in his head. *I know they're coming for me. Both the FBI and Lenny. Shit. Either way I'm screwed.* He'd brought home the money from the safe at the store. That would hold him for a while if he took off for some place. *But I'm sure there's an APB out for me. Exchange the plate on my car with another one. If that bitch hadn't made me leave my phone and wallet in her kitchen. Maybe a little more scotch will help me figure out what to do.*

The bottle was on the table. He poured a hefty amount into his tumbler. Before long he was sound asleep, snoring on the sofa. The persistent loud ding-dong sounds of his doorbell finally jarred him awake. Tony considered not answering the door but decided he might as well. He was going to have to face the music at some point. He shook his head, trying to get rid of the scotch webs. After unlocking the door, he opened it as far as the chain would go. Lenny. Why did it have to be Lenny?

"Hey, Len, what are you doing here?" asked Tony as he unlatched the chain and opened the door. Lenny strode in and sat in the well-worn brown recliner. There was no smile or "How ya doing."

"What do you mean? I expected you to be at the shop so I could pick up the items I have for sale there. Why aren't you working there? I left you a text that I was coming. And what happened to your arm?" Lenny stared at him, his dark eyes, looking to Tony like little dark tunnels to hell.

"I guess I missed the text," Tony answered. "Been kinda busy, you know, what with what happened to Pete and all. Had a cancer on my arm taken off." Tony fidgeted with the mess on the coffee table. He wasn't about to say who had his phone and wallet.

"A cancer on your arm, huh? So, have you cleaned up the shop? Taken out all items that shouldn't be there? You know the law will be checking it out. After all, Pete was your partner, and you saw him last."

"I know. I started to pull out the guns that would implicate us, but Pete blowing up like that got me shook. I've got more to do." Tony tried to look full of remorse. He wasn't about to mention going to Fort Myers with Doreen. All he could hope was that she hadn't said anything about their little trip.

"What else have you heard about the accident?" asked Lenny.

"Nothing, except what I told you. I know Doreen's upset about someone being in the camper with him."

"Listen, Tony, I want my belongings. You go to the shop and put them in a big bag or box, and I'll pick them up in about an hour. Give me Doreen's address. I'm gonna make a quick stop to see her. Offer my condolences and find out what she's heard. Somehow this all sounds kinda fishy. And I really don't like liars. Are you sure you don't know more than you're telling me? By the way, when I stopped at the shop a good-looking woman with long blonde hair drove up wanting to see you. Said she's done lots of business with you. Sounded like she knows you pretty well. What's that all about? How involved with her are you?"

Lenny had stood up and loomed over Tony.

"What are you talking about? I don't know anyone like that who's been in the shop often. Did she say what's she's been buying?"

"Yep, silver. She was all decked out in silver jewelry."

Tony thought the only one who could be screwing around with him was that bitch of a dog walker. "Tell me more about her. What she looked like and so forth."

"Average height, couldn't see her eyes since she had sunglasses on. In good shape, nice voice."

"What's a nice voice?" asked Tony.

"Husky, really sexy. You'd have remembered it."

Tony felt the blood drain from his face. His eyes swiveled everywhere but at his guest, and his hand shook when he picked up his scotch glass.

"You know her, don't you?"

"I don't know any blonde who has bought silver from the shop, honest," he stammered.

"Like I said, I don't like liars. As a matter of fact, I hate them. I'm taking off."

"Wait a sec. I'll get you Doreen's address."

Carlos and Ruben finished pulling up the plants from behind the barn and dumping them in the shallow pit. All but one plant that is, which they managed to sneak into the van to take with them to Miami. After that they went into the house to find Tina setting the table for dinner. She had removed the stacks of tabloids from the table as well as the ashtrays.

"Wow, I don't remember the table being this big," exclaimed Carlos. "Is this a new one?"

"Of course, it isn't. See the ring you made when you put the . . ." She sighed. "Never mind. We're going to have a nice dinner. Ruben, you get the grill out of the barn and clean it up while Carlos takes his shower. And Carlos, when you're done showering you can peel the potatoes."

Ruben looked at Tina and said, "And what are you going to do?" Wrong thing to say.

"Listen stinkweed, who went to the grocery store, bought the groceries, set the table . . ." Tina slammed a pot on the stove.

"Okay, okay." Ruben put up his hands defensively. "I know how hard you work, and this will be a great dinner. I'll go take care of the grill right away." He was out of the kitchen in a flash.

Carlos was too. Staying near Tina when she was on a roll wasn't advisable.

After he finished showering and putting on clean clothes, Carlos quietly walked into the kitchen. No one there. Three big potatoes were on the counter. along with the peeler and a pot. Guess this was his job.

He had just finished peeling the potatoes when Tina walked into the kitchen. She was dressed in a long, multicolored sleeveless dress and her flip-flops. Her black hair was pulled back in a ponytail. The black hair dye was starting to grow out, which didn't create the best look.

"See you got the potatoes peeled. Now cut 'em into chunks and start cooking. I'm gonna use the bigger pot for the corn on the cob. I'm taking the steak out to get warmed up," Tina explained.

"We're gonna have steaks?" asked a totally amazed Carlos.

"Yep, they had this round steak on sale. I got a big one. Should be plenty for all of us. I'll have Ruben put it on the grill. He should have it cleaned by now." Tina took the meat out of the wrapper and slapped it on a plastic plate. "Carlos, watch the veggies while I take this out to Ruben."

The "special dinner" didn't turn out quite as special as they'd hoped. The corn was a little mushy, the potatoes a bit crunchy, and the steak beyond help. Ruben didn't want the red wine. It had to be beer for him. Other than these issues it turned out to be a pleasant dinner. No arguments, shouting, or stomping out of the room.

"Okay, guys, there's one other thing we're going to do tonight. I want you to take three beach chairs out of the barn and haul them to the pit you put the plants in. Don't put the chairs in the pit, just around the pit. Also, bring the gas can you use for the mower over there. Ruben, there are two six packs of beer in the fridge, and Carlos, you take a bunch of the old tabloids. We'll use them to get the fire going. I've got a bag of chocolate chip cookies and some Fritos that I'll take."

"You know, Tina, the smoke from that fire might make us a little, well, you know," Carlos pointed out.

"You two have a problem with that?" asked Tina. "I thought you were more sophisticated than that. Being such worldly men."

"Absolutely not, Tina, no problem at all. It's a great way to end the evening. Isn't it, Ruben?" asked Carlos.

"Yup, real good. Let's get going." Ruben went to the fridge and got the beer while Carlos grabbed an armful of the tabloids.

As Carlos and Ruben carried the chairs to the pit where they had dumped the plants, Ruben said, "Know what? Maybe on the way to Shonalee's shop tomorrow we could give the puppies the rest of the steak. There's quite a bit left. That would keep them quiet."

"It sure would. But by the time we dropped them off, all their baby teeth would have come out.

"Yeah, you're right. Let's stick with the doggy treats."

After getting all items needed hauled out to the pit area, the three of them finally sat in the rickety beach chairs, drinking beer, passing around the munchies, and breathing deeply of the smoke wafting up from the fire pit. The strong smoke from the marijuana plants burning created a relaxing atmosphere. Life couldn't get any better.

Chapter 51

Charlie talked Scottie into staying at his house until Tony was apprehended. She provided him with numerous reasons why she should stay in her own home, but Charlie was so persuasive she finally agreed.

"Charlie, I'm not going to call them anymore. They never call me back. They could at least let me know if the info I give them is any help," complained Scottie as she and Charlie were driving to his house.

"I'm sure the FBI guys have a lot on their plate. Your case is probably one of many they're working on."

"You're right. It's just I find myself getting anxious, stressed out, wondering what's going to happen next. I even told Kevin to do some nosing around. He really hasn't been involved in this case. Possibly, because I'm a relative. Maybe, someone at the police station heard a rumor about what's happening."

"Staying at my house for awhile is definitely the best way to get your mind off that wacko."

"Do you think I should get a big dog like Mr. B? He sure did a job on Tony's arm. Did I tell you that stinker insisted on sleeping on my bed?" Scottie chuckled. "That Mr. B is something else."

"Tell you what. When I'm staying at your house there will be no big or small dogs in bed with us," declared Charlie as he winked at Scottie.

Doreen was totally surprised to see Lenny at her door. "This is a surprise. Guess you've been talking with Tony. Come in." Doreen waved him in and led him into the living room, where they sat down. She had on pink shorts and a white T-shirt, her hair pulled back in a ponytail.

"You're looking good, Doreen, considering what happened to Pete," said Lenny as he checked her out. "Speaking of Pete, just what did happen? I didn't get much info from Tony."

"Oh, Tony is a big mess. I'm surprised he told you anything. Like I said on the phone, he's lost it. The idiot loses his phone, his wallet, and gets bitten by a dog. And the dog bite was really bad. He expected me to fix it up, but jeez I'm not a nurse. I did the best I could. He should've gone to Urgent Care or the hospital. I hope he did. Hey, you want a drink?"

"Guess I'll have a beer," said Lenny.

"Be back in a jiff." Doreen put a little extra swing in her walk as she went to get the beer. She turned back slightly to see that Lenny had a slight smirk on his face as she walked away.

Doreen strolled in with two beers, and handed one Lenny.

Lenny took a swig of beer and moved forward in his chair. Giving her his laser look, he asked, "Doreen, when did Tony lose his wallet and phone?"

"Boy, Len, I'm not sure when he lost them, but he didn't have 'em when he came to see me. If he told me, I forgot. I wound up paying for everything when we went to Fort Myers. What a fiasco that was. We were having breakfast when I got the phone call about Pete." Tears formed in her eyes. "It was the worst call ever. You can't imagine."

Lenny's laser-eyes widened in shock. "What the hell? Are you having an affair with Tony?"

"Good Lord no! No way would I ever mess around with him. Give me a little credit." Doreen picked up her beer and took a big gulp.

"So, what were you doing in Fort Myers?"

"Tony thought a little getaway would be good for us, and I think he was also worried about some guy coming after him," said Doreen, her voice shaky. Being questioned by Lenny could make a person kinda scared.

"Did he say who the guy was?"

"I dunno who the guy was. We got into the scotch big time when he came over, plus I didn't pay much attention to what he was saying. He kept going on about his arm and the dog biting him. Maybe he said it was the owner of the dog who was after him. That was probably it."

Lenny looked at his watch. He couldn't stay much longer.

"Okay, Doreen, tell me what the cops told you about the accident and Pete."

"I don't know what you've heard, but the camper blew up, as well as Pete and whoever was with him. The thing is, Lenny, I never for one moment thought he was stepping out on me. I guess it's true, the wife is always the last to hear about it. The FBI and some police detectives interviewed me. They wanted to know what was stored in the camper because the explosion was so fierce. I told them I had no idea. That camper was a total piece of crap. Much too small. That's why I didn't stay in it at the rally this year."

"So have they identified the bodies already?" asked Lenny. "You're gonna want to know who was with him."

"You got that right. Not yet as far as I know. They want to interview Tony, and I'm sure they'll want to see you too. I mean, you're sort of involved in supplying the shop with merchandise. Pete never told me much about it. I guess I'll be working with Tony now that Pete's gone. I've got a lot to learn."

"Are you saying you gave the Feds my name?" Lenny spoke quietly and calmly, but the dark expression on his face and the tautness of his body showed how he was feeling. A spring ready to snap.

Doreen shrugged. "Well, I had to. They wanted the names of all of Pete's friends and relatives. It's no biggie. They always do it on TV shows."

"We're not a goddamn TV show, Doreen. Do not ever mention my name again. Got that?" Lenny fixed her with his trademark stare.

"Okay, okay. Not to worry. My lips are sealed. Are you seeing Tony today?"

There are times when changing the subject is a good idea.

"None of your business. I gotta get out of here now." Lenny was walking to the door already.

"I'm glad you stopped by. I'll probably see you at the shop from time to time when I start working there." He wasn't listening to her. He was already out the door and hurrying down the sidewalk to the van.

Lenny's thoughts were spinning wildly. *I know now she gave my name to the Feds. What a dumb broad. This could mean big trouble. She pissed me off so bad I forgot to ask if Tony found his wallet and his phone. I'll get my guns from the shop, and Tony boy better be there. I've gotta get on the road. The ship from Argentina should be docked by now. I've gotta get the merchandise off the ship asap, or I know how the captain will be.*

Tony had parked his car behind the pawn shop and used the back door to get in. He was busy tossing the guns that belonged to Lenny into a cardboard box. He also purposely put a couple of knives, including the knife he had used on Pete. Lenny probably wouldn't even notice they weren't part of his inventory.

Suddenly there was a loud pounding on the front door. And then a voice demanding that he open door.

Tony stood still. *Christ, it's Lenny. Stay calm, stay calm.*

He unlocked the front door and opened it wide to let Lenny enter.

"Good to see you again, Len. I've got your box almost ready to go. You on your way back to Miami?" asked a nervous Tony.

"Right, I'm in a hurry. Speed it up," said Lenny.

"Will do." Tony hurried to the back room and tossed in the remaining guns that Lenny owned. He put the box on the counter. "Here you go."

"I just need to get my money and a receipt for what was sold," said Lenny, staring at Tony.

"Ah, it's like this. Since I didn't know what happened to Pete, I took everything that was in the store safe and put it in my home safe. Who knows, there could have been a break-in here. Maybe the person in the camper with him was a guy. Pete could have been doing some extra business on the side we weren't aware of."

"I doubt that. This all sounds mighty weird to me. If I wasn't in a hurry, I'd take more time to get to the bottom of what's going on. Have a cashier's check and my receipt in the mail tomorrow," demanded Lenny. "You don't want me to have to come back here for it. By the way, did you find your phone and your wallet?"

"Oh, I had just misplaced them at home. Like I said, this Pete issue has thrown me for a loop."

"If you hear more about Pete, I want to know." Lenny gave Tony a dark level stare and walked to the door.

"Sure, no problem, Lenny." As the door closed, Tony wiped his clammy hands on his shorts, then turned the sign on the door to CLOSED and turned off the lights. He stood watching the van leave the parking lot, travel down the street, and round the corner. *I'm still alive,* he thought. *At least he hasn't killed me yet.*

After going out the back door and locking it, he drove down the alley behind the shops and headed for home.

Chapter 52

Lenny was in a foul mood as he headed down the highway mumbling his random thoughts out loud. "Boy, I thought I'd never get on the road. But I needed to talk to them. I had to see Tina to get my merchandise out of the storage units and give her keys back. Pete was last seen on her property. I've always helped her with the rallies. Maybe I shouldn't have. She'll probably get a visit from the law, but I'm not too concerned about her. That woman is sly as a fox. Doreen sure didn't know anything useful, at least not yet. Tony is the one that worries me. He's totally lost it. Something is going on he hasn't told me about. No telling what's going to happen there. He'd better not mess up again. Doing in the FBI guy was a major mistake."

Tina, Ruben, and Carlos slept late the morning after the fire pit party. Really late. It had been a fun time. Marijuana and beer, what a combo. They had laughed and laughed, especially at all the off-color jokes Tina had regaled them with. Ruben proclaimed, after the fire went out and they were staggering back to the house, that it was the best party ever, and Carlos had seconded it. Even Tina agreed, saying it was the best party she'd ever put together.

The next morning Tina's mobile phone rang, the ring tone of barking dogs rudely waking her up. She considered throwing it against the wall but then decided she'd better answer it.

"Lo. Whaddya want?"

"Well, good morning, Ms. Sunshine," answered Shonalee cheerily. "Don't tell me I woke you up. I thought the guys would have the puppies here at the boutique by now. I can't wait to see them. I've got that potential buyer coming in about one o'clock."

"They'll be there." Click. (I like this. Very effective way to end the call.)

Tina's mood didn't improve when she couldn't get Carlos and Ruben up and moving. Pounding on the bedroom door brought no results. She finally bellowed outside the door, "I'm coming in there with my cattle prod if you're not in the kitchen ready to go in fifteen minutes. And guess where I'm gonna use it."

They were in the kitchen in fifteen minutes, looking like the walking dead.

"What's for breakfast?" asked Ruben, sitting at the table, sporting an unbuttoned bright red and orange print shirt and a baseball cap on backwards. Carlos was rummaging around in the fridge trying to find some possible breakfast items. He shook his head at Ruben's question. Some people never learn.

Tina gave Ruben the finger. "Get those dogs cleaned up and take them to Shonalee. She wants them NOW." With that directive she left the room.

Carlos fried himself a couple of eggs, made toast, and slathered it with peanut butter. He placed the plate on the opposite end of the table from where Ruben sat. "I'm getting my cup of coffee. Don't you dare touch my food."

"Could you at least bring me a cup of coffee? I have to put something in my stomach," whined Ruben. "It's a pretty sad state of affairs when no one will make me breakfast."

"I made my own, you make your own. And you'd better hurry. You know what Tina said. Here's your coffee."

Ruben made a big show of getting out of his chair and walking over to the counter. Finding the chocolate chip cookie bag from the night before, he dumped the cookies on a plate. Pieces of four broken cookies. "Guess this is what I'll have."

"Guess so," snickered Carlos.

A short time later in the barn they gave the puppies a quick brush, yanked out the rest of the burrs on the one, and put them in their cages.

"We have to remember to give them the treats after we get the van loaded," said Ruben.

"Right. But remember we can't give too many or it'll seem like they're in a coma, and Shonalee won't take 'em," admonished Carlos.

"I know that."

They moved their personal belongings, including the one marijuana plant, to one side of the van and put the crates with the puppies on the other side, along with the rest of the dog paraphernalia that was in the barn. Some of the items Shonalee was going to donate to charity and some would go with the puppies when they were sold.

Tina made one last check around the barn before they left to make sure they'd taken all the dog things. Fortunately, she didn't see their belongings in the van.

"Okay, guys, say hi to Shonalee, and tell her I'll see her soon. Be careful with my van, and I'll see you tomorrow when you bring it back," said Tina.

"You got it. You know you're going to be lonely without us," claimed Ruben sitting in the driver's seat. Carlos, glared at him, poked him in the ribs, and whispered, "Why the hell would you say that?"

"There won't be time to miss you. You're only going to be gone one night." Tina gave a quick wave and walked back to the house.

As they drove down the road from Tina's house, Ruben glanced over at Carlos. "There's nothing wrong with what I said."

"She might think we're going to be gone a long time."

"Well, we are."

"Just forget it and drive."

The day after Carlos and Ruben left, Tina put on her blue and white dress and went to see her new attorney. She was there to sign the papers selling her property, minus about an acre where her house and barn were located. The Hi and Higher Company, the medical marijuana group, had found Tina's property to be the right size and location for what they had in mind. The amount of money they offered Tina was way more than she could ever have anticipated. Way, way more.

Tina was savvy enough to realize she needed to have an attorney involved to make sure, as she put it, they weren't going to screw her over. After much bickering (at which she was extremely good) with the representatives of the company, a final selling price was decided upon. The contract was considerably more lucrative than the first offer. Both she and her attorney were extremely happy. This money would allow Tina to do something that would be a helluva lot better than trying to raise chickens. She hadn't figured out what yet.

"Those puppies are just the cutest little things," gushed Shonalee. "I know they'll sell quickly. I'd be tempted to keep one for myself, but I'm never home." The dogs were sound asleep in their crates.

"We didn't have a chance to get them as well trained as last time, but they seem pretty smart, so they should be okay. The ride in the van just put them to sleep," Carlos informed Shonalee.

Ruben checking out Shonalee said, "Tina says to say hi, and she'll be seeing you soon."

"Really? I thought she was super busy. Did she say if she was coming here?"

"Nope, that's all she said."

"We gotta bring in the rest of the things from the van. Come on, Ruben," ordered Carlos. He could see Ruben ogling Shonalee. That could go on forever.

After depositing all the doggy items from Tina's barn in the boutique, the guys said goodbye to Shonalee and began their journey to Miami.

Tony was feeling sorry for himself. Everyone was out to get him. Lenny, the cops, the friggin' FBI, that crazy dog lady. Hell, he was just trying to keep the business together, make a decent living.

I'm really a good person, he thought. *If Pete hadn't convinced me the FBI guy was dangerous, I wouldn't have done him in. Same with Pete. I knew he couldn't keep his mouth shut. It was just a matter of time before he blabbed to everyone about everything. So, he had himself to blame. Maybe I should go to the area on the rally grounds where I left him. Nah, I couldn't stand to look at him. He'd be pretty gross by now. What a dumb idea. It's bad enough that his smirking face keeps flashing in my brain. I'm gonna hunker down at home, drink some more scotch, and forget about it all. I'll watch some sports. That's what I'll do. Whatever happens, happens.*

Chapter 53

Tina couldn't help smiling to herself. She'd done it. Using part of her newfound wealth, she had bought a unit in the same building that Shonalee's rich boyfriend had his condo. It wasn't as big as his, but it did have the same great water view. She dug around in her bright green pleather purse until she found the key to her new abode.

Once inside Tina couldn't help herself. She danced around the empty great room and then into the two bedrooms and finally out to the deck. What a view! Tina was in heaven and couldn't wait to see Shonalee's face when she saw the condo. Time to give her a call.

"Hey Shonalee, Tina here. By any chance are you at your friend's condo?"

"Yes, as a matter of fact I am. Why? What's up?" asked Shonalee. "Are you at my boutique?"

"No. Do you have about twenty minutes? I've gotta show you something." said an excited Tina.

"Where the heck are you? Are you outside in your truck?"

"No, listen. Come down to the third floor, to unit 310."

Tina was standing outside the open condo door when Shonalee arrived.

"Come on in," said a beaming Tina. "Whaddya you think?"

"It's great. Are you renting it?" asked Shonalee, wide-eyed.

"Hell no, I bought it."

"You—you bought it?" stammered Shonalee, her mouth hanging open. "But how, why? I don't understand why you would buy a place here."

"Why not buy a place here? I like it."

"It is lovely, and I'm sure very expensive."

"Guess I didn't tell you. I sold the farm. Well, not all of it. I still own the house, the barn, and the land around it. I'm thinking of renting it out."

"But what will you do? And what about Carlos and Ruben?"

"I'm not sure what I'll be doing. And the guys, well they're in Miami babysitting. I don't know what's going on with them. I have a feeling they may stay there."

"Weren't you and Lenny sort of business partners? Isn't he going to be upset? You won't be able to hold the rallies unless you make a deal with the new owners."

"Lenny knows there won't be any more rallies, and I just called and told him I sold the property. He and his buddies have plenty of other businesses they're involved in."

Shonalee didn't need to know what Lenny and his friends did, Tina thought. Actually, she didn't know what all he was involved in herself, and didn't want to know. She was just glad he got all his stuff off her property. She wished Pete was last seen somewhere other than the rally site. The Feds knew about where Pete had parked his camper. But hey, she didn't own that part of the property anymore. Anyone wanting to check it out again would have to ask the new owners. Maybe they already had.

"Earth to Tina. Are you there?" Shonalee was waving her hands in front of Tina's face.

"What? Oh, I was thinking I'm going to need furniture here. Not sure if I should bring some of what I have or buy new."

"I would think you'd want new. Maybe a nautical look," suggested Shonalee. "Would you like me to go shopping with you?"

"Sure. I'll let you know ahead of time when we can get together. But I am going to look around the house first to see if there are a few things that I can bring here."

"Listen, I gotta go. I've got a ton of stuff to do. This condo is really great, Tina. I hope you enjoy it," said Shonalee as she walked to the door.

"Yup, it is nice." Tina agreed as she accompanied Shonalee.

Scottie heard her phone ring. Taking her phone off the kitchen counter she was surprised to see it was Agent Myer. "Well, this is interesting. As it happens, I don't have any more information for you yet," smart-mouthed Scottie.

"Actually, I have some for you. I believe we've apprehended the guy who attacked you. We'd like you to confirm this is the correct individual."

"Wow! That is good news. Just tell me where and when and I'll be there," said an elated Scottie.

Agent Myer proceeded to give her the information and that he expected to see her the next day.

After the phone call, Scottie excitedly told Charlie about what she had learned from Agent Myer and her upcoming appointment. "I can't wait to see that creep and tell him what I . . ."

"Scottie, you might not get to say anything to him," cautioned Charlie. "He might be on the other side of the one-way glass."

"You're right. I hadn't thought about that. It doesn't matter as long as I don't have to worry about him anymore. It'll be like a weight has been lifted off my shoulders. You know, I feel like that already. It's got to be him. I'm so relieved, I don't know if I can wait until tomorrow. I've got to do something."

Charlie looked at Scottie and smiled. He motioned to her in a come-hither way and said, "I know what we can do."

Chapter 54

Lenny was in big trouble, thanks to Scottie. The license plate number she'd given the FBI taken from his white van led to the record of Lenny's past offenses: jail time for breaking and entering, car theft, and drug dealing. Most arrests dated from when he was younger, with no recent activity on his rap sheet. Doreen had given Lenny's name to the agents. They figured pulling his van over might be helpful.

Doreen also mentioned that Lenny was from Miami, and he was headed back home. So, Florida Highway Patrol officers stopped the van halfway to Miami at the request of the FBI. They soon found the various firearms, drugs, and Lenny's motorcycle in the van. Not good for Lenny. Additional patrol officers were called to the scene. Lenny was arrested, and the van and the merchandise were confiscated.

Carlos and Ruben were rather enjoying staying with Carmen. Ruben did have to do some babysitting. But for him it was easy. Just give the kids whatever they wanted to eat and let them play as long as they wanted. Carmen's work hours varied, so if she happened to come home late, she would find the children still racing around the house. Of course, getting them up in the morning was difficult.

Carlos got a job within walking distance to Carmen's house. The job was at a small neighborhood grocery store, helping unload supplies from delivery trucks, stocking shelves, cleaning the floor, and making occasional deliveries using the owner's truck. Most of his small income was given to Carmen for room and board.

Scottie was in Shonalee's Boutique, looking for a birthday present for Missy, Bonita's dog. Although Missy wasn't having any friends at her party, Bonita was. Missy really didn't like other dogs. They would tear up your toys and sniff you all over. Ick.

"I'm here to get something for Missy," announced Scottie after giving Shonalee a quick hug. "It's her birthday, and Bonita is having a party."

"I know. I've been invited too. I've never been to a dog birthday party before. I'll have to mention the idea to my customers. Did Missy like the dress that Bonita bought for her? If she doesn't like wearing things, just stick with treats or maybe a toy. I got some new ones in the other day." Shonalee showed her the rack with the new toys.

"By the way, do you know if she invited Tina, you know, my cousin?"

Scottie shook her head. "Not sure, she never said who'd been invited. It'll be a fun time, I'm sure." She picked out a squeaky toy and a bag of peanut butter treats.

Scottie arrived right on time for the dog birthday. The same group of ladies who had been at Shonalee's luncheon were together again. They all brought little birthday presents for Missy, who was only interested in the treats, especially the peanut butter ones from Shonalee's shop.

"This cake is delicious," exclaimed Harper.

"And so is the champagne," added Shonalee. "By the way, did you hear about the camper that blew up? They finally identified the people who were in it. It wasn't the owner after all. There's a possibility that it was stolen. It was on the news this morning."

"What about the owner of the camper? Where's he?" asked Scottie.

"They didn't say much about him. Just that he's part owner of a pawn shop, and he's missing," said Shonalee. Tina downed the champagne in her glass in a single long gulp.

"Did they say who the other owner or owners of the pawn shop are?" *It's got to be the same pawn shop where I went to find Tony*, thought Scottie. *I wonder what happened to the other owner. I wouldn't put it past Tony to do him in.*

"I didn't hear the whole newscast because I was in a hurry."

"I'll have another glass of bubbles," said Tina, as if trying to change the subject. "How often do you all drink champagne?"

Bonita laughingly said, "Whenever there's a special occasion, and I can always come up with one."

Scottie's mind was racing. "Tina, wasn't the guy who went missing last seen at your rally? I think I saw that in the paper. Has law enforcement spoken to you about it?"

"Yep, I heard he was at the rally. And yes, I was asked about it. Didn't have much to tell 'em. Plus, I sold the property, but did keep the area around the house and barn. Shonalee, tell the girls about my new condo." Shonalee gave a detailed description of the condo.

Scottie barely heard a word of Shonalee's effusive narrative. She was too busy trying to put all the information together: how she had been harassed, the missing guy from the rally, the pawn shop, and the dead guy she saw in the yard who had vanished. And of course, Tony trying to kill her. There had to be some connection.

It wasn't until the women had finished their cake and champagne and were getting ready to leave that they noticed Missy sound asleep in her bed with the bag of treats torn open. It was obvious from the amount left that she had enjoyed quite a few.

The following day at the police station, Scottie did confirm to the FBI that the man they were holding was Tony (Diablo), who had tried to choke her. They had arrested him at home for attempting to murder her and was being held in jail without bond. The attorney he'd contacted was quite concerned about his mental stability. Apparently, Tony constantly mentioned he was seeing Pete's face grinning at him. Also, Tony had developed an annoying tic on the side of his face which, along with his sore arm, wasn't helping his mental condition. And he insisted on signing his name Diablo, much to his attorney's dismay.

Lenny wasn't doing any better than Tony. He was in jail too, arrested for selling illegal firearms, drugs, and suspected human trafficking. Several other individuals were also arrested. Lenny squealed about their involvement. He even let slip about a ship from Argentina docked in Miami with the guns, gun parts, and drugs that he was scheduled to pick up. Lenny knew there were several groups throughout Florida and beyond that would miss the services he had been providing and would be extremely concerned about the consequences of his arrest.

When Doreen learned that Pete wasn't in the camper with some woman, she was both relieved and angry. She was glad he hadn't been blown up, but now she had to keep wondering where he was. Plus, his mother would be calling all the time, asking if she'd seen Pete. He still could have run off with somebody. Well, she wasn't going to wait around for him to show up. Going out with her single girlfriends and having fun was definitely going to happen.

Doreen had received another shock. Tony's attorney called her to let her know he was in jail. She knew he had issues, but jeez, trying to strangle a woman! What was he thinking? That meant having to quit her job and run the pawn shop. That might be okay. Hopefully, she'd be able to get some info from Tony about running the shop if she was able to see him. Maybe she could use part of the shop for women's clothing consignment. She'd get a friend to help her run it. Yep, it'd be great. If there were a lot of guns in the shop, she could call it "Gunning for Clothes Pawnshop."

Chapter 55

It was late afternoon, and Carmen had just started her shift at three, but the beginnings of a migraine headache sent her home shortly before five. She didn't get them often, but when she did, they really put her out of commission. When she stepped into the living room and looked at the scene in front of her, the headache went into high gear.

Her five-year-old son was sitting on the floor watching *Naked and Afraid* on television with a large bag of potato chips, a bag of gummie worms, and a Coke can next to him. On one end of the sofa sat Ruben, sound asleep, snoring with a beer can between his knees. On the other end of the sofa her four-year-old son was also sound asleep with a beer can between his knees. Between them the two-year-old was leaning into Ruben, also asleep.

Poor Carmen. She picked up the chip bag, the gummie worms, and the soda can, and hissed in her son's ear, "Go to your room." It would hurt too much to talk in a loud voice. The little boy, seeing his mother's face knew he'd better do what she said. Walking over to Ruben, Carmen gave his foot a fierce kick. She would have preferred to kick something else. Letting a little kid drink beer!

"What the hell," squawked Ruben, waking from a sound sleep. "Wow, Carmen, you're home early. What's up? We were just taking a little nap here."

Ruben's talking woke up the two-year-old. who upon seeing his mother squealed in his high-pitched voice,

"Mommy, mommy" and ran full throttle to her. Carmen almost fell over. The pounding in her head was intense. She knew she had to get to bed. Now the four-year-old was awake. The beer can between his knees tipped over, spilling beer on his pants, the sofa, and the rug.

Carmen stood looking down at Ruben, pointed her finger at him, and said quietly, "I have a migraine headache and I'm going to bed. Clean up the mess here, feed the children some decent food, and take them to the park. I do not want to hear one sound. When I feel better, we will be having a serious talk." With that she left the room, softly muttering in Spanish words Ruben was glad he didn't understand.

It didn't take long for Tina to realize that condo living wasn't all that she had imagined it would be. After she and Shonalee had outfitted the condo with the basics—furniture and kitchenware—she got bored. One can only sit around the pool so much. Plus, she really didn't have a lot to talk about with the ladies she met in the complex, except for Shonalee, of course. It was just by chance that she met Hank. She had taken her truck to Ben's Service and Repair Shop to have the brakes checked, and there he was, having his truck worked on. They hit it off right away. He was a big burly guy, with lots of tattoos and a hearty laugh.

Hank lived in the Cortez Fishing Village and had a fleet of charter fishing/party boats. He and his work team took people out on nearshore and deep-sea fishing trips and off-shore party boat cruises. The first time Hank invited Tina on a fishing trip she fell in love with both fishing and Hank. She found being out on the water absolutely exhilarating.

It didn't take long before Tina was spending more time at Hank's apartment than her own. The apartment was spacious and, to Tina, beautiful. The décor was all nautical, and the view from the west windows overlooked the docks and the boats. As from her condo, the sunsets were gorgeous. Life was wonderful.

The apartment was located above Hank's shop named Cortez Sea Adventures, where tickets were sold for the various sailings. In addition to tickets being sold, the usual sundry items such as hats, T-shirts, and sunblock were also offered. Hank owned the building, so it was a convenient place to live and run the business.

The FBI had questioned Tina several times about the missing Pete and the rally. She had her spiel down pat. Yes, she knew Pete, yes, she saw him at the rally, but she never saw him leave the rally or at any time since. End of story. Surprisingly, she was never questioned about Lenny. Apparently, he hadn't mentioned her name. Oh, and yes, she had raised awesome puppies in a previous life.

Tina was also fortunate the young family who rented the farm had tidied up the yard, thoroughly cleaned the inside of the house (which was really needed), painted the walls, and threw out the disgusting carpets and curtains and bought new ones. Tina had suggested that they might want to plant a vegetable or flower garden behind the barn, which they did. Tomato plants, green onions, and several different herbs. Nary a marijuana plant to be seen. Two young children riding their tricycles around. The couple even converted the storage sheds into chicken coops. The farm looked like a happy, wholesome, idyllic place to live.

The FBI had examined the rally grounds previously and found nothing suspicious. Now those same grounds were being prepared for the construction of the new medical marijuana facility. Any clues to Pete's murder that had been there were long gone.

Sometime later a remnant of what appeared to be a large part of a pair a man's "tightee-whitees"was discovered by a kayaker on the Myakka River.

As a couple was peacefully paddling their kayak on the river, the woman suddenly said, "Hey, look what my oar picked up. It looks like a piece of a guy's underwear."

"He must have been at a blast of a party to lose his shorts. Or maybe he went swimming with the gators, and you know what happened then."

"That's gross. All I know is I'm putting it in the trash when we get back. Does make you wonder how it got here, though."

"I agree, but maybe you shouldn't put it in the trash. It might belong to someone who is missing."

"I hadn't thought about that. You're right. We can drop it off at the police station when we get back to town. I think there is a label on it that might help."

Chapter 56

"I really think we should go on a cruise, Scottie," said Charlie. "You basically gave the Feds the information they needed to catch the bad guys. Getting away and just relaxing will do you good."

"I don't know, Charlie. I've—"

"Don't start making excuses. You can get out of your dog-walking chores. They can get along without you for a while. And you don't have any other commitments that you need to be here for, do you?"

"No, I guess not. I do have to confess that I'm feeling so much better, knowing that butthead Tony is in jail. I still can't believe he'd kill his own partner. You know, it bothers me that they haven't found the bodies where he said he put them."

"That's not your problem. It may take some time, but they'll find them. But see what I'm saying? You're still dwelling on the deaths."

"You're right. I am. Your idea of a cruise is starting to sound pretty good. Maybe we could even talk Piper and Jack into going with us."

"Good idea. They're a fun couple. I just got several cruise brochures we can look at."

"Now I'm getting excited. I'm ready to start packing." Scottie's brown eyes were shining as she leaned over and gave Charlie a quick kiss on the lips.

———————————

Tina wasn't the only one who was making changes in her life situation. Shonalee and her boyfriend were becoming increasingly involved with each other. As a matter of fact, he had dropped some major hints about marriage. Shonalee was certainly receptive to this possibility. She liked being married. A good-looking older man with no major health problems, lots of money, who liked to travel and buy her expensive things—what's not to like? Shonalee was just waiting for him to actually pop the question and then suggest they go shopping for an engagement ring. And she already knew the style she wanted. Hopefully he wouldn't buy one without her seeing it.

Epilog

Carmen did have that chat with Carlos and Ruben. She decided they had to leave. She explained her concerns to them and why they could no longer live with her. Ruben ate and drank too much and was much too lax with the children. He let them do whatever they wanted. No wonder they loved him. It had to stop before the kids were totally out of control. And the small amount of money that Carlos brought home barely covered the extra expenses. Also, she suspected Ruben and Carlos were involved in something at Tina's they weren't telling her about. That was fine with her. She didn't want to know.

She had a friend of a friend who was looking for a couple of deck hands to work on his boat, which he was sailing to Mexico. It was a decent sized fishing trawler, and two of his workers had gone AWOL in Miami. Carmen did some fast talking and convinced the owner of the boat that Ruben and Carlos would be just the workers he was looking for.

Ruben was beyond excited. A boat trip to Mexico! He overlooked the part about it being a one-way working trip. His knowledge of Mexican food items, such as tacos, tortillas, enchiladas, huevos, empanadas, and a few others should put him in good stead. Of course, agua and cerveza were also part of his vocabulary. And he had even picked up a few other words from the children. What more would he need?

Carlos was worried about the trip. He wasn't sure exactly what the work on board would entail or if they would earn enough money to get them to a cousin in Cuernavaca. He didn't blame Carmen for asking them to leave. It was easy to see Ruben wasn't exactly doing his job. Carmen had contacted a cousin in Mexico, and she had reluctantly agreed to take the guys in for a while.

Carlos vaguely remembered the cousin. He hadn't seen her in years. She was older than him and had always seemed serious and quite stern. Hopefully she had mellowed into a more pleasant, easy-going person. Otherwise, she might not find Ruben to be the sort of person she would want to live in her house. Carlos was sure they could find work of some kind once they got there. Going back to Florida was not an option.

Tina, being the businesswoman she was, continued to look for ways to enhance her new financial portfolio. She also wanted to include Hank in her latest venture so she could use part of his shop. Tina had decided that since there are always a lot of senior citizens with various aches and pains who were taking boat trips, selling CBD products in Hank's shop could be quite lucrative. All she had to do was convince Hank, who wasn't quite ready to branch out in that direction. Hank was totally enamored with Tina. He loved looking at her tattoos, which were on various parts of her body, and the new gold booby ring. Tina figured he'd agree to her idea of new products in his shop before long. All in all, they were quite happy with their relationship.

Shonalee was ecstatic. Just as she had hoped, she got the engagement ring of her dreams. A platinum band with two good-sized stones, a diamond and an amethyst. They hadn't set a wedding date yet. Shonalee had some decisions to make first. She was debating whether to keep her shop/house or sell it. Or maybe just sell part of it. Another option she was considering was for her to rent the portion of the building where the astrology readings were held and sell everything else. Having built up a small but steady clientele, she would hate to leave them floundering in their life's journey.

Tina had held an engagement party for her at Hank's place, which Shonalee thought was great, until Tina announced she was going to be the maid-of-honor and would be helping with all the wedding plans. Shonalee had inwardly cringed at the thought of suggestions that Tina might come up with. Although she hadn't considered it before, eloping might be best. Her recent horoscopes had indicated that with proper planning, she could achieve what she wanted. It would all work out.

Tony had confessed to killing the FBI agent and Pete. He had no idea what happened to the bodies, which weren't where he'd left them. He was beyond stressed. There was some question as to whether he was mentally capable of standing trial.

Eventually, remnants of clothing and bones were found in the river and tied to the two dead men. It was then Tony did stand trial for the murders. He was convicted and sentenced to life in prison.

Lenny did not fare well after his arrest. The individuals he worked with were upset about his arrest, especially the captain of the ship that he was to meet at the pier. As the saying goes, "Loose lips sink ships." Lenny, remembering how in the past he'd gotten lesser punishment by squealing on his partners, did the same again.

Unfortunately, this time it didn't work. Lenny tried to deny all the charges against him. It didn't work. He was sentenced to a lengthy prison sentence.

Scottie and Charlie took to cruising like flies to a picnic. They started out taking short cruises and discovered they loved sailing. It was great to just unpack your clothes, not worry about cooking, see great entertainment, and visit interesting places. As they started taking longer cruises, it became more difficult for Scottie to conduct her pet obligations. She finally found a woman who was glad to take over her dog-walking and cat-visiting business. While she missed seeing her furry friends and their owners, from time to time she did do some substitute dog walking with those she had previously known. Going on trips with Charlie was great fun. No way would she give that up.

It was on the most recent cruise that Charlie tried to convince her she had been in the wrong business. He teasingly told her detective work was more her forte, which she found amusing and yet thought-provoking. Just maybe.

After a late dinner in a specialty restaurant, they had gone dancing. Finally, after deciding it was getting super late, considering they'd made reservations to take an early tour of Aruba in the morning, they left the lounge on the top floor to go to their room. On the way back they stopped for a moment to look over the railing down to the atrium. It was lovely. The two sets of stairs, covered in crystals, curved to the lower floor. There the shiny marble floor was surrounded with comfortable-looking chairs with red cushions.

Charlie was gazing appreciatively at Scottie. She was dressed in a form-fitting, green cocktail dress that accented her slim figure. As Charlie was admiring Scottie, she was watching a couple across from them. The woman appeared to be upset. First, she had her hands on her hips, and then she pointed a finger at her companion and shook it. Scottie couldn't totally see the person with her, as a pillar partially blocked her view. It did appear to be a male with a dark suit.

The woman turned, and as she was about to take the first step to go down the sparkling stairs, the arm of the person next to her shot out, put a hand on her back, and gave her a shove. She screamed as she tumbled downward, eventually landing upside down halfway to the bottom of the stairs. Her long blonde hair hung below the step where her head rested. Blood trickled out of the side her mouth. The skirt of the long pink, flowered dress she wore now exposed her thighs. One leg was bent backwards at an odd angle.

Scottie had watched all this as if in slow motion. She had seen the hand pushing the woman down the stairs and then the hasty departure of a man in a dark suit and shiny black shoes. There hadn't been time to see his face. Charlie hadn't witnessed any of this. Two of the ship's officers who happened to be walking at the bottom of the atrium heard the scream and witnessed the woman's tumble. They hurried up to check on her. Unfortunately, the fall was fatal.

It was with Scottie's assistance to the security personnel on the ship that the murderer was apprehended. One important clue was the tuxedo shoes. The guy had been wearing a tuxedo and tuxedo shoes. The couple had been part of a business group on the cruise. The woman had been vying for a senior position with the company that her co-worker also wanted. They were both extremely ambitious, and she had warned him to get out of her way. The job would be hers.

Not to be. That was the reason for the shove down the sparkly stairs. None of the other men in their group had worn

tuxedo shoes, so Scottie's information about the push and the shiny shoes meant neither of the coworkers would be getting the position they wanted.

Charlie continued to encourage Scottie to engage in a new profession. *Scottie Shelton, Private Eye.* Who knows? Stranger things have happened.

Acknowledgments

Many thanks to the individuals who have helped bring this book to fruition. My editor, Carol Gaskin, provided excellent suggestions and writing tips. Thanks also go to Susan Layman, Monica Hoover, and Pat Polazzo for their feedback and Karen Creager for her information on motorcycles and rallies. The encouragement of friends also aided in this endeavor. Most of all, thanks to my husband, Don. His technical expertise was invaluable in addition to his support and readiness to hear my writing concerns.

About the Author

The Dog Knows is P. X. Stratton's first novel. A former training director for a major oil company's credit card division, she developed and employed training materials and wrote a monthly column for the company newsletter. The author currently resides, with her husband, in Sarasota, Florida.

Made in United States
Orlando, FL
18 February 2025

58649508R00164